To Johnny
Live Long, & Prosper!
Connie Jasperson

The Last
Good Knight

Connie J Jasperson

ISBN-13: 978-0615515045

(Fantasy Island Book Publishing)

ISBN-10: 0615515045

Credits:

Cover design: Ceri Clark

Front Cover © Tomasz Bidermann/ Dreamstime.com

Map of Waldeyn © cjjasp

Senior Editor: Pamela Brennan

Structural Editor: J. Darroll Hall

Fantasy Island Book Publishing

Contact us at: www.fantasyislandbookpublishing.com

Dedicated to:

My children who encouraged me to write!! You have my love and thanks for all time....

My husband, who enables my addiction to writing....

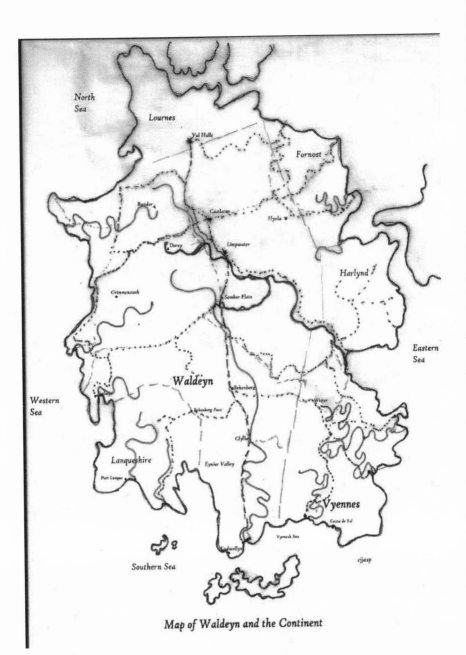

North
Sea

Lournes

Val Halla

Fornost

Bunder

Caaleton

Hyola

Derey

Limpwater

Harlynd

Grimmenstock

Somber Flats

Eastern
Sea

Western
Sea

Waldeyn

Bekenberg

Wister

Behenberg Pass

Clythe

Lanqueshire

Eynier Valley

Port Lasque

Vyennes

Casta de Sol

Ludwellyn

Vyenesh Sea

cjjasp

Southern Sea

Map of Waldeyn and the Continent

CONTENTS

Prologue - How it all Began:

The True Tale of Billy's Revenge, and How the Great Knight Became a Rowdy as told by Huw the Bard:

In a cabin in the woods near the River Limpwater, Billy MacNess, newly-made captain of the Rowdies lay recovering from an inconveniencing wound received at the hands of his rival, Bastard John, captain of the Wolves out of Goober Flats.

And just that morning, unaware that Billy was still mewed up in his bunk, Bastard John had decided to burn the place down, since he had only managed to take off one of Billy's fingers by fighting fair.

Despite his mutilated hand, Billy managed to stab The Bastard in the back before the fire got going. At that point, Billy was faced with the dilemma of what to do with the body. If it got out that he had at last killed his rival there would be repercussions from the Wolves, though they didn't really love their boss.

As he stared at the Bastard's corpse it occurred to him that he should retire from active participation in the trade, and build a proper inn for his Rowdies to live and work out of, for a price of course. 'I could build an inn that would rival the finest inns and then my Rowdies would be the finest band of mercs in Waldeyn. I could do this!'

And so he did, drawing up his plans and hiring the stonemasons to begin the foundations that very afternoon. When the Rowdies all began to trickle back home from their various jobs, the foundations had been laid, and the walls were already going up on the first floor.

"Think of it, darlings: a real bath-house with a side reserved for the ladies, and a side reserved for the gents and two indoor flushing toilets in each! Stick with me and I will do handsomely by you!"

And they did stick with Billy. He was good at finding them work and he cooked well. Plus there was the promise of indoor toilets, and properly plumbed bathtubs; a thing that pleased them all. They were all the rage in Castleton.

And since Billy had built his inn over the bones of his old rival, of course, the only proper name for it was 'Billy's Revenge'.

The town of Limpwater grew up around the inn, and soon it was a thriving town of around five hundred souls.

One dark, rainy night a young bard appeared in the newly grown town of Limpwater and turned up at Billy's Revenge. He liked the place, and so he pulled a stool over to a good spot and began singing for his supper. The good people of Limpwater liked the music so much that within two years the bard, a man with the dark black hair, deep blue eyes and lilting accent of the Eynier Valley by the name of Huw Owyn had enough gold to purchase a cottage on the main street.

Huw's great gift was the ability to spin straw into gold, so to speak; and The Rowdies' adventures gave good Huw more than enough material to work with. Thanks to Huw's skillful molding and retelling, their adventures somehow enlarged and grew into legends;

and if they were not exactly accurately portrayed, they were at least entertaining.

The most popular of his tales involved that most courteous of knights, Sir Julian (Lackland) De Portiers. Lackland was known to be the finest knight in the realm, and so it was an achievement of the most fantastic kind that he should come to Billy looking for work. The knight was exactly what Billy was looking for in a Rowdy: young, intelligent, educated, honorable and, best of all, the man was absolute death on highwaymen. Plus, when something complicated was afoot, there was no one more capable of putting together a good plan, except for perhaps Mags or Lucy.

A cousin of the king and the younger son of a local baron, Sir Julian, had no inheritance to come to, thus the name of Lackland. In the same way as every other child of the landed gentry, Lackland had gone to court at the age of twelve where he had received his education alongside the other children of the aristocracy.

Although Lackland was acclaimed by all as the finest knight in the realm, despite his comparatively low social status, his abilities would have gone to waste had he not chosen to join the Rowdies. Lackland was invincible in the battle-arts, having left many a hardened veteran a bloodied mess on the tourney field before the age of sixteen; the official age of adulthood.

By that time, his place in court had been officially set in stone. Those untalented men of higher birth and lesser ability would always have the positions as tacticians and advisors while he, younger son of a mere baron, would be left to languish on the fringe of court society; his ideas and his abilities being credited to others and advancing the military careers of the pleasant but unabashedly unintelligent sons of earls and dukes.

They had dubbed him 'Lackland' as a way of ensuring that he understood his place, but he had not only embraced the name, he had embraced the concept of what that lack of encumbrance allowed him to do: Julian 'Lackland' De Portiers was a free man. He owed nothing to anyone, save that fierce loyalty that was always due to his royal cousin. Once Julian himself understood that concept, he began treating the upper nobility as if he were not only their equal, but as if he were their intellectual better.

Julian Lackland was young and full of fire. He had no intention of toadying to those courtiers of miniscule ability and lesser wit; and he had accordingly developed a habit of letting the less intellectually endowed courtier know his opinion in his amusing way, often leaving them stunned and gaping at him like landed fish. They were unable to find fault with what he had so politely said.

And they, faced with this force of nature, numbly accepted him in the role he had chosen since he had given them no other option.

Henri fully understood Lackland's position; he'd have done the same himself. The fact that Julian had quickly established himself as a great and highly regarded mercenary knight outside of the court meant that Henri could now openly seek Julian's advice without stepping on his advisors' delicate but incompetent toes.

Henri Dragoran had ascended the throne at the age of nine. His reign had been seen as weak, with his foreign-born mother and her brother acting as regents until his majority. Under pressure from his widowed mother, King Henri had done his duty and married the Princess of Lournes at the age of sixteen and had regretted it ever since. Though he was now very much a strong ruler, he was still hampered by the narrow minded courtiers that remained from the years of his mother's regency, and by his universally despised Queen. It was a marriage made strictly for political purposes, but at twenty Henri still had no heir, and was tied to a woman whose sly, manipulative temperament had for the last two years caused him to avoid her bed at all costs.

Ever the young optimist, Lackland had left the court seeking his fortune. Besides, Billy Nine-fingers had promised that he would have more opportunity to use his true skills as a mercenary than he would at the court, and everyone knew him to be a man who kept his promises. Of course the Rowdies were happy to have a knight of his caliber as one of their own.

However, as one might imagine, Lackland was a unique sort of mercenary, doing it his own way. From the day he first arrived at Billy's Revenge, one heard often of Lackland risking his neck to save the cow of a farmer who could not pay him a copper penny. As often as one heard of his exploits in saving the king's young nephew from a firedrake. In the eyes of the people, young Sir Julian Lackland was, and would always be, known as The Great Knight. He was the Peoples Champion.

In her own mind, Lady Margaret De Leon had never been a proper lady despite her high birth. She had fallen passionately in love with a landless knight, and loathed her life as a lady in waiting. A skilled swordswoman, Mags wanted more than anything to be allowed to swing her sword as a knight. Sadly, though the young ladies of the court could learn to swing the sword and develop the knightly arts as a 'sport', everyone knew that ladies could not be knights. It simply was not done.

Both Julian and Henri knew that Mags was far and away a finer swordsman than most of Henri's Knights of the Realm. However, the climate at court was such that even Henri could not sway the opinion of those who made the rules.

Lady Mags was the only living child of Jules Edward De Leon, third Earl of Bunder, and her tenure as lady in waiting had not only bored her to tears, it had given her an attitude of ingratitude toward her father and polite society in general. Her mad desire to throttle the jealous Queen had led to her leaving the court under a cloud, protected by the king's guard; all of whom shared her desire.

Not long after, on the evening of the day that her father informed her of her impending marriage to an insipid duke from Marionberg, seventeen-year old Mags left her father's house behind her. She had taken her father's old mail shirt and helmet that he had worn as a boy from his armory where they lay covered in dust, and buckled on his old sword.

She left a note for her father and mother explaining that she had decided to commit social suicide and that he should keep the dowry. The horse she rode out on was her own, a gift from her grandmother. Then she had ridden straight to Billy's Revenge where her great love from court, Lackland, was gainfully employed. Mags had taken the first job she was offered, and she never looked back.

Julian had been deliriously happy that she had followed him, and was convinced that she would eventually decide to marry him. He was a man full of noble, romantic ideals and he was determined to be waiting for her when that happened; no matter how long he had to wait. After all, that is what a true knight did in such a situation.

Lady Mags and Sir Julian each regularly took on the bad jobs that no one else would touch, especially if it was for a poor person. Neither one cared a fig about getting rich; they had been that. They just enjoyed the work.

In the early days, it was so easy for Julian to live for the adventure as Mags did; to take each day as it came and to hell with tomorrow. The more the danger, the more she loved it. The rush and thrill of succeeding, when by all rights she should have died, was as intoxicating as the finest wine, and as sweet as the most passionate kiss; and having tasted it once, neither one could walk away from it.

Thus, it was that not long after Julian had joined Billy and his Rowdies it happened. A 'bad' job, taken on for no money at all, turned out to be the first step down a road that would forever alter the course of the eighteen-year-old knight Julian Lackland's life; though he could not have known it. That was the night that Lackland saved the life of young Beau Baker. This was the very boy who would grow up to be both his greatest friend, and the third leg of the love-triangle that would shape the Great Knight's life for good and for ill. That was also the night that Lackland met his first waterdemon.

Chapter 1 - The Messy Affair of the Waterdemon

It was raining cats and dogs, as usual, and the street in front of Billy's Revenge was a mucky mess. Billy was going to have it cobbled when the rain stopped. In the meantime, there were boardwalks built from one end of town to the other, so most folks didn't have to walk in it. However Farroll, the once white but now mud-brown steed owned by Sir Julian Lackland, was plodding through it resentfully, covered in mud to his hocks.

There they were, heading away from the lovely dry stable and out into the misery of a Waldeyn winter's night. Farroll didn't enjoy being a hero, really. His dream was to stand as stud to the king's many mares, but at the rate they were going, it would never happen.

Of course, Farroll knew that a task such as that would be a lot of work, but he really felt that he was more than up to it.

Instead though, here he was slogging through the muck in a downpour looking for some stupid boy that went and got himself kidnapped by a waterdemon.

Bruiser, Slippery Jack's old horse agreed with him fully.

Still, Sir Julian was a good sort, as far as riders went. Slippery Jack was not quite as adamant about seeing to Bruiser's comfort as Sir Julian was when they were on the road. Sighing again, Farroll put one foot in front of the other, and went the direction Julian told him to go in.

"I think your horse is sulking, Lackland," ventured Slippery Jack after they had been on the road for while.

"Do you? I suppose he is. He has delusions of grandeur you know," Julian replied. "His dying ambition is to be put out to stud for the rest of his days, the randy old beast."

"Why I have the same ambition," replied Slippery Jack, winking at Farroll. "I don't suppose there is to be a copper in payment for this job, is there?"

"No, I suspect not, but perhaps we will be fed well. It is old Ben Baker's son you know, so there should be fresh bread for a few days, anyway," Lackland said. "He knows what it's like for us; he was a Rowdy in old Eddie's day."

"What is a smart boy like Beau Baker doing getting caught by a waterdemon anyway? I always thought he was smarter than most of the ten year olds around here. And how do you plan to kill it? We ain't got any Majik, at least I don't," stated Jack. "Too bad Stella One-Eye is out on a job. She has that nasty little lightning spelled-amulet that those water-demons just hate."

"Yes, well, I don't have any Majik-amulets either, but I am thinking arrows. If we can lob a few arrows at him, maybe we can get his attention," Lackland patted his long-bow that was strapped on behind him.

"I dunno," replied Slippery Jack. "I have heard that you can't kill them with a sword, so I don't know how you could kill them with an arrow. But I have only fought the one, and Stella zapped the bugger straight to hell, so…"

"Well, I've never actually seen one, so that is good information," Lackland fell silent, thinking about the problem.

"Too bad we were the only ones in town," muttered Jack. "This is really not my sort of a job, but I couldn't let you go and get killed all by yourself. Someone has to take the bad news back to Lady Mags. Ah well," he said and then he too fell silent. They held the lantern up as they rode, trying to find some sign of the water demon's passing, but the dark and the wet hid it all too well.

The sound of the rain was broken by the jingling of their mail, and the plodding of their horses. Finally they were out of the village of Limpwater and onto the hard-packed trade road, taking the west fork of the road, following the river toward Dervy. Soon they had arrived at the place where it was suspected that the water demon had taken the boy.

There was a strange smell in the air, and Farroll did not like it one bit. It smelled like danger. Why was it that every time Sir Julian dragged him out of the stable on a miserable night like this it always involved some strange and dangerous creature? Farroll snorted, trying to get the scent out of his nose. At least this thing didn't smell like a firedrake. Farroll hated dealing with firedrakes. Bruiser agreed with him, blowing his nose too.

"Damn me if that don't stink. It smells to me like we have found our quarry," said Jack. "I don't think Bruiser likes it much."

They came to a place where a small trail led off toward the river, and even in the dark it was easy to see that something heavy had been dragged down it.

Dismounting, they tied the horses to a bush. "I'll make a quick trip down the path and see what's down there. There should be a hole in the bank if it's a water-demon's den," and so saying Jack slipped off into the dark, while Julian stood companionably with the horses.

In what seemed to be no time at all, Jack had returned.

"Yes, it's a water demon's den down there all right," Jack whispered. "I couldn't see the boy. Mayhap the boy is still alive. These things are somewhat like spiders in that they take their prey when they have the opportunity. They put them to sleep and then eat them later when they have need of them."

"Is there a place for me to fire off a bolt or two?" Lackland was already reaching for his longbow, and pulling his bowstring out of a dry pocket he began stringing it.

"There is, near the river. Lord, yer a strong man, Lackland. I don't think I could pull that bow back, much less string it," Jack commented appreciatively. "That is definitely a bow to be reckoned with."

"Yes, it is that…but I need a certain amount of free space about me, for drawing it unheard in the forest. All I need to do is make the slightest rustle of leaves and then *I* become the target!" Lackland finished with getting the bow strung. "Now we need to make haste. A wet bow string will do us no good. The light of the lantern will draw him out, I am sure of it."

Soon they were crouched before the dark hole in the bank, and the lantern lit the scene before them fairly well. From somewhere to the back of the den, a glimmer of light moved. Suddenly the entrance to the den was filled by the horrifying figure of the waterdemon.

It stood half again as high as Lackland, with a chest shaped like a huge barrel and it glowed in the light of the lantern. The limbs of the creature were somewhat man-like; but not exactly. Nor was its huge, grotesque head much like a human's head. Instead of hair, strands of translucent glowing skin covered his head, each strand waving as if in a separate breeze of its own. Tiny, mean looking silver eyes glared out of its horrific face.

Sniffing the air, it roared its defiance, shaking its head and snarling. The strange glow in the den had come from the beast's transparent, jelly-like skin.

"He don't like the way we smell," smiled Jack grimly, "Shame on him. He smells as sweet as the Wolves' privy in July. You know though, I am not really comfortable with facing him this way; I am a spy, not a bloody knight." He looked at Lackland who of course had paid him no mind. "Julian? Aw, hell."

Lackland already had a huge arrow nocked, and quickly drawing it back, he shot the beast squarely in the chest. The beast yanked the arrow out and came racing toward him. Quickly Lackland fired off another bolt, which lodged in the demon's head. He yanked that one out, swinging it at Jack as if it were a club.

"Now we are done for," moaned Jack, swinging and hacking desperately with his sword. "I could use some help here, Julian." He lopped off a gooey hand, and the demon immediately began growing another. "Julian! A little help! Lackland!"

"You keep him busy for minute," Lackland told Jack. "I know exactly what we need!" Cutting part of his new linen shirt off, he quickly wrapped it about the head of an arrow and touched it to the lantern, setting it alight. Nocking the flaming arrow and drawing it back he aimed for the beast's back, which of course was not facing him.

"Shoot the arrow! Shoot the arrow!" screamed Jack. He lopped off the newly grown hand again, nimbly dodging and ducking as the waterdemon flailed blue-bloody stumps at him, spattering him with jelly-like gore.

"Not yet, Jack; I must shoot him in the back, or he will just yank it out! Get him to where his back is to me," Lackland shouted, aiming and praying that the flaming arrow lasted long enough to cause grief for the demon.

Finally, after a great deal of cursing, hacking and slashing, Jack managed to get the waterdemon's back toward Lackland who quickly fired off the arrow.

The demon shrieked, trying vainly to reach the arrow. Jack scampered out of its way. The beast started toward the river; the inside of it aglow with the burning arrow. For a moment, they just stared at the beast, all alight inside. "Don't let it in the river, for the love of God, Julian! It'll heal itself and we will be dead men," shouted Jack, suddenly coming alive.

Lackland's sword quickly sliced through the back of its left leg, causing it to pause, while Jack pressed forward hacking at its torso and arms, confusing the writhing beast.

Using the last bit of his poor new shirt, Lackland had another flaming arrow ready to go and shot it into the back of the beast's head. It stumbled to its knees, trying vainly to reach either arrow but Jack kept lopping off its arms. Lackland immediately drew his sword again and set to hacking at the brute in aid of Jack. A thin, high screech shredded their ears, as the beast tried to claw at its chest with first one bloody stump and then the other.

After what seemed like hours of chopping and slashing, the beast finally toppled to the earth. First it shuddered and then at last it stopped glowing.

"We must burn this dreadful thing so that it cannot come back to life, by some miracle," Lackland told Jack. He agreed and immediately began trying to find tinder and somewhat dry branches in the sodden brush to burn.

Lackland hacked the beast's head off, completely dismembering it, while Jack found the makings of a good fire. Then the two of them built a roaring fire and burned the carcass, which burned amazingly well. The stench from the burning bits of beast was enough to gag a maggot, but still Jack kept at it. As Jack tossed the last pieces of the beast onto the pyre, Lackland entered the lair, looking for the boy.

Upon seeing the boy, Lackland cursed, thinking him dead, but as he picked him up he could see that he was breathing and only in a deep sleep. Jack carried the lantern while Julian carried the unconscious boy back to where they had tied the horses. Lackland mounted Farroll and Jack handed the boy up to him. The now shirtless and shivering knight wrapped his cloak about himself and the child. They rode through the miserable darkness back to Limpwater, where at last the two stinking, exhausted and gory heroes delivered the boy to his worried parents.

Lackland and Slippery Jack stood in the doorway and handed the boy off to his father, Ben the Baker. His frantic mother, Bertha, begged them to "stay outside for the love of God and please do not drip whatever is causing that horrible stench on my clean floor!"

Rolling his eyes at his wife, Ben ran to get the priestess to see to healing Beau, while Bertha quickly bathed her unconscious and extremely odiferous son. Turning their tired selves toward the warmth and welcome of Billy's Revenge, Julian Lackland and

Slippery Jack silently walked their horses through the mud and back home.

"I'll take yer horses here, lads. I don't want you upsetting the rest of the horses with that stench." The ostler, Cob John, met them at the stable and took the reins of both the horses, waving Julian and Jack off to the bath house. "You stink worse than One-Shot George's boots. Hose yerselves off real good at the tap afore you dirty up the tubs lads, and burn yer clothes." He looked at the two sulky horses. "Don't you be worrying, you two," he told Farroll and Bruiser, "I've got a nice hot bath for you two also."

Farroll and Bruiser both perked right up on hearing that good news. They had not been looking forward to stinking for the next week and being the butt of cruel horsey humor.

Once they were finally sitting in well deserved tubs of lovely clean steaming water, Jack looked at Lackland and said, "Where did you come up with the idea of using fire against him? At least it gave him pause enough so that we could get enough of him hacked apart that he quit growing back."

"It was not very elegant, but it was the only thing I could think of, Jack. When he yanked that arrow out of his head and started to beat you with it, I knew we were done for unless I could find a bit of Majik that we could use," replied Julian. "But I must say, I didn't reckon on how cold a coat of mail gets on a rainy night in Limpwater when half your shirt is gone. I nearly froze my arse coming home."

Stark naked and clutching towels before them, they went up the stairs to their rooms accompanied by the appreciative hoots of the few Rowdies gathered in the common room.

"Lord, Julian, you've a nice arse, and a manly set of legs," called Merry Kat, staring for all she was worth.

"Run a bit slower, lads! Let's have a better look!" added Lucy Blue-Eyes because it was expected.

Finally dressed again, they reentered the common room, where they were greeted with warm bowls of stew and foamy mugs of ale. Merry Kat, with her flashing dark eyes, and Lucy Blue Eyes with her golden hair, sat at the table with Lady Mags whose lush mahogany curls, and the swing of her hip never failed to melt Julian. The three ladies had only just returned from routing a den of thieves for the good King. They had been paid well, and were disposed to share generously, as were all the Rowdies when one of their own had taken on a bad job for no pay.

"… and now I've lost my new shirt and my horse hates me," said Julian as they finished telling the tale to Huw and Billy. "But on the good side, there's one less waterdemon on the road to Dervy."

"I would just like to say that I don't want to do that ever again," added Slippery Jack. "I am a spy, not a demon killer." He shuddered. "I need to get me a couple of Majik amulets for handling that sort of thing."

Despite the lack of remuneration, the two heroes ended up having a merry evening. Julian Lackland and Lady Mags snuck off first, leaving Merry Kat to console Slippery Jack, while Lucy made eyes at Huw as he sang romantic ballads.

At least for Lackland, it was a somewhat happy ending. His heart had steadfastly belonged to Lady Mags since the day that he had first laid eyes on her while they were both 'doing penance' at the king's court. When Mags had so fortuitously become a fallen woman in the eyes of polite society, Julian had felt sure that he had a chance to win her hand. But as they settled in at Billy's Revenge, he had begun to realize that if he ever even breathed the words 'marry me, Mags', she would put twenty leagues between herself and him. He consoled himself with the thought that they were young; he had just turned eighteen, and she was not far behind him.

Lady Mags was never going to leave the trade, despite Sir Julian Lackland's wistful yearnings to the contrary.

Billy and Bess could have told him that, as they later agreed while preparing for bed.

"She's merc to the core, Billy. She'll foster her babes out like Stella, if the herbs don't work; you will see. Julian will never have what he so obviously wants." She disengaged young Brand from her breast, and carefully laid him in his little bed.

"Will I get what I want?" asked Billy wickedly.

"You will, you lucky sot," said Bess as she climbed back into bed.
"I am that," replied Billy happily. "I am the luckiest sot in the world."

Chapter 2 - The King's Whore

The newest Rowdy, Lucy Blue-Eyes, was blond and blue eyed, and as delicate a creature as a man could wish for; unless of course, he ran afoul of her temper and met with grief at the end of her sword. She had a sort of innocence, completely at odds with her reputation; and there was always the occasional new lad that had to be testing her un-ladylike wish to choose her own bedmates.

Lucy was known to be a cruel woman, but they loved her for it. At present, she sat before the fire doing needle-work, looking for all the world like a proper lady. Huw the Bard was madly in love with her, but he was never going to tell her so; with her history it would turn her away.

He and Julian Lackland had spent many a long hour in the saddle, on one or another occasion, commiserating about the fickleness of ladies, and the way that the winds of fate tossed a man's heart around. Huw himself was a fine, handsome man, with thick black hair and a spark in his deep blue eyes that lit his face when any woman, old or young, stout or thin came into his view.

And how the ladies loved to look at Huw, especially when he sang! There was no woman born that could look away from Huw Owyn once he strummed his harp and opened his throat to sing a love ballad.

Julian, on the other hand, was golden haired and blue-eyed, with a noble countenance of chiseled perfection. He was the very image of the knight in shining armor that quickened the heart in each fair maiden's breast; strong, and muscular, with a smile that could turn a woman's legs to jelly. His breeches clung to him just so, and many a woman's eye followed his well-formed arse appreciatively as he walked. Everyone knew he was a lap-dog begging for a morsel at the famous Lady Mags' delicate feet, but that just added to his cachet.

Billy Nine-Fingers looked around his common room, noting that there were three too many Rowdies hanging about drinking up his profits, instead of going out and saving the world as they were supposed to be doing. "Well you're not earning any gold sitting on your arses in my common room," he groused. "This is a sad day, Lackland; a sad day!"

Billy's spirits lifted somewhat when the door banged open and a man in the King's livery stood there, looking around. Seeing Julian Lackland, he ran quickly to him, saying, "Cousin! There's a problem, and you must help me."

Julian had sat up and tried to look somewhat attentive. The man was his cousin, John De Portiers, and he was often given to hysterics. "What is it now, John? Have the sheep gone mad and eaten the nasty Queen's roses again?"

"Yes, how did you know? But that is not why I am here," he said with wonder in his voice. "It's Nell Mackey, the King's Whore; she has gone missing! The king is distraught, but he really can't send the guard after her now, can he... what with the Queen and all! And he suspects that the Queen is behind it; she has that cruel jealous streak. You must find her!"

John finally gasped out the important (at least to Billy) part, "He will pay you handsomely! I have traced her to the town of Somber Flats. They have her in the

Powder Keg. I can't figure out how to spring her, cousin. You must do this!"

"The Wolves! We'll do it," said Billy, happily. "This job is a duty to our King and country, and of course, the Rowdies all know their duty." His face turned stern and he said piously, "It is also our duty to rid the world of Mercs who've turned to kidnapping defenseless whores. Bloody Bryan gives all good mercs a bad name."

"And Billy gets twenty percent off the top, plus room and board!" added Lackland with a twinkle to his eyes. "Bless his little heart; he sees to it that we work regularly!"

That is how Huw the Bard, Julian Lackland and Lucy Blue-Eyes found themselves gearing up to go out and rescue a highly respected whore.

"Tell me again why we are riding into Wolves territory?" commented Huw. "They are considered to be touchy about that."

"It is just a job, Huw. It is a job like any other. I'm good for maybe four or five of them, and I am sure you two are at least as good, so that takes care of twelve. They are sure to all be there if they have taken the King's whore." Julian finished buckling on his sword belt. "She is a prize they will be guarding well."

"Stealth and cunning is what is required in this matter," replied Lucy, with a glint in her eye. "This is woman's work. Leave it to me boys, I will get us in and out with none of our blood being shed AND we will bring out The Whore safely."

"If you say so, Lucy," said Huw. He had only recently begun going out on the occasional foray with the Rowdies. This was his first big job, and he was sure that there was great potential for a good ballad in it.

"You shall be our captain then, Lucy," replied Sir Julian. They mounted up and trotted smartly down the dusty road toward Somber Flats. "You devise the plan and we shall carry it out."

This was Lucy's third job with the Rowdies; she had previously been a young lady of quality whose brother had gambled away the family fortune. Just before he drank himself to death, he had sold his fourteen year old sister in an effort to pay off his debts. Lucy, being a girl with a strong sense of survival had one night slit the throat of the depraved beast who had 'owned' her. He had for two years been selling her body to young nobles with unsavory habits. She left his house that night with her horse and a stolen sword. When she turned up at Billy's Revenge, Bess had told Billy to hire her, despite the fact that she had no experience as a merc. *She has what it takes, and she was born to do this sort of work. If you don't hire her you are a fool. She is worth three men.*

Along about noon, they were approaching the somewhat depressing town of some seven-hundred souls. "How shall we do this? Do we just walk in and say 'Give us the whore, we know you have her'?" Huw looked at Lucy.

Lucy giggled, saying "I will do that part. You two will skulk about in the shrubbery outside the back of the place until I find out where she is being kept. Then we will get her free and get us out of here. But first, we will do it in such a way that they do not realize that they are short one whore, until we are long since gone from here."

Leaving the main road before they could see the Powder Keg, they quietly walked their horses down a dusty side street and around to the field of scrubby shrubbery and pine trees at the far back side of the stables. Quietly they led the horses through the tall brush and hid them where any noises that horses might make would not be out of place, and where the two men had a good view of the back side of the Powder Keg. Lucy left her mail coat and sword on her fine little mare, Pansy.

Checking to make sure her knives were all secure and handy, she pulled out of her saddlebag a flower bedecked bonnet, a lacy shawl and a sweet little beaded purse. She primped her hair and adjusted her skirts. Before their very eyes, she became a featherheaded young lady of quality who was suffering some distress; having lost her horse on the road. Winking saucily at them, she walked around to the front door, entering apprehensively.

The front door of the common room at the Powder Keg swung open and a frightened young lady stood timidly for a moment, before she got up the courage to enter. Staring about the room, the terrified girl finally saw the innkeeper and hurried over to him.

"Sir, have you a room available for a lady? I have come from Bekenberg and have lost my horse on the trade-road, the wretched thing." She looked appealingly at the poor inn-keeper who immediately succumbed to her patented innocent blue-eyed look. "My name is Lucinda...er..., but most call me Cindy...I had to leave without my servants, though I hope that they are following me." She deliberately did not mention a surname, implying that she had run away.

"Call me Bryan, my dear. Aye, lass, we do. We have a room to spare. What does your horse look like?"

22

The inn-keeper was the man known in the trade as Bloody Bryan, for the reason that when he killed a man, he liked to play with him first. Bryan had seized control of the Wolves and the Powder Keg when Bastard John disappeared, and many credited him with killing the Bastard and hiding the evidence, but no one could prove it. He was known to be an unsavory man; dangerous to allow around young girls and boys alike. Merry Kat and Stella One-Eye had left the Wolves and gone to the Rowdies when the leadership changed hands; as had Johnny Malone and all of them refused to talk about it.

"Well, he has a saddle…" The poor girl wracked her brain, "and saddlebags," she added helpfully.

Bryan didn't so much as blink an eye. "I will roust some of these louts to go and look for your horse, while you get yourself settled," and so saying, he grabbed two of his men. "You, Dick, and you, Tom, get your arses out there and find the lady's horse."

"How will we know that it is her horse when we find it?" asked Tom Saunders who had been drinking steadily all morning. "There could be any number of horses out there."

Bryan rolled his eyes, "Yer the stupidest git, Tom. It will be the one with the saddle and saddlebags, all ready to be ridden."

"Oh, right," said Tom. "I knew that."

"Well, git then!" Bryan shooed them out the door. "Off with you! Down the trade-road toward Bekenberg. The damned horse can't have gone too far, you bloody idiots; the lady has walked here! If you come back without it, I will hang you by your nuts, so look sharp for it!" They looked at each other and shrugged, walking quickly out to the stables.

Bryan showed her to her room which was on the corner of the second floor, and of course, faced the rear and the stables, as the Wolves occupied the front rooms. That was well known throughout the trade; the mercs always got the best rooms since they were the bread and butter of any town. He led her down the corridor, past a room that was heavily guarded, taking her to the room next to it.

As soon as Bryan left, she opened the window. She sat for about ten minutes and then she went back down to the common room, walking past the two guards at the room next door. Glancing fearfully at them, 'Cindy' hurried down to the common room.

"Have you any tea? I…don't have my maid so…" she allowed a tear to fill her luminous blue eyes.

"There, there," said Bryan with a comforting leer. "I will send some tea up to you and a maid, though you will have to share her services. Another, er, lady has arrived with no maid only last evening."

"Oh," replied Cindy, "Did she lose her horse too?"

"Aye," said Bryan, momentarily taken aback. With a rather nasty smirk he said, "She did lose her stallion, though we immediately settled that little matter. She now has a better horse to ride."

"Wonderful! Perhaps she would consent to having tea with me, both of us being temporarily alone in the world." Having said that, 'Cindy' went back up the stairs and walked quickly past the guarded door to await the arrival of the maid.

*

Meanwhile as Lucy went into the inn, Julian and Huw settled down in the shrubbery to wait for a signal from her. Soon a window on the corner of second floor was thrown open, the signal that Lucy had been successful in getting herself established.

"Now we wait," whispered Julian. "Once it is dark, she will tell us what to do."

"I just hope she doesn't get herself killed," muttered Huw. "It seems a mad plan."

"You must have faith in the ladies," replied Julian. "They are more dangerous than you can imagine. I almost feel sorry for Bloody Bryan, although he has earned everything he has coming to him."

"We must somehow hobble the horses so they can't come after us," suggested Huw worriedly.

"I don't like to hurt the poor beasts, and the Wolves themselves for the most part are decent enough. It is Bryan that has them under contract and they can't break it; you know the terms. But we could misplace their tack when their ostler and stable-hands all go in for their supper," replied Julian with a thoughtful tone to his voice. "If we hide their harnesses, they will not be able to ride after us since most of them are unable to ride bareback."

"I can't ride bareback either, Lackland," muttered Huw. "I never even had a horse of my own until I came to Billy's Revenge! Where I come from, it's only the gentry can own a horse. But a Bard soon learned to love Shank's Mare, down in the Eynier Valley, before the troubles came."

"Troubles?" Julian was interested. Huw had just appeared out of nowhere one rainy night, two months before, and it had been clear that he was running from something dire, though he had refused to discuss it. "Trained bards are rare up here, Huw. I know by your looks and your accent that you are from the south; all the trained bards are from the south. What sort of troubles?"

"Trouble that would make a stone weep, Julian," replied Huw, with a bleak look in his usually merry blue eyes. "Trouble that could get me killed if it gets out that I am here in the north. There's a reason bards are rare," he met Julian's gaze and held it. "The one duty a bard has, above all, is to see to it that the truth is told."

Julian nodded. "Bards are the only source of news for most people, and have safe passage wherever they may travel because their impartiality is an integral part of their craft."

"Not anymore," muttered Huw. "There's a Grand Duke in the Eynier Valley that dislikes the truth. He has the power to do what he wants, despite the king's laws. He has sent out his murdering thugs to do the dirty work for him. They have hunted down and murdered every Bard in the long valley. I am the last fully trained bard you will ever meet, so far as I know. King Henri will have to deal with him, and do it soon, if he wants to keep the long valley and the southern port."

"Tell me everything you know about this," replied Julian, realizing that this could be the beginning of another clan war in the Eynier Valley. "This poses a threat to Henri's rule, and that cannot be allowed! I will see to it that Henri is made aware of the state of affairs down there. We cannot afford to lose the port city of Ludwellyn, and the Eynier people cannot afford to lose the protection of the crown in the long valley. They will be overrun by Lanqueshire the minute that happens."

"Don't you just know it!" said Huw, his eyes flashing. "But the Grefyn's are notoriously shortsighted."

*

Just as Lucy was sitting at her dressing table, wishing for something to do, there was a timid knock upon her door. On opening it, she discovered a shy young maid standing there. "My name is Mary," said the girl. "I am to help you, Lady Cindy, until your horse is found." Mary was a rather hollow cheeked, underfed looking girl of perhaps twelve. She was rather thick in the middle, and had many bruises on her face and arms. Some were very recent, and some were older. Her mute anguish of a personal nature touched Lucy's heart.

"I am thinking of waiting here for my footmen," she told the girl. "I am sure they are following me, and they will be bringing my girl Bess with them. Then you won't have to do double duty."

"Oh, it is no trouble," Mary replied. "The other lady is no trouble at all, she never asks for a thing, and she just sits and cries all the time, poor thing." Mary clapped her hand to her mouth, looking over her shoulder. "Oh, Miss! I should never have spoken out of turn like that!"

"Never mind, Mary," 'Cindy' said gently. "It is no disgrace to worry about a poor sad lady. Perhaps she and I can share some tea if she would like. Mayhap that would cheer her up. In the meantime, I must write a letter. Can you bring me the necessary items?"

"Of course, my lady," Mary replied, bobbing her head in a curtsey and backing out of the room.

Somewhat later, another knock resounded on 'Cindy's' door. Upon opening it, she found Mary waiting there with the things she had requested. "Lady Nell, the other lady, would like to share supper with you so that you will not have to go alone, down to the common-room. But you will have to dine in her room as she does not go out."

"Of course, that would be wonderful to have someone to talk to," answered 'Cindy'. "I am not dressed properly for dinner, but perhaps she will understand." She allowed herself to appear insecure.

"Oh I am sure she will; she is a wonderfully kind lady," said Mary, smiling tremulously. "She also came away without her trunks, and has only the clothes on her back."

While she waited for the knock upon the door, she busied herself with writing three notes. The first was one for Julian and Huw, which she dropped fluttering out the window, to lay there waiting for them to collect it. The second note which she signed with her true name was to be slipped up her own sleeve, and then given to Lady Nell upon her departure after their dinner, alerting her to the rescue.

The third note was to be sealed and given to Mary for Bryan to post. It was a note to her 'father' in Castleton detailing the dreadful abuse that the husband he had chosen for her (a cretin named 'Lord Reginald St. Clare') had inflicted upon her person. It graphically detailed many perverted acts that should keep Bloody Bryan quite busy with reading it, before he resealed it and sent it on. The St. Clare name should definitely interest Bryan, sounding as if it were a noble house with connections to the throne. Her 'father's' name should interest Bryan too, 'Duke Langford St. Stephen'. There was great ransom potential in the letter she gave to Mary.

Soon Mary's knock sounded on the door, and after handing the girl the letter to be posted, she followed her to the guarded door. She pretended to look fearfully at the two massive guards she entered the room. The guards left the door open, so as to allow the ladies no privacy.

A small table set for two had been drawn up before the fire. Lady Nell sat quietly in the darkened room. As Cindy drew closer, she could see fresh bruises on her face and throat, and broken skin on her shoulder. The dazed, broken look in Nell's brown eyes said that she had been used roughly, and against her will, stirring Lucy's righteous anger.

Lucy introduced herself, saying simply, "I am Lucinda, but my friends call me Cindy." That was said for the guards' sake.

"I am Nell," replied the woman. Her voice was a rich, melodic contralto. She was a dark-haired, fine-boned, delicate woman of high breeding and good education. She might be the King's Whore, but she had been born a squire's daughter. Her kidnapper or someone had decided that she was simply a whore, and they had raped her, more than once by the desolate look of her. "I am just Nell."

As they ate their meal, they discussed all the things that proper ladies discussed when dining with new acquaintances. There was nothing of substance in their conversation, but Lucy found herself admiring this woman, whom everyone knew loved the good king.

After thinking about Little Mary and Nell, Lucy decided that a little vengeance should be added to the evening's events. With only a little small talk regarding her own supposed adventures that day, implying that she would rather not talk about it, she discovered that Bryan was indeed the culprit. The look on Nell's face when Cindy mentioned the 'nice innkeeper' told her all she needed to know.

"Trust no one, Cindy," she urgently tried to warn her. "This place is full of evil men. Trust no one!" Her fear for Lucy's safety touched Lucy deeply, but she dared not try to comfort the poor woman.

Upon leaving, 'Cindy' took Nell's hand and pressed it repeatedly between her own two hands, telling her how glad she was to meet her. Then she exited past the guards and entered her own room, leaving Nell clutching the note and pretending that nothing more than a handshake had passed between them. She shut the door to her room, and locked it.

"Have you saved us any supper, Lucy?" Huw's whisper came from the shadows of the room. Julian knelt in the shadows beside him.

"Here love; it is all I could steal without drawing attention. It should hold you over until we get back to Limpwater." She pulled half a loaf of bread and a large chunk of cheese from the pockets of her skirt, along with an apple; all of which, he and Julian shared between them. "She is in the room next to me, and two brutes guard her door."

"What is she like, our King's Whore?" Huw was interested on a purely professional level, as he was already creating a ballad in his head.

"She is a true lady, Huw; a kind and gentle lady. And our good inn-keeper has not been a kind host to her. I suspect that I too will be receiving a visit from our good host soon, and so back out the window you go.

"Thank you for remembering us when you had your supper, Lucy. You are a darling," Julian whispered. "I will leave the rope as it is for you. Close the window on it and draw the curtains and he will not notice anything out of place. Try to be neat when you gut him, Lucy."

With that they silently climbed out her window and down the rope. She closed the window on the rope, and drew the drapes closed.

Mary came and offered to help her prepare for bed, apologizing for having to divide her time. The poor girl hung her dress in the wardrobe and then turned down the lamp, wishing her a good night with a worried look; saying "Please be sure to lock the door behind me, Lady Cindy, to help keep you safe." Looking over her shoulder, she quickly said, "Don't open the door for anyone. Not anyone!" Lucy patted her hand and locked up after her.

"Mary knows Bryan's ways, I am sure of that," Lucy thought as she locked the door behind Mary. "Poor thing, she has no choice but to do as he says."

Mary's waistline was definitely rather thick and Lucy nodded, saying to herself, "He's gone and got her with a bun in the oven. She can't be much more than a girl, the dirty old bugger. If she has even barely had her first flow, I would be surprised."

*

The two guards at the door to Nell's room stiffened as Bryan walked past them, winking jauntily at them. "I will just spend a few moments to comfort the dear waif in the room just yonder, so if you should hear a bit of a scuffle, pay it no mind."

Lucy lay naked under the blankets pretending to sleep. After Mary had left, she had quickly taken off her chemise and under-drawers, not wishing to bloody them. She had to wear them home and she hated ruining her clothes. She had then hidden her silken belts and her scarf under her pillow, and secreted a special knife under the edge of the mattress near the foot of the bed. It was her favorite knife, good for all sorts of purposes.

Lying in the bed she waited, and smiled inwardly as she heard her quarry's muffled voice saying something to the guards at Nell's door. Then she heard her door unlock itself, and felt rather than heard Bryan slip inside. She listened to the quiet rustle of his clothes, as he took off his breeches and his shirt, and felt the cold air as he raised the blankets and slid naked into bed next to her. She felt his surprise as he found her naked, sliding his hand over her breast and then down her stomach.

"Was you expecting company then, Cindy?" asked Bryan, his surprise turning to pleasure.

"I rather thought you might pay me a visit, to keep me safe from the bad men who infest this inn," she replied. She felt his pleasure firmly against her leg as she turned toward him in a lover's embrace; kissing him passionately, and entangling his arms in the blankets; then kissing his throat, his belly, his manhood and back up to his chest, while he moaned, "Cindy..."

Then she whispered, "I want to give you a treat, because you have been so nice to me. I know you will remember it for the rest of your life. Are you the sort of man to try something a little different?" At his wondering nod, she took her silken belts from under her pillow and gently tied his wrists to the bedposts, using a technique that was her own creation. Each movement he made tightened the bonds a little more. Then she arranged the pillows so that his head was comfortably propped up, but not able to move from side to side. Though Bryan did not realize it, he could only look forward.

Smiling innocently she took her scarf and gagged him, muffling his voice quite effectively.

He had begun to look a bit worried at that, but she gently kissed his throat, chest and stomach, caressing him; and as she progressed downwards he relaxed, rising rhythmically to meet her ministrations.

She had deliberately left his legs free. Each movement of his made the bed squeak, and tightened the bonds that held his wrists.

Then she began working on him in earnest.

Hooking her feet over his muscular biceps she straddled his chest and kissed his belly so that he was looking at her maidenly buttocks spread before his wondering eyes, and unable to look away. Bound and gagged as he was, he could only look and appreciate the roundness and the view.

Gently, tenderly she reached between his legs with her soft white hands, and he soon gave himself up to her, thinking to himself that she was an amazingly perverted little minx; and the bed made some very satisfying noises as Bryan gave it all he had, grunting with the effort.

It was then, that with her soft, delicate hands and sharp little knife, she unmanned him. Shrieks erupted from his throat, but her gag muted them; he actually sounded like a girl being forced against her will. That was a thought that made Lucy smile happily.

His flailing legs made the bed squeak rhythmically, and his feet made desperate thumping noises that were completely in keeping with that which he had planned for her. She allowed that to go on for a certain length of time; all the while his girlish shrieks and howls were muffled by the neat little gag. The more he struggled, the tighter his wrists were bound to the bed posts, and still he was forced to look at her fine, delicate arse spread wide before him, the last view he would ever see.

At last Lucy sat up. Sitting squarely on his face she smothered him with her buttocks, cutting off his air supply. As he struggled, she stabbed her bloody knife into him several times and finally into his heart, and all the while the rhythmic squeaking of the bed rose to a thundering climax.

The guards outside of Nell's door rolled their eyes at the muffled cries and enthusiastically squeaking and thumping bed in the room next door. As the sounds rose to a crescendo, Jim said wryly, "He do enjoy his sport, don't he, Bill."

"Regularly," replied Bill. "Give him an hour's rest, and he'll be at the one in this room again."

"And then he'll be at Mary, poor thing. Bryan's a beast, Bill. Bastard John would never have tolerated his doings. He was a bastard, but he had some class," said Jim with a disgusted look. "These poor gals…but what can we do? We signed the paper when he took over; he's the boss. I'm jumping to a different crew when my time here is up. I don't want to have the reputation this crew has now. We won't get any decent contracts with this hanging over our heads, even if the Queen did authorize it."

Bill agreed with him whole-heartedly, and then said, "He's in fine form tonight; he's been at it for twice as long as usual." Bill's discomfort and disgust were as evident as Jim's.

The squeaking bed, thumping and muted shrieks went on for a while longer and then died off.

As the noises died away, Bill and Jim visibly relaxed, each desperately wishing that there was a legal way out of their contracts.

As Bloody Bryan at last fell silent, Lucy felt no pity on looking down at his horrified face and staring eyes, forever locked on the ceiling as if begging for help. She collected her belts, removed her gag and neatly placed his balls in his open mouth.

Leaving his bloody corpse in the bed, she retrieved her knife and cleaned it carefully so that it would not lose its edge. Giving herself and her scarf as thorough a bath as she was able in the basin on her dresser, she dressed herself and repaired her hair. After checking her appearance in the mirror one last time, she tossed her possessions out the window and climbed down the rope. Julian was waiting for her. He gave the rope a peculiar twist and flip, and then pulled it. Deftly catching the claw as it came down, he coiled it up and silently they moved to the ground underneath Nell's room. Her window was open, just as Lucy's note had instructed her to do.

Standing back, Julian tossed the hook through, and gave it the peculiar twist that secured it. Without any further thought, Lucy climbed up, and gently helped Nell out the window. "Go ahead and climb down, Lackland will not let you fall no matter what, and we are not too high up anyway."

Nell hugged her, asking her if she was okay. "I am fine, Nell. I promise you it was not me who suffered this night," Lucy assured her. "I will tell you what happened once we are gone from here."

"But the noises... Are you sure you are okay?" Nell's worried eyes looked searchingly at Lucy who repeatedly reassured her. At last convinced, Nell turned to the window. Without a sign that she was fearful, Nell bravely climbed out the window, clinging to the rope and losing her grip partway down. Julian caught her, lowering her to the ground. Lucy followed, and once again Julian retrieved the rope.

"Oh Lackland! I am in terrible trouble now. You should have left me," Nell told him miserably. "You should have left me."

"No Nell. Sh… it will be fine, you will see," replied Lackland, holding her and comforting her as she sobbed against his shoulder. "I will see to it that it is all made right, trust me."

Huw was waiting behind the stable for them, with an extra horse saddled for Nell. Soon they were off, traveling through the night towards Limpwater and Billy's Revenge. "How did you know which horse was mine?" Nell asked with wonder, "And my saddle…Henri gave it to me…" her voice broke on Henri's name, but Huw pretended not to notice.

"'Tis a simple thing, my Lady; 'twas the only horse here with the crown tattooed in her ear, and the only lady's saddle and gear in the stable. The women won't work for Bloody Bryan."

"No one will have to work for him ever again," said Lucy grimly. As they traveled, Lucy told the tale of Bloody Bryan's untidy end, finishing her tale with, "The Wolves have lost two leaders in less than two years. I think it may be bad luck to be their boss."

"Who would think that you could do such a thing when you are so innocent looking," said Nell, wonderingly. "When I read your note, I thought you to be audacious, but when I heard the thumping from next door I thought that he had done you, as he did to… me," her voice trailed off, and she shuddered; once again she had that shattered quality that tugged so at Lucy's heart-strings.

"Lady Nell, I swear to you that he will never do such a thing to anyone again," replied Lucy with a glint in her eye and steel in her voice. "He thought he was going to have me, but I had him."

"Remind me to be very polite to you, Lucy Blue-Eyes, when I take leave of your room of a morning," muttered Huw, the whites of his eyes showing in the darkness. "Sometimes you are a scary woman, Lucy-love!"

"You are too decent and innocent a man, Huw. You can't imagine the filth that lies in the hearts of people," said Lucy sadly. "You are far too good for one such as me. I am full to the brim with vengeance and you do not deserve that."

"My Lady Nell," began Julian, but Nell interrupted him.

"I am no lady, as you know very well, Sir Julian. I am just plain Nell Mackey, the daughter of Squire Mackey of Tula; and until yesterday, I was the King's Whore. But no longer; it seems that the Queen has taken exception to my presence in her husband's life." Her voice was hurt and angry as she continued her tale, "The woman could have simply ordered me to go away, and I would have done so. She did not have to give me to that brute. I would not have done such to her."

"My Lady, and despite your protestations to the contrary, you are every inch a lady. You are more than welcome in Limpwater," said Sir Julian. "You will find though, that his Majesty does not know that you are no longer his Whore. It was he who sent us after you, and he whom I think you will find, waiting for you in Limpwater."

Nell was silent, and then she said brokenly, "I am fit for no man, especially as good a man as is my King."

Huw and Julian looked at each other. They had seen that sort of reaction before and knew that only time would heal it, so they dropped back and let Lucy take over, murmuring comforting words to Nell.

Soon they arrived in Limpwater. The lamps were lit, welcoming them back. As they entered the stable, they noticed two fine horses that were unfamiliar to Huw and Lucy.

"'Tis Henri and John De Portiers," said Nell. "What will I say to him? How can I ever make this right? I can't. I signed my own death warrant when I did not have the strength to fight that beast off." She was trembling, and Julian had to lift her down from her horse.

"Nell, it was none of your doing," said Julian. "What has happened has happened and you cannot change it. But you did not cause it, and you should not have to pay for it. You will feel better after a bath, and a change of clothing. Trust me Nell; have I ever let you down?"

Pulling herself together, she said with a peculiarly grim note, "I am the King's Whore, Julian. It is a title that comes with a price, and you of all people know very well what that price is. That price is absolute fidelity. Now that bond between us has been broken, and whether it was my fault or not, I am no longer fit for him. The penalty is death." Her voice shook as she said those words. "That is just as well, Julian. Henri was the first and only man I ever had."

Her voice broke and she trembled violently as she said, "Now I am sullied, and no amount of washing will clean my soul." Tears flowed down her face. "How could I ever again go to the best of men when the worst of men has destroyed me? Dying will be easy, so easy compared with explaining to Henri what that beast did to me. Lucy was too gentle with him." With that she turned and followed Lucy to the women's baths where her own maid was waiting for her.

Julian looked at Huw, and said, "We had best see his majesty first. Baths later, eh?"

Huw nodded. "Mayhap we can still be of assistance to the poor lady. She should not have to pay for this."

And so it was that Sir Julian 'Lackland' De Portiers found himself once again giving counsel to the king. "Where is she? Is she safe?" Henri Dragoran's face and voice reflected his tension.

"She is safe. She is in the women's bath, guarded by the finest guards you will ever know, Sire. But I must talk to you privately; will you walk with me for a moment? Huw will see to our privacy." They stepped out to the front steps, and stood in the pool of light cast by the lantern. Huw followed, standing guard at the door to insure that they were not disturbed.

Julian looked at his cousin and saw that he was grey and ill with worry. "Henri, you know that the queen wishes your relationship with Lady Nell to end. She has gone to great lengths to insure that it does just that."

"How great? Is Nell injured?" Henri's eyes betrayed his worry. "Tell me what has happened."

"She has been violated, which has harmed her more than I can tell you. She is shattered," Julian told him the truth as bluntly as possible, getting it out in the open so that it did not lie festering in the dark unmentionable corners of polite conversation. "Lucy is working with Lady Nell, trying to help her heal somewhat. I think Lady Nell should remain here for a few days, anyway. Lucy and the other ladies of the Rowdies are the right people to help Lady Nell get past the pain and humiliation, and fear of your wrath. But what Lady Nell needs is for you to be a real husband to her, as I know you feel yourself to be. You must tell her that you know it is not her fault; that she did not cause this to happen. She needs to know that you love her."

Henri Dragoran was silent for a stunned moment. "My God, Julian! You don't understand it at all! It is a law, Julian! My own law! The law of my own making, made to protect Nell from that bitch and now she has turned it against me to force me to kill an innocent!"

Henri clenched his fist and slammed it into the wall and then pulled at his hair. "Aaugh!!! Aaugh!!! Tell me that is a lie! Tell me that you lie!"

"Sire, I am sworn to tell you only the truth and that is what I now tell you. What are you going to do?" Julian had stood his ground against the King's rage. "The lady needs you."

"Do? Julian do you understand what that bitch, Queen Morganna of Lournes has forced me to do? I *must* have Nell executed for infidelity now, because that witch arranged it. *I* must be the one to kill the woman *I* love, because that bitch from Lournes has plotted to arrange it in just this way!" Henri paced back and forth, tearing at his hair. "It is not bad enough that she gave my own precious Nell to those bastards to use as a common trollop! She now has forced me into this corner! If I do not execute Nell, I am breaking my own law! Why, tis the very law that I made, so that no one could take Nell away from my side. I was forced to marry the bitch princess of Lournes, for the good of the country, instead of Nell the commoner for the good of my heart!"

"I know of that law. If Nell had gone to this of her own free will, then that would be your right under the law. But sire, what about the law that says that the crown must protect and defend the citizens above all?" asked Julian. "Lady Nell was put into harm's way by the Queen's actions. The Queen has made a mockery of the Royal Obligation to protect and defend by doing so, and has tarnished your own reputation incalculably! You are the supreme source of justice here in Waldeyn. True justice would be for you to take into account that the Queen deliberately sold a woman to a man, who was known to be a sadistic rapist. Her intent was that if she survived his unkindly attentions, she would then be murdered at your hand!"

Henri was stunned into silence by Julian's logic. The light of hope shone in his eyes; hope that two great wrongs could be righted by this debacle.

"Justice... yes Julian, justice is exactly what will be the result of this tragedy. You will see. I will be rid of Morganna of Lournes, and Nell will be my Queen as she should have been in the first place. Had it not been for my late, unlamented mother's meddling in politics, it would have come to pass." Henri clasped Julian's shoulder. "I wish you would come back to court, I need you there cousin. I am surrounded by idiots."

"One day, perhaps. I am not ready to leave the life I have here," replied Julian. "I am not done saving the world."

"You are not done loving Lady Mags, you mean," said Henri with a knowing smile. "She will never marry you, cousin. She is a wild bird. She would see it as a cage."

"I know, Henri," replied Julian. A look of desolation passed fleetingly across his face; so fleeting that one might have imagined it. "But that is of no great matter; we must see to getting you and the lady taken care of tonight."

"What shall we do about the bastard that did this to my Nell?" Henri was still enraged. "Some retribution is in order, I think."

"Ah... as to that... well...how should I put this... it seems that during his attempt to rape our Lucy; the rapist fell on Lucy's knife and accidentally castrated himself before inadvertently stabbing himself through several vital organs and finally the heart," Julian replied, carefully. "He was apparently quite a clumsy man."

Henri stood stunned for a moment, and began laughing. Soon he was roaring, and more than one head inside turned their way, wondering what could be giving the King fits, though he was known to be a most jolly king.

Once Henri had recovered, Julian said, "But now, sire, there is a matter that I have only found out about today, which you must somehow deal with."

When Huw the Bard created the ballad of 'How the Rowdies Saved the King's Whore Twice in One Night' he was rather vague as to the details regarding the demise of Bloody Bryan the Ball-less.

It turned out that poor little Mary was actually Bastard John's daughter, and should have had the Powder Keg as her inheritance when her mother died at Bloody Bryan's gentle hands. King Henri took possession of the Powder Keg, to hold in trust for Mary, as payment for her suffering. It was now a public house and would never house a mercenary company again. He sent a steward to manage it for Mary and her babe until a good husband could be found for her.

The Ladies of the Rowdies took young Mary in hand, and taught her how to be a lady and yet still be able to get the tough jobs done. They also helped her to get beyond what Bryan had done to her. Over the space of the next two years, Mary bloomed into a lovely and genteel woman, who was truly a lady despite the trauma of her past.

Much to his own surprise Dennys the Steward, a landless younger son of a squire, one day found himself in love and married the girl. He raised her daughter as his own, declaring himself to be the happiest man in Waldeyn.

*

Some few weeks after the kidnapping, a crown messenger rode into Limpwater and tacked a notice up on the wall of the chapel. The notice announced that the traitorous Queen, Morganna of Lournes, had been tried by the high council of Waldeyn. She had been found to be guilty of the crime of failing to defend the people of Waldeyn, and for consorting with and employing a known rapist to kidnap and rape Nell Mackey. Her efforts were to compel the King to abandon his duty to his people and murder the woman he loved.

It was announced, that therefore, the marriage of Henri Dragoran, hereditary King of Waldeyn, and Morganna Maria Siones, youngest daughter of King Carlos of Lournes, had been annulled. The former queen had been summarily executed. Her father had sent his deepest apologies, and ten kegs of his finest ice-brandy as recompense for his daughter's perfidy.

The same messenger also posted a bill announcing the marriage of the King to Nell Mackey, who had lately been known as the King's Whore. There were celebrations all over Waldeyn on hearing that great news.

Lady Mags had smiled grimly upon reading that. Her days in Morganna's court had been quite enlightening as to the foreign woman's true nature.
One year to the day after Morganna's demise, the people celebrated the birth of twins, Harry and Lucinda Dragoran to good Queen Nell and King Henri; the best King and Queen a country ever had.

Chapter 3 - The Ladies Clean House

That same day, while Julian, Huw and Lucy were down in the town of Somber Flats rescuing the King's Whore, the ladies of the Rowdies were taking the long road to the nunnery at Hyola, but not as a pleasure trip.

Not three hours after the three had left to rescue Nell, the ladies returned from guarding the book merchant, Evan Fallon, on his journey to Castleton and back. While the ladies were still in the baths, Billy Nine-Fingers had received an urgent visit from the Fat Friar.

This time, Friar Robert was not only stone cold sober, but in severe distress of a religious nature. A lone survivor had stumbled into the chapel, gasping that the nunnery had been attacked and burned to the ground by a band of foreign mercenaries who had come into Waldeyn from Lanqueshire. "They were holy women, Billy! Who will tend to the wounded, the sick and the poor with no other refuge? Sister Genevieve will stay here and try to build an infirmary, but who will stop those beasts?"

Apparently the marauders were no longer welcome in Lanqueshire. In an effort to avoid the hangman's noose, they had emigrated to Waldeyn, but had neglected to inform either their own former government of their departure or the Waldeyn Census Taker of their new residency.

As soon as the ladies had bathed and eaten, they were on the road again, this time heading to the mountain nunnery of Hyola. Chicken Mickey had outfitted them while they bathed, and Mags had gone through the list of supplies and signed off. With fresh horses under them, they had immediately headed to Hyola. Lady Mags was leading, as was usual, accompanied by Merry Kat, Annie Fitz and Babs Gentry.

Although they would have enjoyed a night in their own beds, there was no one else available for this job. Sometimes it happened that way; you came in, cleaned up and went right back out. Other times, you spent a week languishing in the common room waiting for a job. It was all of a piece.

Lady Mags wore her new scale-armor, a brigandine specially made for her by Gertie the Smith. It was the product of an idea that Gertie had for a while. It had cost four golds, but it was more than worth it. Gertie was sure the other gals would buy their own, once they saw how well it did for Mags. Unlike the armor that she made for the men, this was lighter than a mail shirt, made to fit a woman. It protected the shapely torso that left the boys speechless and dry-mouthed when she walked past them. The ladies of the Rowdies were women and proud of it, none more so than Lady Mags. Gertie was a master-smith, despite the fact that her father had never accorded her what she was due. The Rowdies were proud to have her as their armorer.

Lovely Ethel, Limpwater's own dressmaker, had been a Lady Rowdy, but she had married Bert the Tailor when he had lost his left leg to a highwayman's sword and had to retire. Ethel made the ladies their special riding outfits, that in no way pretended to be boy's clothing. Outfits showing off as it did, the fine, fit figures of the fighting women of the Rowdies. Full, divided ankle-length skirts, over high-heeled riding boots, showed nothing a lady would not wish to show, and emphasized everything that she did wish to flaunt. Ethel had made their bodices specifically to be worn under mail or armor, and yet it was stylish and very flattering in every way when the lady was not wearing mail or armor. Her surcoats were to die for, completely hiding the fact that the lady was armored; and each of the ladies owned at least two of the embroidered creations.

Everyone in Waldeyn traveled by horse, and there was not a woman at the Court of King Henri who would not kill to have a dress like a Rowdy's riding dress. The dressmakers at the court blatantly copied Ethel's designs, but her flair was evident, despite their best efforts.

Lovely Ethel had also created special hats, working with Gertie the smith. Wide-brimmed to keep off the sun and the rain, but lined in the crown with Gertie's best steel. These hats were helmets, and nothing less; though that was a secret known only to ladies. Lovely Ethel had padded and covered the steel helm inside with good felt and out with silk and velvet. She then created new fancies for them, every now and then, so as to disguise and lend a variety of style to them. What one saw, when one looked at a Lady Rowdy's hat, was a confection of silk and velvet. The Ladies of the Rowdies were known by all to be as stylish as they were effective.

As they rode out of town, they made a colorful and gaily decorated group of ladies. One would never have suspected that they were anything but well-heeled ladies on a pilgrimage to the nunnery. Taking the southern fork of the Hyola road out of Limpwater, the ladies rode until dark, making camp near the banks of the River Limpwater. It was Babs' turn to cook; a job that none of them were particularly good at, and at which Babs was particularly bad at.

Early the next morning, they were on their horses and riding west toward Hyola before the sun was fully up. Hyola Nunnery was the spiritual center for the Sisters of St. Anan; healing priestesses, all women with the gift of healing Majik. It was the place that they went to be trained in the use of their gifts before they went out into the world.

Hyola was also a refuge for the abused women of all stations in society, those who had no other place to go.

It was late afternoon when they clattered into the courtyard of the Nunnery. They were met with nothing but still faintly smoking ruins and bloated corpses, exactly as they had expected. The chickens had been scattered and now wandered aimlessly, wondering where their ladies were and who would feed them.

The marauders, had of course, violated every one of them including the children, and then murdered them. All that was of value had been looted, though there was little enough of that, and then the buildings and outbuildings had been set afire.

"All of this was done for the sake of a few golden holy-relics," murmured Mags as she surveyed the ruins from her horse Dove's back. "If you combined all of them in one bag, they did not equal in value the least of these lives."

Only the youngest full sister, Sister Genevieve had survived. She had been out back feeding the chickens, and had run to the woods; hiding as the outlaws rode into the compound, shrieking their own personal war-cries and riding down any poor woman who tried to run.

Two old men had been in the men's barracks; they too had been butchered as they tried to defend the nuns. It had taken Genevieve four days to reach Limpwater, deeply in shock and ill from not being properly dressed. She had spent three nights exposed to the cold and rain. Billy and Bess were caring for her, as well as they could, and had sent for the healing priestess in Somber Flats to come and tend to her.

"Well ladies, we must bury these good women," Mags told the girls grimly. "One large common grave will have to do it." It was long after dark before they finished praying over the cairn for the souls of the fallen. The four ladies were in a dark mood indeed by the time all the work was done.

Merry Kat had two chickens roasted for a late supper, though none of them were hungry, being depressed by the stench and appalling brutality of the scene. They would take the cold remains with them in the morning.

"Now we must discover where these deadmen have gone," Lady Mags announced. Her voice was a steely tone as they drew water from the well and bathed themselves and washed their clothes up by the light of the smoking torches.

Her words, in referring to the marauders as 'deadmen', meant that Lady Mags had tried and convicted them and was going to see the sentence carried out; a sentiment echoed by the rest of the ladies.

"They are obviously men of great ability and confidence, that they would dare treat holy women and their pensioners thusly." Annie Fitz was a hard-faced woman of few words and lightning reflexes. She rarely discussed her life before the Rowdies, but she had come from a wealthy family; it was evident in her speech and her demeanor. Something had happened, something that turned her brittle. As had most of the ladies, Annie Fitz had seen too much, too young. "They will soon see the error of their ways."

"Yes, I think they need to be made to understand the way in which a decent man treats holy women. They must be taught respect," replied Merry Kat, whose name reflected her taste for ale, pretty lads and song. She was as grim as any, at seeing the sad remains of the holy women, whose mission had been to feed, clothe and shelter orphans and abused women. No one, child or woman, was turned away; even needy men were fed and housed, outside the gate in the men's barracks, until they were strong enough to leave, or they remained there working to support the nuns.

The next morning found the ladies slowly walking their horses down the road, with Annie Fitz tracking the deadmen. "These tracks were made by horses poorly shod in the style of Lanqueshire," she said, "I think that they will not be hard to follow; they have not made any effort to hide their tracks. Blind Sheila could follow them without her specs." Blind Sheila had worn thick-lensed spectacles to see, giving her a somewhat bug-eyed appearance. She was now married to the book merchant that she had guarded extremely closely on several cold nights, finding herself with a bun in the oven, as sometimes happened.

After following the tracks for most of the day, it was agreed that the murderers were definitely headed toward Tula. But as that village was a four-day ride, it was doubtful that they were going that far.

"They have a bolt-hole somewhere around here," said Lady Mags, decisively. "I would bet that there is a farm nearby that has recently changed hands."

"Aye, changed hands at swords' point," agreed Merry Kat. "Mayhap they buried the corpses this time, instead of leaving them for us to take care of. We will still have to dispose of these deadmen some way or another."

"Don't worry too much over it, Kat; I say we simply leave their carcasses for the crows and the other carrion eaters to have at them," said Babs.

"I was thinking we could bar the doors and windows on the outside, and burn it down," said Annie Fitz. "I could pick them off with my bow if any decide to leave the party early."

Lady Mags shuddered inwardly, but said, "A good idea, if we could implement it without their knowing. We will have to resort to less simple methods, I think." She was turned around, rooting about in her saddle bags. "I have just the thing here. Ah, here it is," she said as she held up a dark vial. "Tinctura Coniine." Smiling smugly at the others' shocked looks; she shrugged and put it back in her saddle bag. "There is enough there to poison an entire company of twenty five. Judging by their tracks, there seems to be only ten or so of these deadmen, so all we have to do is get it into their soup, or porridge. This particular seasoning has been specially distilled so that it won't leave a bitter taste in their mouths; and has added appeal in the fact that it won't bloody my dress. It seems the logical solution, at least to me."

"Where did you find an apothecary to...never mind," Annie's finely plucked eyebrows had risen into her hair. It was a death sentence for an apothecary to distill potions that had only one purpose; to kill. "I will just pretend that you found it lying along the road."

"Actually, that is exactly what happened, in a way," replied Mags with a crooked smile. She distilled her own tinctures and herbal concoctions for every need, but did not feel the need to share that information. "So, what we need to do now is find a way in and out that will not draw unfriendly attention. Once we see the lay of the land, we will know how we are going to season things for them."

"I think we should ride up bold as brass, and simply take over. If we do it just before breakfast, we can confuse them long enough to get them to take their medicine," ventured Babs. The others looked at her, interested in hearing more.

"Go on, dear. You obviously have been thinking about this," said Lady Mags, beginning to feel in good spirits about things.

"Well, you know that men have notoriously limited attention spans." Everyone nodded. Babs continued, "Think about it; these deadmen are so desperate for women that they have pillaged a nunnery. They are strangers in our land, and they are somewhat unfamiliar with our customs. So this is what I say we should do." She proceeded to lay her plan out for the others. With every bold stroke of color as she filled in the picture, the ladies' smiles became wider. At last, Babs finished outlining her plan.

"Well! This could be fun after all," said Merry Kat with a wicked gleam in her eye. "This will give us each two to focus our attention on with a couple to spare."

"Count me in! This is the perfect capper for this sorry venture!" Annie's normally solemn face had broken out with a rather wolf-like grin, which was not much softened by the cold gleam in her dark eyes.

"It is a plan, then, ladies!" Lady Mags was quite pleased with Babs' ability to create a plan that played to their strengths.

Billy Nine-Fingers now left the yea or nay on all the new recruits to Mags, though that was not widely known, since he had made a few errors in judgment. Two dead bodies put a bit of tarnish on your reputation. Mags had warned him about them beforehand, and so after the wake for Tangle-Foot Ernie and Red Dorothy, Billy decided to screen everyone, man or woman through her.

The only way she would accept a lady into the Rowdies was if the lady had no scruples about cheating to win. There was no such thing as a fair fight in her opinion; only winners and losers. More than one hopeful lady had been gently turned away after stoutly declaring that she fought with honor. Billy would then tell them that he was full up on girls, but if an opening came up he would consider them, though that was a polite lie.

The Ladies set to searching carefully for the bolt-hole, and after several hours they followed the tracks to a once prosperous farm. It had recently acquired a decidedly neglected look to it. They looked in the grimy windows, seeing that the place was a disgrace and the men looked even worse. They were a slovenly, unkempt lot who were laying about the filthy place, drunk or playing cards. They had posted no guard, and were completely oblivious to the women who watched them so closely.

Peering at the poorly tended midden heap, Mags discovered that whoever was cooking for the deadmen was a worse cook than even Babs, and that was saying something. "Well, they will enjoy what we are planning for them, I think. Judging from what they have been eating, they have much lower standards than we do."

"We won't be using that stable for our horses," said Annie decisively, after a brief glance inside it. "They will be much better off picketed, and one of us can come out and see to it that they are watered. Once the work is done, we can come back for them." The others agreed wholeheartedly. The stable was worse than anything they had ever seen.

Merry Kat could turn out a nearly decent stew or porridge, and Annie was more or less a dab hand at making biscuits, so they turned back to the forest to camp for the night, and to plan their assault on the Deadmen's bolt-hole.

As she sat her watch that night, Mags considered her situation with Julian. She loved him, she was sure of that, but why did that mean she had to marry him? He had never asked, but it was obvious that he did expect that they would marry one day. *'Not even for Julian!'* she thought angrily, stirring the fire. *'I will not give up the sword ever! But I love him and it isn't fair to him that I am this way.'* She looked through the branches to the stars above, thinking about the nuns and what they had suffered at the hands of men. *'I only wish to see to it that the fallen innocents are avenged, and the weak have some sort of a voice. It is my duty as a lady-knight, and my duty as a noble-woman to care for them. If I were to marry Julian, my sword would be sheathed; there would be one less champion to defend these innocents!'*

Mags watched the low fire, thinking of Julian's warm lips, his strong arms holding her so gently. *'Why do we have to marry? Why can we not go on as we are, doing some good in the world and what we love? Why do I feel so terrible for wanting to live my life, in my way?'*

The next morning, they were up before dawn. Mags had the lantern out and lit, warming the curling irons. She and Merry Kat curled Annie Fitz's hair and then each others. Annie took a comb to Babs' naturally curly hair, carefully wrapping each curl around her fingers just so. They inspected each other carefully, and put a star-shaped beauty patch on Annie's cheek to hide the scar that her late husband had given her, the very morning of his accident with the axe. They straightened their skirts and made sure they had easy access to all their knives.

Then they rolled their mail shirts up and put them into their saddle bags; while Mags put her armor in the bottom of her saddlebag. She and Gertie had made sure that it would fit when Gertie was designing it. Since the ladies all had rather large saddlebags, as compared to most of the gentlemen, it was not a problem.

Leaving the horses picketed by their camp, they started off to the farm house. As they approached, they could see that it was silent.

Just as the sun rose, Lady Mags knocked on the door.

There was no answer.

She knocked again.

After she had resorted to pounding on the door, a bleary eyed, rather squinty man with shiny, bald pate opened the door a crack to see who was knocking. On seeing the four ladies standing there with smiles on their faces, he shut the door quickly, saying, "Bloody hell, Pete! There's wimmen at the door!" He opened it a bit wider this time and said, in as polite and winning a manner as he could muster, through his hangover, "And how can Bob Smalley be of service to you fine ladies this morning?" His smile was rather lacking in teeth.

"Well Bob, we understand that you boys are looking for a few good women to cook and clean and provide you boys with the comforts of home, so I have come with my crew to do just that! For a price of course," Lady Mags smiled right back at him. "We are here to get started, don't you know."

"Um, just a moment if you will, dear," said Bob, and he closed the door again. The ladies heard him saying, "They want to cook and clean and comfort us, for a price." They heard a voice say something muffled, and then Bob's voice saying, "I dunno, Pete. I'll ask 'em."

The door opened a crack, and Bob's gap toothed smile beamed at them. "How much is your price?"

"Just the usual guild rate - two silvers a week for the four of us, and the comforting happens after the cooking and cleaning are done for the day," replied Mags. "We can't comfort well in a dirty house, and I am sure you would much rather that we comforted you well."

"Well, I think it is fair enough, but I have to see what the boss says," and Bob shut the door again.

After a muffled discussion, the door opened and a rather seedy and dissolute looking fellow, who might once have been an exceedingly handsome lad, stood at the door, smiling graciously. "Welcome, ladies! You are just in time; we are auditioning cooks this very morning! I am Lord Peter Selnes, captain of this...er...mercenary company... Yes...we are mercenaries."

"Well, Peter, we will just get started, then, shall we? I am Maggie, and these fine ladies are Barbara, Kate and Annabelle," and so saying, the ladies pushed their way inside and began tidying up on their way through the door. "Kate, you get the porridge going and Annabelle you start the baking! Barbara and I will get started mucking out the kitchen and clearing the table off!"

"Could we have some comfort now? It is a lonely life, out here," asked Peter hopefully.

"You are so amusing Peter," Maggie patted his unshaven cheek, "Surely you know the guild rules, or are you testing us? Ladies, tell good Captain Peter the Golden Rule of the Cleaners and Comforters Guild."

Barbara, Kate and Annabelle snapped to attention and saluting Maggie they declared in unison. "Cook and Clean first, Comfort last! Cook and clean with attention to detail, and Comfort with a will!"

"See? You are a lucky band of Mercs; my crew is the best at comforting in the whole guild! Now, you boys get out to the horse trough and wash up. Breakfast will be on the table in no time," said Maggie firmly. "Shoo! Use some soap boys, you smell like you have been rolling with the pigs!"

There were several new cakes of soap, in a basket near the sink, that had never been touched since the day the 'Mercenaries' had taken the farm, judging by the dust that covered them. "See what the Goodwife has left for us," Annabelle said in low tones to Maggie, who nodded; a steely look in her eye. They looked around the kitchen, seeing her hand in the details that were buried by the filth.

Barbara found a drawer with lovingly made aprons in it, and shared them out. The beautifully embroidered dish towels and folded cleaning rags had never been touched since the last owner had put them neatly there; and vengeance rose even higher in the hearts of the ladies, as they thought about the Goodwife whose pride and joy had been this home. Knowing what her fate had been at the hands of these ten slovenly, doubly-dead men, they vowed that the vengeance would be painfully drawn out.

Maggie found a shovel and Kate found the broom, and between the two of them, they cleared the floor in the kitchen and scoured the table. Then they set to scrubbing the crockery with sand to scour it clean, and after that was done, they set the table. Placing the pot of porridge in the center of the table with a huge platter of biscuits, Maggie called out the door that breakfast was on the table and to get their arses in to eat.

The boys had been lounging on the porch and were falling over themselves getting to the table. The noises they made, as they slurped and smacked their lips over their food, were quite gratifying to the chefs. "What sort of work do you boys normally do?" asked Maggie, her hand on Peter's shoulder, toying with his oily hair.

"Work? Oh! Ah...well...we go hither and yon rescuing and protecting folks'...um... valuables," replied Peter, with an innocent smile that was completely at odds with his unshaven, hung-over countenance. "Why just last week we rescued...a poor lost...er...lass...and her sheep. Yes... it was a lamb that was lost." He looked around the table at the boys for confirmation, and every head nodded. "Mary, her name was. She had lost her lamb."

Maggie laid her arm across his shoulder, and kissed his cheek, rubbing her breasts against his back. "You boys are so brave and wonderful," she pinched his cheek just a shade too hard. "And just how do you call yourselves? All the famous mercenaries have named their bands…what name do you fine looking men go by?"

Peter looked around the table, desperately trying to think of a good sounding name for them, not having any idea what they should be called. Mercs went by the name of their clan in Lanqueshire. They had each been kicked out of their own clan for one reason or another.

Nine pairs of eyes (well actually eight pairs of eyes; Blinky Bill had only one eye) stared back at him. Bob Smalley shrugged at him.

"We were told that this was the home of the Deadmen, ten brave souls who were death on evil-doers," suggested Babs helpfully. "Our guild does not let any brave band of mercs go uncomforted. It would be so sad if those who do so much for so many others should be going uncomforted."

"Um…yes," replied Peter gratefully. 'Deadmen' sounded quite dangerous to him, completely in keeping with his view of himself and his band of thugs. "We are the Deadmen, and quite proud to be so, are we not, lads?"

Nine heads nodded in agreement.

Annabelle's eyes hardened and her smile grew brighter. "Oh, it is an honor to be cooking and cleaning and comforting for the Deadmen. We will be the envy of all the other Cleaners and Comforters in the trade!" She sighed, kissing Bob Smalley's cheek and saying, "To think that you care so much for the poor, down-trodden lasses of the world."

"We does our best to care for them," Bob said, turning red.

"We will just get the laundry started while you boys finish your breakfast," said Barbara, kissing cheeks and pinching bottoms as she walked around the table, startling the rank and file and causing them to jump. "My goodness, but you boys are jumpy!" she laughed, as she and the ladies hauled huge armloads of reeking clothes to the horse trough to wash them.

Staying in character, they quickly and efficiently washed and hung the pathetic rags that the Deadmen called clothing, hanging it over the line to dry. Then they turned back to the house, where the boys were done savaging the porridge-pot, and were lolling about with stuffed bellies, preparing to go back to sleep. Not a drop of porridge was left in the pot.

Mags surveyed the sorry-looking lot sprawled about the kitchen before her. "We don't want to interfere with your usual work, mucking out your stable and tending to your horses, so you boys tend to that while we finish mucking out in here," said Maggie, smiling broadly, pinching Peter's bottom and kissing his startled cheek. "We know how much you mercenaries value your horses! The sooner the cleaning is done and the cooking is done, the sooner we can get to the comforting, if you know what I mean. Rules are rules, right?"

After a moment of stunned amazement, there was a mad rush to the stable, and the ladies cleared the table. Maggie and Barbara washed the crockery and Annabelle and Kate took the shovel and the broom and continued with shoveling the debris that filled every room out the back door. Once that was done, they burned the pile of refuse, while Maggie and Barbara scrubbed the floors.

"There are two shallow graves out by the burn-pile," Annie whispered to Mags as they vigorously swept the wide front porch and broad steps. "One was a man, the other a woman with two small children."

Mags nodded grimly.

Out in the stables, the 'Deadmen' stood around looking at the filth. "Well don't just stand there, you lot! Get mucking! You, Ted, and you Big Jack; you tend to the horses; get them curried up all pretty. Look sharp!" Peter found a likely looking pile of hay and flopped down on it.

"Why the hell should we be mucking the stable? That's scut work!" Bertie Binns stood with his hands on his hips. "I ain't no scut!"

"Yeah, Pete. This place ain't been mucked since we took it from the geezer what had it first!" Blinky Bill stood blinking at Pete. "There's two months worth of mucking here!"

Leaping to his feet, Pete's knife was at Bertie's throat before Bertie could whine any further. "Look you stupid git! I aim to get some comforting after supper, and you ain't gonna stand in my way. They think we are mercenaries. WE are going to play the part, at least until we get down to the comforting," he leered at them. "Muck boys! Muck out or the only comforting you will get is a nice warm kip in the dirt!" Bertie sullenly turned to the task.

"But they expect to be paid for it!" Bob Smalley was already picking up the tack and saddles that were tossed about, all skippety. "I ain't got the money. Do you have the money?"

"Are you nuts? WE ain't going to pay for nothing," said Pete. "They will see it my way after the comforting starts." He laughed a nasty laugh, and thumbed his blade meaningfully, before he sheathed it. "This way we get a clean house, some clean shirts and a couple of hot meals out of them too!" The others also laughed, feeling much better about things. They set to mucking out with a will, and Pete flopped back down on the pile of sour hay to catch up on his sleep.

Inside the house, a flurry of cleaning and dusting had been undertaken with great enthusiasm. Once the dust had settled, Kate and Annabelle started cooking the stew and doing the baking for supper. Maggie and Barbara finally got the five actual beds made with clean linens, and straightened up each room, carefully putting away the gold and other valuables that they came across for 'safe-keeping'.

The rough pallets that were strewn on the floors upstairs and the possessions around them had gone onto the fire. Then Maggie brought in the rest of the laundry, while Barbara dusted, and set the table for supper.

Finally, as the sun was heading toward the horizon, the 'Deadmen' finished mucking out the stable. It looked almost like a proper stable. The surprised horses had been curried and groomed with more attention than they had ever had in their sorry lives. As a group, the men trudged to the house, looking forward to a fine meal and some comforting, more than they had ever looked forward to anything in their lives. Pete was well rested and feeling quite chipper.

Bob Smalley started to enter through the front door, his feet covered with muck from the barn. Maggie grabbed him by the ear, and turned him back around, with him squealing 'Ow Ow!' all the way, saying firmly, "You get those boots scraped clean before you come in here, Bob Smalley or there'll be no comfort for anyone. The guild rules are clear: Clean house first and comfort second! Now get washed up for supper!" The other men glared at Bob and headed straight to the horse trough to get cleaned up.

The 'Deadmen' were all sitting as quietly and well behaved as ladies at a quilting bee on the front porch. Each and every one of them had used soap. Beards had been combed and some attempt at getting the spots off their shirts and breeches had been made; and every pair of boots was brushed clean.

"Supper, boys," said Barbara, from the door. "Soon it will be time for comforting, so eat hearty, to build up your strength!"

"We take comforting as seriously as we take cleaning, so conserve your strength, boys," Annabelle patted bottoms and pinched cheeks as they filed past her to the table.

Once again, the sounds of slurping and the smacking of lips, accompanied by much belching, was a welcome and cheery sound to the cooks, who tidied in the kitchen while the boys ate with gusto. After scraping the pot clean and eating every crumb of biscuit, they all filed out to the porch, to eagerly wait for the cleaning to be done so that the comforting could begin.

The groaning began just about the time the dishes were all done. Barbara calmly scrubbed the table, while Maggie swept the floor under the table and made sure that the floor was spotless.

As the groaning escalated, the ladies finished washing the dishes and made sure that everything was put away nice and neat. Then they gave themselves a quick wash and took off their aprons so that they could begin the comforting. The groaning had become muted screams.

"It sounds like the boys are in desperate need of comforting," said Maggie, winking at the girls as they walked out to the porch. The convulsing men had soiled themselves, being unable to control their bowels, now had progressed to the stage where they were slowly suffocating. They arched and writhed and shit all over themselves with their seizures; and all the while they struggled to breathe; with each breath coming harder than the previous.

Ten horrified faces, covered in tears and spittle, stared helplessly at the ladies.

"Why did you do this to me? Why?" Peter's face had turned a shade of blue, and his eyes were wild and terrified. "What did I ever do to you?" Pete's voice had a pathetic wail to it as he suffered a particularly violent paroxysm.

"Hyola, Peter my dear," replied Lady Mags, pinching his cheek. "You raped every man, woman, girl and child in Hyola, and then murdered them and left them to the crows. They were not the first that you had done so dirty. There were children, little girls and little boys; and women of God, Peter; and old men. What had they ever done to you? What did the goodwife, whose home here you appropriated, ever do to you to deserve to be gang-raped and dumped in a shallow grave? What did any of your victims ever do to you?"

"I told you, Pete!" gasped Bob Smalley. "I told you it would come back on us. They was Holy Women! It is your fault! It was you that brought this on us!" His heels scrabbled vainly on the wide wooden porch floor. Several of the boys had fallen off the porch in their paroxysms and lay helplessly in the dirt; jerking and twitching in their spasms.

"You...promised us comfort..." Pete convulsed again. "You promised! What about your guild vows?"

"I do offer you some comfort, Peter. Soon you will rest in the arms of the one final lover you will ever have. Death waits for you and longs to hold you in her arms, and feel your breath on her cheek, then draw your body inside of hers. Isn't that a comfort to you? It is to me," Lady Mags stroked his cheek tenderly, and patted him. "Since we mustn't have a dirty house, we are going to drag your carcass to the field and let the crows have at you, instead of burning your wretched corpses here and now. I take comfort in knowing, that in death, you will have benefitted so many, while in life, you were naught but a boil on society's ass."

"Who...are...you..." Peter's question ended on a wail.

"We are the Cleaners and Comforters, Pete. We see a mess and we clean it up. Sometimes that means we find Lady Death a new lover, dear man, so we are also Matchmakers," Mags whispered to him. "Don't worry, I have been told that I will find my own match one day in Death's arms. That should comfort you some."

Lady Mags, Babs and Merry Kat stood guard, making sure that each of the boys got on with their uncomfortable dying effort. One by one, as the deeply penitent 'Deadmen' finally stopped convulsing, the ladies stabbed each one through the heart to ensure that the dying was done.

Horrified eyes watched helplessly as the ladies got on with finishing their work with the same grim efficiency with which they had cooked and cleaned. Terrified eyes glazed over as they each one finally received the comfort of death's embrace.

While the other ladies tidied up the corpses and found the ropes for dragging the bodies to the field, Annie Fitz went back to their camp and retrieved their own horses and their possessions. Soon their horses were stabled in the nice clean stable

Using one of the Deadmen's horses, the ladies dragged the bodies out to the field and left them for the beasts and birds to fight over.

Then they cleaned themselves up in the kitchen, and sat at the table, watching the sun rise. At dawn's light, they collected all the horses, and began the long trek to Limpwater.

The horses that the deadmen had owned were in bad condition. They couldn't push them too hard, which meant an extra night on the road. Toward noon, they rode into town, and rousted Cob John and Chicken Mickey out to take care of the extra horses.

"Where did you find these poor things?" asked Cob John, looking at the pathetic beasts. "When did you four take up horse rescuing?"

"These are for the church, John," replied Lady Mags. "A band of marauding deadmen has just yesterday offered them up as their death-gift to the martyrs of Hyola. We will deliver them to the Fat Friar tomorrow, along with various other offerings from the same deadmen."

"Gertie will have to see to their feet, before we send them to the Fat Friar," said Cob John, looking closely at their feet. "They haven't been reshod properly since they were stolen in Lanqueshire, I would wager."

"You would be right. But their place of origin is no longer an issue; nor the cost of their upkeep," replied Lady Mags. "The deadmen also offered up every bit of their gold to cover the costs of healing these nags for the church."

"I see," said Cob John, and indeed he did see. Each one of the ladies had that cold look about them that said they'd had an unpleasant task to do, but had done what was necessary. "It was only justice, then."

"Yes, as much justice as we could squeeze out of them," she replied as she turned and headed to the ladies baths with the other girls. "They did the little boys dirty too, at Hyola, John. I know how you feel about that."

"As I said, it was only justice, Mags. If you want to talk about it, I will be out here," said Cob John, looking at the poor nags that were now in his care. "I know you hate to have to be The Matchmaker, but they were vermin, girl. You just did what had to be done."

She looked sharply at John, and then just nodded.

At supper, they told their tale, and then they listened to Lucy, tell of their adventures in rescuing Nell Mackey, the King's Whore. Huw the Bard wracked his brain trying to find a way to turn their tale into a decent ballad. But somehow, ten men writhing and shitting themselves to death on a porch just did not make for a good ballad, so he tweaked it a bit, just to lend it a bit of interest.
The finished ballad, which was called 'How the Ladies Cleaned House', ended nothing like the actual event, but it was quite humorous, and became one of his more popular comic tales.

Chapter 4 - The Dragon and the Daisies

Seven years had passed since the Rowdies had rescued Nell Mackey from the clutches of Bloody Ball-less Bryan. Queen Nell had produced another daughter for proud papa Henri, and was expecting yet another child. A son and two daughters was quite an accomplishment, in his opinion. However, he had little time to enjoy them, what with the war with Lanqueshire and the resulting disorder in the Eynier Valley.

Julian Lackland was now twenty five and in the prime of his manhood. He had become even more golden and handsome than ever, with his ready wit and charming smile elevating him to 'mouth-watering', in the opinion of most of the women. However, Julian was still in love with Lady Mags and always would be, although she had turned cold to him the previous fall. He currently sat in the common room at Billy's Revenge and polished his boots, waiting to be assigned a job.

The exposed steel on Lackland's new scale-armor was as polished as it was ever going to get. It had cost him seven golds, but it was well worth every penny. It was far and away, the finest armor that Gertie had ever turned out, and that was saying something. It was light and sturdy. Mercs from all over Waldeyn were starting to come to Limpwater to have their armor made by Gertie the Smith. Even good King Henri had come to Gertie for his new brigandine.

Gertie had taken on three new apprentices and another journeyman, making her armory the largest in Waldeyn. In the eight years since she had opened her smithy, she had gained the reputation for being the finest armorer on the entire continent, despite the fact that she seemed to have a child every other year or so.

A few of the other Rowdies, hanging about the common room, were also engaged in various small housekeeping tasks: Lucy Blue Eyes was sharpening her knives; Percy Longstride was mending a slice in the sleeve of his best surcoat, and no few others were simply drinking and playing cards or tossing the dice. As was usual, Lady Mags was reading a book of poetry in the corner, enjoying the day her own way; while Huw the Bard and Davey 'God's Gift' Leweyllyn argued politics.

Davey and Percy were new to the Rowdies, but they fit in well. Billy would have it no other way. Davey was far and away, the most beautiful man that ever walked on the earth, and every eye must always be on him when he walked into the room. All the ladies in the entire town of Limpwater lost their tongue when he passed on the street. The tragic part of this was that he was completely unaware of his effect on the fair sex. Alas for them, he was not exactly a ladies-man, preferring to enjoy the company of lads, most often partnering with Percy Longstride (Lord Percival St John), although he had not really settled down yet. Percy loved Davey, despite his inability to remain faithful, though he suffered terribly from jealousy.

Percy was, as was Julian Lackland and several others of the Rowdies, a younger son with only a minor inheritance to come to. Rather than hang about the court and make a marriage of convenience, Percy had struck out on his own. He soon found his old childhood friend, Sir Julian De Portiers. There was some tolerance at court for those who were not inclined toward the opposite sex. But nevertheless, they were expected to marry well and breed children, no matter what their true preference in the bed might be.

The mercenary culture had no such scruples. They cared not one whit who you slept with, or where you came from. True names might be known or might not be, but the name that mattered was the one you answered to. Percy was the tallest Rowdy, taller even than Lackland, who was quite tall; and therefore, he was Percy Longstride and content to be known as such.

The Lady Rowdies loved to travel with Percy and Davey since they never pestered them, as the occasional new lad was wont to do until he had shed blood over it once or twice.

The door opened and closed, and messengers came and went all morning long. Various Rowdies were selected for various jobs, and the common room gradually emptied, until it was just Lackland and Mags left. They were the last, since they had both been the most recently returned from their tasks. Lackland was now playing nursemaid to young Brand and his two little sisters, while Billy and Bess handled the tasks that came along with owning an inn of quality.

Mags was now doing needlework, a task she rather enjoyed. She was making a tapestry depicting a rather bloody battle that the King had recently won with the neighboring land of Lanqueshire; with whose people the land of Waldeyn had been forever at war.

Bess was supervising the new laundress, while Billy handled a plumbing emergency in the men's bathhouse. Over the course of time, Billy had become quite knowledgeable as to the vagaries of modern plumbing; though it was a constant source of grief for him. Still the hot water and flushing toilets were what elevated his Inn and the Rowdies to the top of the list when a customer needed either a merc or a bed for a night on the road.

Lackland was now crawling about on his hands and knees with young Brand on his back, with Cissy and Letty whooping and laughing in a mad dance about him; all of them having a merry time of it.

Just as Billy returned to his post at the bar, the door banged open and a man in the livery of the king's messengers stood peering into the gloom.

At last seeing what he was looking for, he hurried over to Billy, saying, "We have a problem that requires your help." He plunked a pouch of gold down before Billy. "There's no one else available to handle this. The King and his men are down at Bekenberg Pass stamping out the land-grabbing bastards, but now this situation has arisen."

Billy looked at the pouch suspiciously. When the customer led the negotiations with gold, it was likely to be a nasty job that could end with a funeral and a wake for a Rowdy. "What sort of job? We are a little short handed right now. You should have come this morning; I had a full house then."

"I am sure that whatever help you can send will be fine," replied the messenger, looking quickly around the room and spying Lackland on the floor in the corner with the children, spinning them a tale. "It is the sort of task in which numbers matter not, but which will require a certain amount of cunning and guile."

"Um...exactly what is the problem, then? Surely there are some of the king's guards available for a small task such as you are describing." Billy had a bad feeling about this job, but the gold was real: twelve gold pieces, by the weight of the purse. "What are you asking of the Rowdies?"

"There is a beast holed up in the Grimmenstock Mine," replied the messenger. "There is no one to spare to deal with it; you know what is going on with the Eynier Valley. They have been unable to open the mine for half a season and we are running low on ore. The armorers cannot make armor without iron."

"What sort of beast? There are many different varieties of beast, and they all require different methods of removal. This may not cover our expenses," Billy said, looking at the full pouch. "We don't do dragons; that is a job for the king's men."

"Ah...I have no idea what sort of beast it is, but it has closed the mine. This is a deposit; just to get the hero on the road," the messenger said. "The King's Chamberlain told me to tell you that you could name your price, but you must do this. The mine must be reopened, or the war to the south will go badly and we will lose the Eynier Valley. The iron is desperately needed."

"Well...I can send someone, I suppose. But if this turns nasty, your deposit is forfeit," replied Billy, tucking the pouch into his shirt. "I will send you the bill when this is finished. And if it turns out that it is a dragon, the fee will be quite high."

"The Lord Chamberlain said it would be thus. Send the bill, but rout the beast, please!" and with that the messenger turned and left.

"Lady Mags! Lackland!" shouted Billy. "Roust your arses and hit the road. I've a job for you two."

Mickey's parting admonition to "boil the water afore you drink it in those mountains, or you'll be dying from the shits" was fresh in their minds as they trotted smartly out of town. "Yes Mother," they had both replied, laughing.

"You two fools can laugh, but Johnny Malone boils the water now, ask him if'n you don't believe me," Mick had said as he finished ticking off the list of supplies and the two pack ponies he'd outfitted them with. "I swear, Lackland; you've more luggage on your poor beast than the entire company of ladies took with them."

"It is the new armor, Mickey. It takes up a certain amount of room, and needs a saddle bag of its own," Lackland had replied ruefully. "I'll not be wearing it until we get there; the brigandine is much more comfortable for traveling."

"Lady Mags don't have so much luggage, and she has her armor in a bag with two dresses and an extra surcoat," groused Mickey. "Are you leaving home? Everything you own is in those bags, Lackland."

"Lay off, Mickey. I have what I need, right? I swear, you are worse than my mother," Lackland had retorted firmly, as he secured his longbow over the top of everything and settled his quiver where it would be handy. He'd checked his pockets to be sure his bowstrings were handy, and then looked at the list of supplies. After showing the list to Lady Mags, they had both signed off on it. He then mounted Farroll and began trotting out the gate and down the lane to the trade road.

"Good Bye Mother! Good bye Father!" Lackland had taunted happily as they left, receiving rude gestures in return.

As they trotted, the horses were feeling a wee bit frisky, having been cooped up for two days. They made good time, entering the gates of Castleton just as the sun set.

They soon found their way to the Inn that the Rowdies all favored, The Queen's Garter. It was on a quiet side street, not too far from the Castle. They sat in the common room and listened to all the gossip, partaking in none.

Lackland hadn't blinked an eye when Mags ordered two rooms. He had expected it. She had turned away from him the previous fall in the months before Yuletide, telling him that she felt it was for the best since she could not give him what he wanted. Though it bothered him terribly, he simply accepted it for what it was because it was her right to do so. For a brief time, he had thought that perhaps she had found another lover, but now they were entering the warm days of high summer and so far as he could tell, she had not taken any other to her bed; though it would be her right and no say of his.

At Yuletide, a month after Mags had so suddenly turned cold to Lackland, she had gone home to her father's house; most Rowdies did go to visit family at Yule if they had any to visit.

Lackland had allowed himself to find comfort elsewhere on occasion, when someone offered it to him, but he never sought out a partner. His heart wasn't in it. He couldn't let go of Mags until he knew for sure what had happened to turn her away from him, and that was all there was to it.

But Mags went several weeks early, and didn't return. And later, in a letter from his own mother, he heard that her mother had passed away at the end of March. Mags ended up staying there for two full seasons. When she returned to the Rowdies at the end of May, Mags had remained cold to him.

Lackland had his suspicions, but he had no right to ask her about it.

Still, he obsessed about it, his cheerful nature taking a somewhat dark turn. Some of the Rowdies who knew him best were worried about them both, because the drastic change in both of their natures was hard to accept. She refrained from confiding in him any more than she would have One Shot George, Little Fred Scutter or any other Rowdy. Lackland took comfort in the fact that at least she did not treat him with anything less than courtesy. She was unfailingly friendly, polite and professional.

At last, Lackland had resorted to gossiping with the garrulous wine merchant Ned Wells when he was guarding Ned on a trip to Dervy. Ned told Lackland that Bunder town was in mourning, as their Earl's wife had suddenly passed away. Lady Mags' mother had died in childbirth, having become pregnant at the old age of forty-five. That she had died of it was no surprise to Ned, as she was thought to be well past it, and it was an iffy thing for an older mother to have a late-life child.

Still, Ned was happy that the old Earl had finally gotten the son he had thought he would never have. Though the people of Bunder were glad to finally have an heir, they were sad for the loss of their beloved Lady. The black bunting hung in every window and over every door to show their mourning, which Ned thought was quite touching.

Ned had also told Lackland that Lady Mags had gone home to nurse her mother through the pregnancy. It had looked to him like she was still grieving when she had ridden guard for him soon after her return. She had been very quiet, and not at all merry, as she was known to be. When Ned had offered her his condolences on her mother's death and his congratulations on her brother's birth, she had thanked him. She then told him she had helped her father find a wet nurse for her little brother; staying with him until her father was back on his feet. Once her father was situated, she had returned to the Rowdies, but she had certainly not been the merry lass that she had been previously, in Ned's opinion.

Ned Wells had been Lackland's only source of information, since Mags was just as close-mouthed to the rest of the Rowdies, as she was to him. Although everyone was very curious about each other, and sometimes discussed what they might know of another Rowdy's life when talking pillow talk, no one pressed anyone for information or spoke about it in the common room.

Lackland had no other source that he could discretely pry information out of, and it had nearly driven him mad. But as always, he buried his questions and suspicions under a veneer of lighthearted banter; a commentary of nonsense and fluff, though at times there was a hard edge to his humor. The very last thing that Lackland wanted to do was to have his own turmoil affect the rest of the Rowdies. He did drink a little more seriously, being unable to fall asleep without a little 'extra for relaxation', as he thought of it. As long as he didn't get sloppy, no one would say anything and Lackland himself had too much pride to become a drunk.

Thus it was that on departing Billy's Revenge on this particular job, Lackland and Mags had kept the conversation cordial and polite, but little of substance passed between them. Oh, they joked, laughed, and said all the things that they would say to any Rowdy that they were on a job with, but it felt all wrong. Still, Lackland did not press for anything more from Lady Mags, although he was full of questions and desperate for answers.

When Fair Ellen, a lady of the mercenary group known as the Ravens who operated out of Bekenberg, invited Lackland to her room to 'see the new book she had just purchased for her collection', he was just drunk enough to go with her, and they passed a friendly enough evening. He made every effort to leave her happy and content when he slipped back to his room in wee hours of the morning. Indeed, the next day as she and her crew took the road east guarding a merchant, she was happily describing the extent of her contentment, to the awe and appreciation of her fellow guards.

But Lackland did not seek out companionship; in truth, he was a bit apathetic about it. If it sought him out, he might or might not take it. The fact was, it felt hollow to him, and though he had certain drives that sometimes led him into brief encounters, there was no great joy in that aspect of his life any more.

Though he did not realize it, Lackland's reticence and polite lack of effort in capturing the interest of the opposite sex had the effect of inflaming them. They hunted him, like wolves stalking a wounded deer. He was used to the boldness of women; it had been thus since he had struck out on his own, at the tender age of eighteen, full of ideals and dreams. His quick wit, handsome smile and diffident charm, combined with his physical magnificence to make a challenge that women could never resist.

But no matter who he dallied with, they were only a poor attempt to fill the emptiness left behind by the loss of his one great love.

Lady Mags knew what was missing in Lackland's life, but she had her reasons for her coldness. She would never leave the trade; not even for Lackland, whom she loved with all her heart.

In the common room at The Queen's Garter, Mags sat stewing in her own juices; telling herself he was better off taking his comfort elsewhere, because all she could offer him was a shadow of what he really wanted, and it was wrong for her to lead him on.

Lackland had never asked her to marry him. He had never pressed her to leave the Rowdies and take up the life of a goodwife, but she had sensed it in him. He yearned for a home and a family. Lackland was the marrying kind.

Whenever she saw him playing nursemaid to Bess and Billy's children or to Gertie's little ones, it cut her deeply that she would never see him play with her children that way. But Mags was a mercenary to the core and children did not come into it. You couldn't save the world or guard a caravan with one babe at your breast and two more tied to your apron strings. Lady Mercs who found themselves with a bun in the oven either fostered them out or left the business to raise them, it was that simple.

Mags was like many of the lady mercs, in that she had absolutely no maternal instinct. She didn't know how to properly care for a baby; the thought of having such a tiny, helpless thing that depended, so completely on her, made her panic; she wanted to run as far and as fast as she could.

There were herbs that a woman could take to prevent that from occurring, but nothing was sure.

She would often look at Gertie and Dame Bess. They couldn't be happier in their respective occupations and they were raising their children, but they were off the road, and out of the best part of the trade.

Mags only wanted to carry a sword and travel the roads; making a real difference in the world and being a part of something important. That was all she had ever wanted to do with her life: to protect the innocent or even the not so innocent, as some of her clients turned out to be; but no matter what it was, the job brought with it a thrill that was indescribable.

Lady Mags craved that thrill, it was better than any romp in the sheets that she had ever had. It was the excitement of the adventure that she loved; the thrill of waking up alive after a job had gone bad, and she had to pull it out of the fire by the skin of her teeth. It was the occasional opportunity to avenge the innocent and rid the world of vermin who preyed on the weak and helpless. It was making a difference in the often bad world; making some small good happen in the midst of the misery.

It was the thrill of knowing that tomorrow the job could come along that might be the one that took her into Lord Death's arms as her final lover. Each time she escaped him, she felt that indescribable delight. She was as addicted to that feeling as the lowest street slut was addicted to daze-spice. She had to have that thrill to know that she was alive.

Once she got comfortable with a danger, it ceased to be a danger, and so she had to move on to the next madly dangerous venture to feel the thrill, and that would be her downfall; she knew it.

And so, despite the fact that she had been angling to never be paired with Lackland, she now found herself on a long job with him. If she didn't know better, she would have said that bloody Billy Nine-fingers had done it on purpose, though she knew he had not. The jobs were handed out depending on who had just been out and how many were needed; or as in the case of this job, how many were available to send out. The rotation had simply fallen out this way.

All the Rowdies were aware that she and Lackland had cooled towards each other. They simply accepted it, knowing that they would behave professionally and never put anyone else in jeopardy because of any trouble that might lie between them; nor would they make the others uncomfortable. This was the way it was supposed to be done; they were professionals.

And so, Lady Mags and Lackland kept strictly to the pretense and soon it was easy to believe that it was true.

Now that they were traveling alone though, Mags worried that Lackland would try to rekindle their relationship; or at least want to know what he had done to drive her away.

And that was the trouble.

He had done nothing; nothing at all. It was Mags, and Mags alone, who was at fault.

It was her own complicated mass of fears; and then with what she had done at House De Leon, and her mother dying so suddenly... well she just couldn't be honest with him; despite the fact that she owed it to him. She had started out by not telling him the truth. She was a coward and an idiot, but there it was: she could not be honest with him. She couldn't even be honest with herself.

Lackland was too simple and good. He would have accepted what Mags should have told him with mute suffering, and it would have shown all over him. Then she would have had to look at him and everyone would know that she had driven the knife into his heart.

But who was she pretending to fool? They all knew it anyway, or suspected.

Bloody Huw the Bard would make a ballad that would wring tears from a stone over this, if he ever found out the truth.

Now Mags had to calmly watch Lackland go upstairs with Fair Ellen, a lady merc of decent enough skills. Lackland was fairly drunk and he was laughing at whatever it was that the woman had said to him.

Mags knew that lust did not drive Lackland, and so she didn't feel jealousy as one might think she would. She did feel some strange emotion whenever he bedded another woman, but even when she looked honestly at herself, she knew it was not jealousy.

What Mags felt so keenly was a deep and desperate sadness, both for herself and for Lackland. Lady Mags was fully aware that it was broken-hearted loneliness that drove him into the arms of other women.

Or men, perhaps; she had never asked him.

One didn't ask, but the unwritten code of the road said that you took comfort where you found it; and she had occasionally shared a pillow with a Lady Rowdy or two in her younger days.

She had never asked Lackland, but right after she returned, she had noticed that Davey God's Gift Leweyllyn watched Lackland with soft eyes. She had returned only a day or so after they had come back from a long trip up north. It was purportedly to Marionberg, but everyone knew it was a mission into Lournes for the

King; though of course no one said. The situation had been grim at one point, and Lackland had been wounded in the shoulder. Despite the trouble, they had escaped and managed to keep Henri's name out of it by pointing the evidence toward Lanqueshire, whom Henri was currently fighting a war with.

And of course, no one said a word about Davey and Lackland; no one would; but Percy Longstride had a burr under his saddle, until Lackland and he had been assigned a job guarding a caravan to Tula. At that point, everyone seemed happy enough; Davey and Percy were together again, so whatever had gone sour between the three of them had been buried.

The road was lonely, everyone knew that; and it was trips that involved only two Rowdies that were the dangerous ones. Three or more on a job was not dangerous in that way. Long evenings around the campfire with nothing to do but talk… well, folks found themselves sharing everything about themselves; hopes, dreams, ambitions, everything. Often that could lead to sharing a bed; it happened. It had happened to her on occasion.

Besides, she had turned cold to Lackland, and had never told him why. He had a right to ease his pain however he chose. Mags understood heart-sore loneliness; no one knew it better than her.

But that didn't mean that she wanted to see him go up the stairs holding hands with Fair Ellen, unconsciously smiling that killer smile that set Mags' heart to thumping. Still, she had sucked it up and put it out of her mind; at least until the next morning when they were all down in the stables preparing to leave. She had overheard Fair Ellen's smug voice describing Lackland's prowess.

That was when Lady Mags' own blood began to boil.

"Now *this* is jealousy," she thought wryly, as she stuffed it down and mounted Dove. She forced herself to bid a cheerful farewell to the stable boy, trotting out into the sunlight of a bright summer morning ahead of Lackland and his white stallion Farroll. All the while, she was seething with jealousy, and angry with herself for suffering so needlessly.

Farroll had gotten Dove with foal on more than one occasion, the randy old beast, but Dove seemed to like him anyway. The way he was sniffing at her, she was in a fair way to be getting that way again.

Now they had left the main trade road that went to Waldport, and were on the long road west though the back country. In good weather, it was a five day journey from Castleton to the Grimmenstock Mine. As it was the long, dry, first week of July, they would most likely be there by Sunday.

There were no inns along this way that she knew of. There were shelters, at intervals, for the great ore-wagons to stop at, but they were simply thatched long-houses. Each with shuttered windows, six bunks, a rough table and two benches, cold stone floors and a fireplace for cooking and heating. The shelter building was divided in two, separated by a stone wall; one half was for the teamsters, and the other was a barn for the animals. Through a connecting door, you could enter the cabin area from the good sized shelter for the oxen. The long-house could shelter the teams, wagons and drivers of three wagons at one time, though it was tight quarters when that was the case. A well stood uphill for use when the snows had melted, and a fairly clean privy stood down the hill a ways. The teamsters kept the places well stocked and the privies clean.

Each shelter was stocked with firewood and feed for the teams. On the way up to the mines, the teamsters carried in the supplies with which they stocked the shelters. They made the trip every week, to and from the mines, with mail and supplies for the miners and bringing the great cartloads of ore back to the smelters at Bevey. You brought in your bedrolls, and any meat you wanted to eat, and you left the place clean. There were plenty of dried beans and a few other staples for the drivers to eat, if they were snowed in for any length of time. But God forbid that it should stretch for longer than a week, since cabin-fever would kill them, long before they ran out of beans. The teamsters mostly had to fend for themselves, but the long-houses were very warm in the winter.

This was the King's Forest; hundreds of leagues of wilderness protected by the King's Right of Privilege. The only people you would meet would be patented foresters. Those with a patent were allowed to hunt on the king's land. The wood-gatherers, with the king's patent, would be cutting fallen trees and limbs. Anyone could apply for a patent, but few would brave the wilderness.

For days, the road would be empty, and now began the part of the journey that Mags was dreading.

Lackland was not very talkative either, as he too was dreading the next few weeks. "How am I going to remain polite and professional with her? I must not look at her. I must not think of her." That is how his mind spun for the first three or four leagues as they traveled west. As they rode, the silence stretched, and soon neither one knew how to break it politely.

Farroll trotted along, wondering what had gotten under Lackland's saddle this time. "Lackland is an idiot. Horses are so much smarter than humans," he told Dove. "We just do what comes naturally and we are much happier for it."

Dove snorted her agreement. "Mags is a good human, but she is very confused about what is important."

"They think too much, humans do," replied Farroll, "I am not much for thinking. I'd rather be doing." He leered at Dove, who winked back at him and flicked her tail saucily.

Soon they had entered the forest. Though the trees hid the sky and they rode in deep shadow, it was still warm enough that they rode without their surcoats.

Toward evening, they stopped at the first shelter, and as was usual when anyone traveled with Lackland, he did the cooking. Mags' snared the pheasants and dressed them out, while Lackland roasted them with his own special mix of herbs. Part of the necessaries that the pack-ponies carried were Lackland's specialty cooking tools and spices. Everyone who traveled with Lackland knew that they were in for a treat when he cooked.

"I've brought along something so that we shall not have to boil the water to drink it," ventured Lackland as he uncorked a bottle of wine. "Chicken Mickey was right about the trots you know, but I will never tell him that; the old thing enjoys mothering us so. It would take away the joy of nagging us to death, if he thought we were able to care for ourselves." He poured two mugs for them, and though the meal was a lot merrier for it, things did not warm up excessively between them.

Finally, after a long evening, that Lackland spent reading romantic poetry by the lantern's light and which Mags spent writing letters, they went to their own beds.

The next day they breakfasted on the remains of their previous night's dinner and continued on their journey through the deep forest. They climbed ever higher into the Great Western Mountains toward the king's mines.

That was the way the next five days and nights were spent: traveling the dark forest road, and stopping at the shelters until at last they arrived in the mining town of Grimmenstock. It was a town, in the sense, that there were six or seven houses, a general store of sorts and the barracks for the miners in a few small clearings at the end of the road. Giant trees grew between the buildings, spreading their dark branches over them, as if protecting them from the sky.

If you wanted to buy something, there was a small store out of which was sold the necessaries: bacon, cheese, flour, honey, salt, pepper, a few spices and a few other things that a person might need for the long journey back to Castleton. The storekeeper also provided a large room above the small store. This was for the teamsters to stay in when they came to pick up a load of ore and then take it back to the king's smelters. There were six bunks, a small round stove, a window and a table with four chairs. There was no common room, and the storekeeper's wife brought their meals up to the room. The privies were clean, and there was a large bath-house, serving the entire community with one tub, and a bucket on a rope for a quick shower. You hung the 'in use' sign out, and had to draw the water from the well to refill the water heater, but most places were like that.

The stables were clean and large, built for housing the huge oxen who pulled the great ore wagons.

Lackland and Mags arrived at dusk, and the storekeeper, Geordy Jackson was glad to see them. "We were told that the king was sending someone, but we didn't expect you two! Now we will be famous, for having had Sir Julian Lackland and Lady Mags staying with us!"

The master-miner, a short, dark, dour man named Colin Macre, said with obvious relief, "Now I know we will be rid of the beast soon. I was afraid they would send the castle guard, instead of someone with brains."

As they ate their dinner, Mags and Lackland questioned the master-miner closely, wondering what sort of beast they were dealing with.

"Didn't they tell you? We are sure it is a dragon of some sort," said Colin, with some surprise. "I told the messenger that it was most definitely a dragon. The damned thing bit poor Jakey in half! I have never seen anything like this beast, but it is every bit as most bards describe them: wings, large head, hundreds of teeth, long neck and tail, and as big as a house. I am sure that you will agree that it is a dragon."

"Ah..." said Lackland. His serious blue eyes met Mags' worried brown ones. "Ah." He cleared his throat, "Well, this could take a while then." He looked at Mags again. She gave the slightest of shrugs. "How far into the mine has it made its lair?"

"I would say about half a furlong," said Colin. "Not too far. I have a map ready for you." He placed the scrolled map on the table.

Lady Mags unrolled it and flattened it out. Then she, Lackland and Colin pored over it. "So, would it be just about here then?" she pointed to a place not too far inside.

"Yes. It can come and go fairly easily from there, but it doesn't stay gone when it does go out for a meal," muttered Colin. "It is regularly poaching the King's deer, hunting without a patent as it is apparently doing."

"It has to hunt deer, because there are no cattle anywhere near here, and we keep the horses stabled," added Geordy. "Of course, the deer are much bigger than most miners are, so we are not high on the menu. But it did have poor Jakey for a snack, and we are not going to trust that it prefers venison."

"It flies out, every three days or so, to hunt and then it doesn't budge out of there for nothing, until it goes out to hunt again," finished Colin.

"When does it fly out next?" asked Lady Mags.

"Well, that should be tomorrow, sometime after midday," replied Geordy. "The beast is fond of a long lie-in in the mornings, the slothful creature. When it does finally roust its arse out of its slumber, you won't even hear an insect call. When it is flying about nothing else will show itself; the birds don't fly and even the bears hide."

"Right. Well then," said Lackland, wracking his brains for some sort of a plan to deal with the dragon. "We will get on with laying our plans for dealing with this. We will let you know what we are going to need after we decide how we are going to do this."

After some more small talk, and much smiling and bowing, the two men left them to get on with planning the routing of the dragon.

"I think we will definitely need some explosives," said Lady Mags, "Or perhaps a cart of coal."

"I think I see where you are going with this, and it is a good idea," replied Lackland, noting the items 'dynamite' and 'coal' on his list.

"You will need to bring your long-bow, and I will need to see what sort of plants we have around here," Mags said thoughtfully. "If we can't blow up the dragon, we are going to be in for a long fight. Maybe we can poison it."

"I don't know what sort of poison would work on a dragon," Lackland mused, "And I must say, I doubt that my bow could penetrate a dragon's hide. Regular arrows just bounce off, you know. It may help if I sharpen the arrowheads to a razor edge."

"Do that. Your bow is no common thing, Lackland. Your bow may be what saves the day here." Mags bent her coppery curls over the map. "What about a back door? That could be useful." After looking, they saw that there was indeed a back door, but it was much further to the south. It was the old entrance to the worked out part of the mines, and some of the shafts were marked 'dangerous'.

After they finished planning the job, Lackland courteously offered Mags the first bath, and they spent the rest of the evening as quietly as they had spent the previous evenings, Mags on one side of the room and Lackland on the other; both pretending that they were quite busy with their own tasks.

The next morning after breakfast, they found Colin and asked for some explosives, if any were available. "Ah…I am not really comfortable with that notion. How much do you want?" Colin's face had 'no' written all over it.

"Well, you know how big he is. How much do you think it will take?" Lady Mags was at her charming best.

"He is big enough that I think that if you were even a hair off on how you placed the explosives, you would collapse the shaft and kill yourselves too," replied Colin. "I don't want to be the one to go and kill such beloved heroes as you two. There must be a better way to do this."

"Well there is, but the king's men were unavailable," replied Lackland, a trifle sourly, but doing his best to hide it. "So here we are, wracking our brains trying to figure out a way to kill your dragon instead of letting the king's men get on with it, as they should be doing."

"Well... he should be flying out sometime today, so perhaps, if you get a good look at it you can see what you need to do," said Colin. "I take it that you were surprised to hear that it was a dragon."

"Yes, and no," replied Lackland with his glorious smile. "Yes, the messenger lied to us, but these things happen, so it was no real surprise about the lie. We just don't usually deal with dragons, because the standard method is to keep throwing men at it, keeping it busy while other men hack away at it. You usually lose five or six before the damned things grow tired enough that you can swarm and kill them. Mercenary companies are not able to support those kinds of losses. This will cost the King dearly, and I feel sure that upon his return, Henri will take it out of the pockets of the recalcitrant knights who have shirked this duty."

"Oh," said Colin. Everything fell into place in his mind now. "I see why the kings' messenger was less than honest with you. The real soldiers are down south fighting like they ought to be and all that is left to guard the castle are the parade soldiers, am I right? The ones that are the useless noble sons of suspect bravery, those that no one trusts on a battlefield. They aren't going to stick their necks out for the likes of us. The Lord Chamberlain could not offend their fathers, but he had to do something and so he settled on the lot of you."

"You have the right of it, I suspect," said Lackland, grinning widely at Colin's accurate assessment of the situation. "Well, there is nothing for it; we two need to sit somewhere and wait for it to fly over us. Maybe we will get a good enough look at it, that we will be able to find a weak spot in its defenses, but the forest is too thick, even here. Is there a field nearby?"

"There was a farm a half a league from here," replied Colin. "I can set you on the trail. Though the forest has reclaimed some of it, there are still meadows there. But are you sure that you want to be exposed like that? What if he swoops down and eats you?"

"Why then, you will have to tell the king's messenger that his plan failed, and that he will need to find twelve stupid lordlings to do the job properly," replied Lady Mags with a twinkle in her eye. "We shall leave the horses here; they are large enough and tasty enough to draw attention that we would like to avoid."

"Don't worry about us," added Lackland. "We will make a blind, as if we were hunting ducks."

"Aye, that will do it, then." Colin felt immensely better that Sir Lackland and Lady Mags were there to handle it. They had taken everything into consideration.

They were consummate professionals, who would never allow themselves to be eaten by a dragon.

Geordy's wife, Lena, packed a basket with a good picnic lunch and Lackland tucked two bottles of wine from his saddle bags into it, and their mugs. Lady Mags took her map case to pore over the maps, and a notebook along with a charcoal pencil for drawing; just something to do while they were waiting for the dragon to fly over them. Lackland had stowed his book in his pocket when they set out to find the farm and a good place to watch for the dragon.

After walking the path that Colin had set them on, for perhaps, half an hour, they came to an abandoned farm.

Feeling as curious as children, they peered into the cracks of the shuttered windows, but nothing had been left behind; no clue remained of the previous tenants. Now only birds nested in the attic, and the roof had places where the sky shown through. It was sad somehow, but this abandoned farm was so far away from civilization and so lonely, that it was not surprising that they had not stayed, whoever they had been.

The small barn leaned heavily to one side; it would collapse soon; if not this winter, then the next. They walked past the old buildings and down a long unused path through the brush, and rounded a corner. Both of them stopping with a sharp intake of breath upon seeing what lay before them.

A wide field of daisies lay spread out before them, as thick and white as snow; contrasting sharply under the deep blue sky. Bemused by the beauty that lay waist high all around them, they walked to the center of the field. "Oh…" breathed Mags as they looked about them.

"This is how I have always imagined heaven to be," said Lackland, his blue eyes full of wonder and appreciation as his gaze met hers. "I say to hell with the blind. Let us enjoy the day; and the dragon be damned. We will see it better from here."

"I couldn't agree with you more," she replied, awed by the splendor about them.

Lackland spread his cloak and courteously gestured for her to sit upon it, which she did. After settling the basket, he too sat down. The tall daisies formed green walls about them, and the peace of the field seemed to soak into them. The wide blue sky, dotted with puffy white clouds arched over them; making them feel small indeed.

Soon Lackland stretched out, looking up at the sky, and watching the clouds. "Look, there's a cloud shaped like a horse," he said, feeling completely at peace; at last more fully relaxed than she had seen him to be for far too long. Mags watched him laying there, his long golden hair shining in the sun and his eyes bluer than the sky. The perfection of his face, and his heart-stopping smile took her breath away. *'How I love him'* was all she could think.

Without thinking about what she was doing, she leaned over and kissed him, gently.

Julian's arms went around her, and he kissed her with all the love and pain of the last year pouring out of him. "Marry me, Mags," he said, holding her closely and tenderly stoking her hair. "I love you. With all my heart, I love you." She could feel the beating of his heart; feel the life pulsing in him as he held her so lovingly.

"No, my Julian," she replied. "I won't marry you. I can't leave the trade. Not even for you." Her voice broke and she found herself crying. "I am so, so sorry Julian. I love you but I can't marry you." The tears flowed down her cheeks and she could not stop them.

"Sh, sh...don't cry, my darling; it will be fine. I knew you would not. Nothing has changed, I still love you," Lackland cradled her, tenderly kissing away her tears. "I will always love you, my beautiful Mags. I would not have you any other way." Her unhappiness tore at his heart; her fear, of not being able to pursue the life she loved, was the driving force behind their tragedy.

"Julian, I owe you a confession. I must tell you something that will change how you feel about me," she said, her dark eyes full of pain and sadness. "There is no easy way to tell you this. You will hate me."

"Then tell me, and let me bear whatever it may be as well as I can. Nothing will change how I feel about you," Lackland had an idea of what he was about to hear. He had had this notion since she had gone to House De Leon; her father's house.

"You have a son," she said, her dark eyes full of tears. Pain, loss and heartache were written across her face. "I have left him for my father to raise because I can't do it. It broke my heart; but I left our baby with my father, Lackland."

"I know," said Lackland, his ideas confirmed. "I have suspected such since the day you left." He held her close and kissed her forehead. She started sobbing, and he just held her until she had cried herself out. "Nothing has changed, Mags; it is only that I know now for sure why you turned away from me."

"I didn't tell you, because...because..."

"You didn't tell me because I would have begged you to marry me," Lackland finished for her. She nodded, and his arms tightened about her. Turning her chin up to face him he said, "You were right. I would have pressed you to marry me." He kissed her eyes and her cheeks. "And I know that you aren't the sort who can give up the trade and be a goodwife, no matter what I would wish for us. Does your father know that I am the boy's true father?"

"Yes," she said, sniffling a bit. Lackland handed her his handkerchief. "He said that he knows you are an honorable man, and that I have done you a terrible wrong by hiding this from you. And he is right. I have done you great wrong, and I knew it was wrong when I decided to keep it from you." Mags started crying again.

"No, no, darling, don't cry over this. What is done is done and given the circumstances, it may be that it is for the best. You must remember that I have nothing to offer him now; I come by the name of Lackland honestly. Will your father allow me to be a part of the boy's life?"

"Father also said that you would ask that, and that I should tell you yes," she said, hiccupping a bit. "My poor, poor mother. They were putting it about that she had been blessed with a late life child, as sometimes happens. They had posted it in Bunder town, and the whole town had prayed for her safe delivery. They were still celebrating his birth when she passed away, and they took it hard. She was so looking forward to him, and so was my father. She had made the most beautiful swaddling clothes for him.

"My old childhood nurse had helped us to find a wet nurse. Since ladies of breeding don't nurse their own babies usually, Mother had nursed me herself and also my siblings that she bore." Mags found herself to be babbling now, but she could not seem to stop herself. "Five babies; my sisters and brothers. They all died within hours of their birth. Mother was overjoyed to have our son, so healthy and strong, to ease the pain of her losses. But my mother had suffered from weak lungs for years. She took a chill and died three weeks after young Jules was born. At least she got to see him for three weeks. Bunder town is desolate that she should die and not get to see her long-awaited son grow up."

"Jules? You have given him my name?" Julian felt a stab of joy pass through him at that thought. "My mother calls me Jules; it is her pet-name for me."

"He is named Julian, after you in my heart, though he will be known as Jules Edward De Leon IV. It is the family name of the Earls of Bunder. My grandfather was Jules Edward De Leon, as is my father and now young Jules. Our Jules is my father's heir, and no taint of illegitimacy will touch him," she told him. "My father wished desperately for a son and an heir, but all he got was me: a wild scapegrace and fallen woman, though he has long since forgiven me. Now Father has our Jules to be the scion he always dreamed of, and he is pleased that the estate and the title will continue in his bloodline after all."

"Huh... my son... an Earl," mused Lackland, smiling wickedly at Mags, "Fancy that! Here I am... a poor landless knight, and my father was only a baron. Now, my ever so snooty, brother will find himself giving way to my son at court someday, and I will enjoy that immensely!"

"I am sure you will!" Mags laughed; the first truly free and joyous laugh that she had laughed in many months.

"I have missed the sound of your laughter, my dear. I have missed you so." Holding her gently Lackland kissed her lips, and she responded, leaning into his kiss in a way that sent the blood racing through his veins, and scattered his thoughts the way no other lover could.

At last Mags pulled away, and said sadly, "But now, I also have to tell you that we can never have the sort of relations that we once enjoyed. I can never go through that again, my dear, dear man. Leaving him was more than I could bear, though it was for the best. I can't count on the herbs to prevent pregnancy."

"Ah. Well, I have had somewhat the same notions. Not long after you returned to House Leon, I made a visit to an apothecary in Castleton that my royal cousin recommended to me. It is a man's responsibility, I know this now. The little glove takes some of joy away, but the little jar of salve helps and it is better than risking trouble." He reached into the pocket of his cape, and held something up with a wry smile. "I do exactly as the apothecary instructed me, and I feel better about things. She tells me they are made from the sap of a tree that she acquired some years ago from a far-off land. Now she has a green-house with a small forest to make her special gloves. I simply stop by her shop when I am in Castleton and she supplies me with what I think I might need."

She looked at what he was holding up and started laughing. Throwing her arms around him and kissing him, she began to unlace his shirt, saying, "Oh, Julian-love; I have missed you for so long, and it was my own foolishness that caused it. If I had only talked to you in the first place, these last months could have been warmer between us."

"Not only your foolishness, my dear." Lackland was a man who faced his own failings and admitted to it. "I could have gone to House De Leon and forced the issue; I nearly did so, countless times. I didn't because I respect you and I believe that you *do* know that what you are doing is the right thing for you. I was afraid of what you would say. I couldn't bear it if I had forced you into marriage, just for the sake of convention, and then you had run away." Lackland looked into her warm brown eyes and tenderly touched her burnished curls, saying, "And I have missed you desperately. No matter where the wind blows us, you will always be the love of my life." He took a deep breath, and said the words that he never thought he would ever say to Mags. "I love you, Margaret De Leon. I hereby set you free of any perceived contract that may once have bound you to me. I set you free to live your life the way you wish to live it."

They held each other, tears of joy and sadness mingling on their cheeks. They both felt the joy that they had made things right between them, and sorrow that their love story was never going to end the way love stories ended in Huw's tales.

Kissing her, with all the love he held deep within him, Julian let his lips trace down her throat, to her breast and her belly and back to her shoulders; and then kissed her throat again. His hands moved with a will of their own, and as her hair came down, he once again kissed her breasts. Mags sighed, touching him gently, lovingly, her hands caressing the face she loved so much. She kissed his shoulders, his throat, marveling at both the strength of him and his gentleness; breathing in the unique wonderful scent that was his alone.

Her body rose to meet his lips and his hands; she gasped as his hands parted her legs, stroking down her thighs to that most pleasurable of places. His gentle fingers sent a fire singing in her veins, and she arched to meet his questing mouth. The beauty of the sky and the quiet of the field seemed to sweeten the release when it came, and she lay completely at peace, as he kissed her belly and her breasts.

He sat next to her, stroking her skin, drinking in the beauty of her, his touch rekindling the fire that burned within her for him. She pulled him to her, wrapping her legs around him. With her demanding hands firmly grasping his buttocks, she arched to meet him.

Hungrily, passionately, he made love to her; bringing her to ecstasy again and again before allowing himself the joyous release that his body demanded.

At last they lay sated, lost in the joy and the pleasure of loving each other.

They spent the rest of their time that day loving and giving love with all their hearts. There was a poignancy that tinted the overwhelming beauty of the day with a fairytale quality.

There both knew there would be no happily ever after for Sir Julian Lackland De Portiers and Lady Mags De Leon, although they would live and love each other to the fullest, taking each day as it came.

Forever afterward, that day in the field of daisies, under the deep blue sky shone in each of their memories; a piece of heaven to hold close to their hearts, no matter where the storms of life sent them.

Near sunset, they returned to their room over the store, quite sunburned in delicate places, but with happy smiles and lighter hearts, holding hands and looking to all the world like lovers, as the ballads claimed them to be. Geordy and Lena smiled at the sight of them, and found themselves reaching for each other's hand.

When Colin and Geordy came by to see what Mags and Lackland had discovered, they had a plan to show them. They had indeed seen the beast, twice as it passed over them; once on the way out to hunt and the second time flying back with a fat buck in its mouth.

"We will need some small explosives, but not so much as we thought," said Mags. "We are going to give the beast a fatal case of indigestion! If that is not enough to kill it then Lackland will shoot it full of arrows with his great bow, and I do assure you, that in his hands, that bow is quite effective."

Geordy said with a wry smile, "Lena told me that this job needed a woman's touch. There are some jobs that must be done with finesse, and that is woman's work!"

"Explosives are not finesse, Geordy!" Colin was aghast, but he finally agreed to give Mags the dynamite.

Lackland spent the next day, on a bench outside the general store, sharpening his arrows, carefully filing the edges to a razor's sharpness. Mags asked Lena for a pot to brew medicine in that could be thoroughly scrubbed out afterwards, one that she could use on an open fire. "I need to brew a... health tonic," she said, since the men were listening.

Lena looked over at Lackland filing his arrowheads and smiled knowingly, and without a further word she fetched a light weight enameled kettle that bore the signs of similar use. "I make some of our own medicines. It seems to me to be a wise course of action, and one I would have recommended. You might need some water, to get the consistency right," she said as she handed Mags a skin of purified water. "A good health tonic must be of the right consistency, thick but not too thick."

Mags went out into the forest to find a local poison to dip the arrows into, looking for one plant in particular. She found a large amount of nightshade and immediately set to brewing a concentrated concoction right where she was in the woods, so that no one would have to keep a secret about how she had come by it.

All they needed to do was get it into the dragon, if the other plan failed to work. Lackland would have to be very careful to not touch it if he was forced to resort to arrows; but then, Lackland was always careful.

That evening she came home, carrying her pot of 'health tonic', which she immediately took up to their room and set in a corner, covered with a cloth. Lackland immediately set the business ends of his specially sharpened arrows into the bucket to soak.

"If these penetrate the hide, the shafts are soaked in the poison as well as the arrow-heads," Lackland told her. "I just suspect that they will not be useful against him, with his thick hide. His chest is well armored."

"We must hope that we do not need to resort to them," Mags agreed.

The next day Lackland and Geordy went hunting, while Lady Mags and Colin prepared a special stuffing to spice up the dragon's meal.

When, in the late afternoon, two hunters came trudging up to the camp wearily dragging their large old buck. Colin's crew quickly placed it onto a hand cart and carried it down to the cold-cave in which they kept their meat. There it lay, ready to be stuffed and sewn back together.

Colin reluctantly brought her several sticks of explosives, muttering all the while.

"Um...Lady Mags...I think this is the most dangerous thing you could possibly be doing. You will blow us clean to heaven if you make even the slightest error. That is enough, please," he pleaded as he watched her. "This is enough to collapse the tunnel if it is placed wrong, and we don't want that. Stop now, please." He looked at the carcass, the whites of his eyes showing. "You have enough to do the job and then some."

Mags looked at the explosives that she had packed into the buck's belly, and then added one more. Then she sewed the belly up with twine while Colin carefully backed out of the cold-cave, muttering that she was crazier than any woman had a right to be.

The following day, when the beast next flew out to hunt, Mags and Lackland would take the booby-trapped buck to the dragon's lair. A long fuse would trail out of the buck's belly, and it would lead to the entrance of the mine, where they would light it. The plan would probably not work as well as they hoped, but it was better than nothing.

"All that we need is for the dragon to just eat the buck carefully, swallowing it whole. Then the touchy beast must completely ignore the hissing and sputtering fuse, as it creeps toward him," muttered Mags. "But I can't think of anything else that we could do that would be any less iffy. We will be resorting to hacking and slashing sooner or later in this job, I fear."

"Well, me and the boys will back you up, if it comes to that," said Colin. "We have been talking in the barracks. We think it's a dirty shame that two of you are all that was available to be sent to rout a dragon. My brother works for the seneschal there; last month he told me that your brother, Mortimer, is at court wearing his armor and proudly declaring himself to be defending the realm while the king is away." Lackland's eyes rolled on hearing that. Colin continued, "We owe you two that much. Besides, we owe the beast retribution for Jakey, so say we all."

Lackland and Mags were quite taken aback by this declaration of support. "Well, let us hope that it does not come to that," replied Lady Mags, hoping fervently that it would not become a bloody massacre as dragon hunts were wont to do.

The next morning, Colin and two of his boys watched the entrance to the mine. As soon as the beast lumbered out and took off, flying low over the forest everyone leapt to action. Mags and Lackland carefully pushed the booby-trapped buck into the mine, pushing the cart all the way to the beast's lair. Mags covered their scent with scent from the buck's musk gland and carefully unrolled the fuse on their way out.

Everyone hid once again, only this time, they were fully armed, though the miners were armed with picks and axes and any other sharp implement they could find. Once the dragon returned to the lair, everyone would immediately move to battle stations about the entrance.

Lackland had his longbow strung and his special arrows were at hand, though he really did not want to have to use them. He had set up, opposite the entrance, where he could shoot his bolts at the dragon's torso and soft underbelly if he had to. He had never tried to kill a dragon with his bow before; hopefully the arrows would pierce the skin and the poison would have an effect, if the explosives had not done their job completely. The special arrows were placed in a quiver that he had made out of the bark of a cedar tree especially to carry them in, so that they would not be accidentally used until they were needed.

Soon the dragon landed in front of the entrance to the mine, carrying a rather smallish doe. "Good, whispered Lackland. "He will still be hungry when he finishes his kill. Hopefully he will eat the bait in one bite, and get indigestion. Then we can swarm him and finish him off."

Of course, that is not exactly what happened.

Mags crouched just outside the entrance, peering inside and watching as the dragon devoured its kill in two bites, before turning around three times like a dog preparing to lie down. As it did so, the dragon let go of a rather substantial fart, which seemed to linger in the atmosphere of the lair.

Suddenly the dragon noticed the booby-trapped carcass.

Intrigued, the dragon looked closely at it, with first one eye and then the other; looking, for all the world, like an inquisitive bird examining a worm in a hole. Then it sniffed at the carcass several times, before it finally came to a decision and licked the buck's head, sampling the scent of it with its long tongue.

After farting loudly again several times, the dragon ate the torso section only of the buck, and then licked the buck's now severed head once again; not noticing the fuse that dangled from the corner of its mouth.

Quickly Mags lit the fuse, and darted away from the entrance, making not a sound, and took her place at Lackland's side. "I think venison doesn't agree with him, poor thing," she said. "He is farting up a storm in there."

"Too bad, poor thing," agreed Lackland. "I don't know what they normally eat; probably horses or cattle."

They stood watching, and waiting.

For a long moment, nothing happened.

Just as Colin was getting ready to have a look see, there was an ear splitting shriek and a thunderous roar as the dragon exploded. The concussion knocked everyone to the ground as bloody bits of gore, followed by flaming hunks of burning dragon, flew out of the entrance to the mine, followed by a whoosh of flame which drove everyone back. The buck's now antlerless and blackened head rolled out of the mine like an oddly-shaped ball, sucked along by the trailing edge of the explosion.

Leaping to her feet, Mags whooped with joy. "I want to do that again!" she shouted, dancing and turning a cartwheel in her excitement. "I want to do that again!" Throwing her arms about Colin's neck, she exuberantly kissed his startled cheek. He stared at her, aghast as she danced and shouted with glee. "That was so much fun! What else can we blow up?" she asked, looking around, disappointed that there seemed to be nothing that needed blowing up. "I want to blow something else up!"

"She is barking mad," Colin said faintly. "She should be locked away for everyone's safety."

"You have ruined your dress, my dear," said Lackland to Mags as she capered about. "I do think that you have routed the dragon though." He was terribly proud of her. "Let's not play with the dynamite any more now, Mags; you are making poor Colin nervous."

Disappointed, Mags settled down, behaving more like the competent lady that people normally saw. Soon she was picking up the buck's head and blowing the cinders off it, looking it over.

Colin stood looking into the reeking mine, with a stunned look on his face. "Who is going to clean this mess up? There are bits of bloody, burning dragon everywhere!" At last, he pulled himself together, but he kept looking out the corners of his eyes at Mags, obviously concerned about her sanity.

They all waited until the air had cleared before they went inside. "Well, our work here is done," said Lackland cheerfully, as he looked around at the mess. "I think that was one of the more interesting jobs that we have ever done. Who knew that dragons were so explosive?"

"I told her that she added too much dynamite to the buck," muttered Colin after he had had a chance to examine things. "We are just lucky that the shaft is still stable." He beckoned to his crew, telling them to get their arses moving and clean up the mess.

Fortunately, the dragon's body had absorbed most of the initial explosion. The Shaft had channeled the explosion when the other gasses ignited out the entrance, like smoke going up a chimney.

Once his crew had cleaned up the mess and he had gotten over his initial shock, Colin had gradually gained a better outlook on things. He was inclined to be a bit more charitable toward Mags.

"It may have been that dragons are naturally explosive," Colin sagely told Lackland. "I suppose we will be able to handle our own dragons now that we know what to do." He looked sideways at Mags who was engaged in an animated conversation with Lena. "I will go a bit lighter on the dynamite next time, though." Colin looked at Lackland, and said shrewdly, "She is a handful, I would guess. But she will never marry you, laddie. What are you going to do about that?"

"One day, when I am ready I will probably go to my royal cousin and help him win his war," Lackland replied, seriously. "After that, I've a notion to teach a certain young nobleman and his cousin the art of the sword; they should be just the right age for it by then." There was a faraway look in his eyes as he spoke. "Henri's boys will need instructing, and also my nephew, whom I will not allow my brother to ruin; and Lord De Leon's infant son will need instruction when he comes of age for it, as it would not be seemly for his sister to instruct him, though she is as fine a sword-swinger as any you will meet. I will stay busy."

*

Three weeks had passed by the time Lackland and Lady Mags returned to Billy's Revenge. The crowd was sitting about the common room moping, as they were suffering a temporary lull in employment.

Billy was thrilled that the beast had indeed been a dragon, and immediately sent a bill to the Lord Chamberlain for one-hundred gold pieces. Everyone celebrated their safe return, and every detail of the routing of the dragon had to be told over and over again.

Only Huw the Bard seemed a bit put out. "How am I supposed to make a decent ballad out of that mess? You went on a dragon hunt, for God's sake, Lackland! I was so looking forward to a really good heroic saga, and all that you bring me is a dragon that farts from eating too much venison and then explodes." His head dropped to his hands, as he said in the most tragic of tones, "Why me?"

The room erupted in laughter.

Chapter 5 - The Bad Year

Ten years had passed since the summer of the dragon and the field of daisies, and many changes had happened in Julian Lackland's life. Lackland had, for most of the last eight years, divided all his time between House De Leon and King Henri Dragoran. As Henri's Arm's Master, he was busy with duties for his majesty, and the rest of the time he spent with Edward De Leon acting as his estate manager, and handling the education of the young heir to Bunder. Even while he was away from House De Leon, he managed to keep things running smoothly via letters and short visits. The only time he was unable to help Edward was when he was in the south, fighting, but he still kept in close touch through daily letters.

During the campaign in the Eynier Valley, Lackland had made a name for himself as a sharp tactician and a wily general who fought for his king fiercely. On the battlefield, he was known as The Great Knight, and was well known to be Henri's right hand.

He was an eligible and desirable catch, eagerly sought after by hopeful parents wishing to marry their daughters off to so well-loved a knight as the great Lackland. However, his well known, unrequited love for the wild Margaret De Leon was his shield against such importunities.

The old Earl loved him like a son, feeling that their arrangement was the only right way to deal with the situation; and for the most part, Lackland was happy there. He was still very much alone, though he did occasionally have brief love affairs while on the road.

He was always honest, stating at the outset that, just as the songs all declared, he was unequivocally in love with Lady Mags and would marry no one, if not her. Lackland refused to make any sort of commitment that would interfere with his arrangement with the Earl.

Henri understood the situation and rarely asked more of him.

During the first war council that he had sat in on, he had been shocked by the incompetent but enthusiastic generals. Their loyalty to Henri had far outstripped their abilities to plan a war against the sort of nasty fighting that the Lanques were used to.

It was a tricky situation; he was their friend and compatriot, but there was not one man among them who was qualified to plan a christening, much less plan a war. With his sunny disposition and warm humor he somehow managed to offend no one, simply taking over as if they had been waiting for him all along. Indeed, they had been waiting for someone, and everyone agreed with relief that Lackland was the most qualified soldier in Henri's court. Lackland had devised strategies that would eventually crush the Lanque forces.

His exploits on the field of battle had become legendary, and Henri had made him his Master-of-Arms, relying on Lackland to train up his courtiers, and make them into a fighting force worth their pay. Lackland was in the process of doing just that, but he had a long road ahead of him. However, he had a plan which he would implement in the fall of the next year.

It was the end of November and an oppressive atmosphere had descended upon the town of Limpwater. There had been four wakes for Rowdies since the previous Yuletide, but the wake they had held that day had been the worst.

It had started in January. Grumpy Jake McGrath had been killed when the caravan he was guarding fell under attack, just inside the border of Lournes. There were six of them on that trip: Percy Longstride, Lady Mags, Little Fred Scutter, Johnny Malone, Davey 'God's Gift' Leweyllyn and Grumpy Jake McGrath. The north of Waldeyn had become somewhat of a haven for highwaymen, what with the king being occupied in the far south for most of the time these last ten years. They had hired two extra guards, which had turned out to be prudent.

Grumpy Jake had never even seen the woman who gutted him while he was occupied with fighting off her companions. Percy had 'cut her hair off at the neck' over the incident, but Jake's death had set the tone for rest of the year.

Two years previously in the high summer, Lucy Blue Eyes had at last married Huw the Bard and settled down in the sweet little cottage that he had bought some years before. Her sudden capitulation had surprised everyone, Huw most of all, but he had been over the moon with joy. Lucy had made the cottage into a tiny paradise. Her happiness was complete, when at long last she found that they were going to have a child.

Lucy had been overcome with joy; she had been thirty-two when she had finally married Huw, and had been afraid that she had waited too long to have a child. But two years after they were married, she had been thrilled to find herself pregnant, and the baby was expected to arrive toward the end of May.

In the first week of March, just as the warmth of spring had begun to quicken the world around them, Lucy went into premature labor and they couldn't stop the bleeding.

They had buried Lucy and the baby under the blossoming apple tree that Huw had planted for her on the day they were married.

Huw had fallen into a deep depression that Billy feared he would not come out of. The bard could not make music for weeks, but at last he began to come out of it, writing and singing some of his most touching love ballads, all written for his Lucy Blue-Eyes.

Just as Huw began to recover, Cob John suffered a heart-attack and died. One moment he was there, grooming the horses and grousing about their owners and the next he was gone. Poor Chicken Mickey was bereft, but he confessed that he had been worried about John for months. "He's been short of breath, and pushed himself when he shouldn't. He was sixty-eight, and not as young as he wanted to be. I tried to tell him, but he wouldn't listen."

When broken Huw tried to console Mickey, he had raised his tear-filled old eyes to Huw and said, "Don't shed a tear for me, laddie. I had thirty years with him. That is a good life by any measure. I have my memories to keep me company." For some reason, Mickey's fortitude in the face of his loss had helped Huw in dealing with his own loss more than anything.

The other Rowdies had pulled together and supported Huw and Mickey through the dark days as the summer had progressed.

However, today they had buried both Davey 'God's Gift' Leweyllyn and Percy Longstride, laying them together in death as they had been in life. The tragedy was more than the poor old fat friar Robert De Bolt could take; he was drunk as a lord, in his corner of the common room at Billy's Revenge, and he was not the only one. Old retired Rowdies had made the trek from wherever they had drifted off to. If it had been a more cheerful crowd, it would have been a good party.

But it wasn't a good party. There was a sense of anger and helplessness that made the grief even worse.

Huw sat on his stool strumming his harp, unable to sing a note.

One cold dark day, just two weeks previously, Huw and Percy had returned to Limpwater from the little job they had taken to eliminate a nest of just-hatched firedrakes for the King. It had been a troublesome job, but they had managed it.

They had just handed off the horses to Gertie's oldest daughter, seventeen-year old Betty Smith, who had taken over the stables after old John's death. She had always been mad about the horses and had been John's helper for several years, working harder than any boy he had ever had as a helper. Betty had never taken up her sword; instead, she insisted on being the Rowdies ostler and had just recently married Tom Stanton. At twenty five, he was still on the road but had been helping Mickey with provisioning for several years and was gradually taking over for him.

Huw and Percy were still in the courtyard, laughing at a joke Mickey had told, when the wagon rolled into the courtyard. Johnny Malone and Little Fred Scutter brought Davey back, all of them bloody and unrecognizable; but Davey was hurt most grievously.

By the next day, everyone but Percy knew that Davey was dying.

Davey had been on a trip with Little Fred Scutter and Johnny Malone guarding William De Vayne to Val Halle, the crown city of Lournes and back. De Vayne was a cloth merchant, and though Billy had told him that he really needed to hire three more guards, De Vayne had demurred in favor of his profit margin.

They had been on the final leg of the journey, coming through the Psalter Pass, half a day's ride from Limpwater, when they were ambushed. It wasn't a regular hit and grab-the-loot sort of ambush; it was personal and directed at Davey. The attackers had lain in wait for them to come through the narrow pass on the trade-road. Shrieking epithets and slashing with long-knives, two of them had taken on Davey while the other two held Fred and Johnny off with swords. Little Fred and Johnny had killed the murdering bastards and saved the client and his merchandise but they had nearly lost Davey. The ride home had been an ordeal. William De Vayne had gently loaded Davey into his wagon, binding his gut wound up as best as he could, and then Fred and Johnny had climbed on. He had driven for Limpwater as fast as he could, with their horses tied to the wagon. As it was, Davey was so injured that he never spoke again; slipping into a coma on the trip home.

Bess had sent for the priestess to work her healing Majik to try to save Davey's life. "I have never seen anyone cut so badly, and still live," Bess had told Billy as Davey somehow hung on to life.

Billy himself had stitched up Fred and Johnny, and Bess had dosed them with poppy. They had then been placed in chairs near the fire, somewhat in shock, but recovering. Each held a mug of soup in his shaking hand while he told his part of the tale.

Neither man knew for sure why Davey had been attacked. It was a black mystery. Fred and Johnny both swore that the bastards knew him. "They was screaming at him in that language they all use down there, and they was dressed like Eynier, but it felt wrong. But they hated him, for what I don't know, unless it was because he liked the lads," Johnny shook his head slowly. "They kept calling him by his surname, Leweyllyn; only they was saying it wrong, calling him 'Dukweyllyn', sneering it at him."

Huw's ears had perked up at hearing that; it had reminded him of something, but he couldn't pull himself together well enough to think about what.

The only thing that anyone could think of was that it must be a clan feud, since he was from down in the Eynier Valley. While they were always at war with Bloody Lanqueshire, there was a lot of in-fighting among the great families. Some of the feuds had been going on for generations, sometimes even between members of the same blood-lines.

Huw was from down in the Eynier Valley too. He said that the use of the long-knives meant that it was a ritual revenge killing. "Long-knives are the signature of a Clan Grefyn assassination. Davey's name was Leweyllyn, so he came from the northern valley, and clan Weyllyn. Clan Grefyn has the southeastern valley, almost to Ludwellyn, the port city. The crown holds the western valley and the port city. If you look closely into it, you will find that Davey's relatives are disappearing or dying all over the place. That is one reason why I left the long valley. I can't live that way. Davey couldn't either." His voice caught, but this time he didn't break down. "I had to run from the Valley because I was a bard, and the old Grand Duke Grefyn was 'cleansing the valley' of troublesome, truth-telling bards by murdering them wholesale. I may be the last one left who was properly trained in the craft."

Huw's deep blue eyes held the same bleakness that everyone's eyes seemed to hold. His voice had a note of grim satisfaction as he said, "At least Fred and Johnny got the bastards that did it. Now, whoever sent them will never know if they were successful or not, and they won't be able to bury their own dead. Denying them the funeral is going to hurt them as much as losing their mates. The Black Grefyns live for funerals down there; it seems as if the very soil is soaked in blood simply for the love of a good funeral."

It had surprised no one that Percy had gone mad when he saw them bringing Davey home, unrecognizable and unconscious. Tom Stanton and Huw had had to restrain him. Once they got him calmed down, Percy stayed at Davey's bedside, refusing to do anything else or let anyone other than the priestess and himself care for his love. He tenderly sewed his mutilated face back together and tried to keep his gut-wounds from killing him.

The healing priestess had done her best, but she was frank in her assessment of his prognosis. "I can't heal his gut wounds, or the punctured lung; if he survives them, it will be a miracle. Even if I had been there when he was attacked, I would not have been able to do much for him. These wounds were meant to kill him. There are things we cannot mend and this is one of them. All I can do is ease his suffering."

She had given Percy her best healing and pain-relief Majiked potions, and came every day to cast her spells of 'heal' and 'ease' on Davey, but he never did improve. For two weeks, Davey lingered, hovering near death, while Percy stopped eating, stopped speaking and stopped living for anything but Davey.

At last, just before dawn one morning, Davey opened the one eye that could still see, and looked at Percy. Then he heaved a great sigh and passed away.

Percy had lovingly prepared Davey's body for burial himself, allowing no one else to touch him. The others made a beautiful bier for him down in the 'ladies' parlor' where he was laid out in state, and the black-notice was sent to all the retirees.

Once his last task for Davey was done, Percy spent the rest of that day holding Davey's cold dead hand, sitting in the cold dark parlor, refusing to leave him, speaking to no one and eating nothing. Though Mickey tried his best to get him to rest, he refused.

At some point toward midnight, Percy had looked up at Mickey and asked, "Why Mick? Why? Who had he ever hurt that he should have been treated so? He was the most beautiful of men, but I can't even remember what he looked like before they hurt him. All I can see is what they did to him. I can't live this way."

They found him the next morning, lying next to Davey on his bier with his arms around Davey's cold dead body. Percy had slit his own throat rather than live with the memory of what had been done to beautiful Davey. He'd rather die than live without him.

Huw couldn't pull himself out of the pit of depression long enough to write a tragic ballad.

But now with Percy's death, there was a problem that none of the others would ever have foreseen. It had fired all of them up, like nothing else could have.

Everyone had thought it odd that Babs Gentry and Annie Fitzgerald had taken the tragedy exceedingly personally the way that they had; and now with Percy's death they were openly and angrily talking revenge. Both were mothers of young sons born within two days of each other. Despite their rage, it was unlikely that they would be making that sort of a foray any time soon with the babies nursing still, both of the boys being only nine months old.

In a very unusual move, Billy and Bess were going to be caring for the boys while their mothers worked, once they were weaned since both ladies refused to name the father of their babes, nor would they leave the trade. "I have to make some sort of arrangement. If I don't, I will lose two Rowdies. There is no one to replace them. I need the help and they need to support their babes," Billy had said when the unusual arrangement had become known. The two ladies were making short runs now, and soon as the babes were weaned, they would be back on the road with the rest of the Rowdies.

And now with Percy's death, it came out that Davey had 'done them a favor'. The ladies had each of them wanted a baby, but since they shared a pillow it was just not going to happen. Though they had both once enjoyed the lads, they had cemented their own relationship five years before and had no desire to alter it.

But now at the age of thirty-four, if they did not do it soon they would never have children. The same had gone for Davey, because of his nature. He had on occasion mentioned that he deeply wished he could have a child and wished at times that he had been created differently. On more than one occasion, he had confessed that he had never ever been with a woman, which as he had wryly admitted, was a requirement for those who wanted children.

A year and a half previously, while the three of them had been out on a little task for the Lord Chamberlain they had found themselves discussing their mutual problem around the campfire. The solution had seemed so obvious. As they talked in the light of the campfire, it came to Annie that the solution was staring them in the face. Who could possibly be better than 'one of the ladies' to help them with solving their problem? There was no one that they could trust more than Davey, and after thinking about it, he agreed to the mad scheme.

Davey was the very last Rowdy that anyone would ever suspect of fathering even one child, much less two born within days of each other. And so they had all gotten a wee bit drunk and settled the issue then and there. Over the course of the week-long trip, they had made quite sure that they would get their babes out of it.

Davey had never told Percy about the arrangement. Percy was a mad-jealous man, and wouldn't have understood how badly Davey wanted a child.

It had worked out well, too. When they returned, the three of them told Billy what they had done. He reluctantly agreed, despite the fact that the ladies would be off the road for at least a year once they got too big to work. At first Billy and Bess worried privately that Percy would find out and kill them all, but it had gone exactly as they had planned. That was until the day Davey was brought home so wounded.

The Rowdies consoled themselves with the knowledge that Davey had at least seen his children born, though it had been his own secret. Childlessness was a secret pain that every merc suffered from. All the Rowdies loved the children that Bess and Gertie kept bringing into the world, so two more were loved by all. Every night, they had passed the babies around, playing with them; just generally enthralled with them, Davey and Percy as much as anyone. If Davey had seemed particularly fond of them, well, it was well known that men became quite foolish about babies as they entered middle age, especially childless men.

However, now that Percy was gone, there was no reason to deny who had fathered the boys.

Interestingly enough, the contract that all parties signed when engaging the services of the Rowdies was specific and strictly enforced; now William De Vayne owed a death-geld of five golds each to the two ladies.

He would have been better off hiring three more guards. Poor William sat in the corner crying harder than any. Everyone was sure that he would take Billy's advice from that day on, when it came to hiring guards.

The common room almost looked like the old days. Lackland had returned from wherever he had been on business for the king, grim and grey with anger and grief; he had been very close to both Davey and Percy. Slippery Jack was back, along with Merry Kat and their young ones who were happily playing with the other children. All the old Rowdies were together again, but it was a miserable old time.

Toward the end of the night, Lackland found himself sitting opposite Mags. She was alone for the moment; her lad, Beau Baker had left to help Huw carry the Fat Friar home.

Mags looked across the table at Lackland and felt the old feelings welling, but as always when they met nowadays, they kept it strictly cordial. "My father says that you are his good right arm these days. Is he as well as his letters claim?"

"Perhaps not quite as well as he wants you to think, but not terrible; he refuses to go to court now, preferring to stay home and run his estate. This next year, he is going to send your brother in his stead." Lackland's thick blonde hair had begun to go silver at the temples. He was leaner and stronger than she remembered him ever being; with laugh-wrinkles at the corners of his eyes, but somehow he was even more handsome for those changes. Her heart thumped wildly whenever she looked at him, as did many another ladies' heart.

Lackland continued, "The lad is doing well, and will benefit from his time at court. He is already quite smitten with young Rose Dragoran, who in turn is smitten with him. Henri and your father are planning a marriage there when the time comes." His pride as he said that was quite evident."Henri is quite pleased with the prospect of the two families being joined."

Mags' eyes had warmed as she eagerly listened for all the news about her 'brother'. "I sent him a new mail shirt, did he like it?" her eyes begged to hear that he did, and Lackland was able to tell her that indeed, the boy had been over the moon that his 'sister' had a shirt made especially for him by the famous Gertie Smith.

"It was all he could talk about for a month," he told her with a twinkle in his eye. "The lad is mad for fighting, as they all are at that age."

"Well, I think I will send him Dove's next foal, if it is a male," she decided. "He will need a sturdy mount." At thirty four, there were some silver threads in her mahogany hair but Mags was still the beauty that had forever claimed his heart; only riper and more polished. His mouth still went dry and his mind ground to a halt when he watched her walk.

"Ah. Good old Farroll is now living his dream; he is happily employed in the 'service' of the King's Mares," laughed Lackland. "My new mount, Strider is a sturdy enough fellow, being much younger and much more interested in traveling, as I do so often now."

"Where are you off to now?" she asked, wishing that he would tell her that he was rejoining the Rowdies.

"Not too far this time. I am headed home to House Portiers, to school my nephew over the Yuletide," he replied. "The boy is showing some promise and I don't want him completely ruined by Morty's notions of a proper upbringing."

"How is Morty? Still got a face that looks like he has a sliver festering in his arse when he smiles?" Mags did not have much use for Mortimer De Portiers.

Lackland grinned widely at her assessment of his brother, the humor at his brother's expense lighting up his gloomy countenance. "My pompous ass of a brother says that young Melvin will be going to court this next fall too, and I've a hankering to see my mother. Next fall when the season begins, I will return to court as Henri's Master of Arms as I do each year, teaching the young men what they must know to survive. You know why I will be at court; it is not my great love of the courtiers' life, I do assure you." His voice carried a note of determination as he promised her, "As much as I can without drawing attention, I will be where ever Jules is until he is a man; guiding him and giving him the training that he must have to survive. I have promised this to your father."

"I know you will, and I am greatly comforted knowing that you will be there, when he is surrounded by idiots like Morty," she replied, laughing. His wry grin and the spark in his bright blue eyes tugged at her heart-strings. There was no chance that he would return to the Rowdies unless Mags changed her mind and that was not going to happen.

"Will you go home for Yuletide? It has been two years and your father and Jules both miss you. I promised them that I would ask." Lackland tried not to sound like he was pleading with her, though he was doing just that.

"I will, since it means so much to you; if father doesn't mind me bringing a friend," she said reluctantly, though she wished she had not agreed as soon as she said it. "I want to see them both. So badly I wish to see them, but I have done neither one of them any good. I don't feel worthy of them."

"Stop that, you are being ridiculous. Your father just badly wants to see you, Mags. He and Jules won't care that you have brought Beau with you; they will like him quite well, I think. Edward knows that you are never going to be anything other than his mad, merry daughter." Lackland's smile eased her fears about his acceptance of her lad, Beau. Mags couldn't bear to be alone and Lackland knew that. "HE loves you just the way you are, and Jules worships his sister."

Lackland had yearned to be a part of Jules' life, and Mags knew that as well. In order to do that, he had set Mags free ten years before, and he had meant it when he did it; though he had stayed with her for nearly a year afterward.

Edward De Leon was a wise man, and had conspired with Henri to devise a plan that was the best for everyone under the circumstances. Lackland returned to the court of Henri Dragoran, and when he was not at court he was residing at House De Leon, as a 'dear family friend and instructor' of young Lord Jules De Leon in the arts of knighthood. Lackland had become a son to Edward, who deeply wished that his daughter would just marry him and be done with it. "She doesn't have to live with you, for heaven's sake. She could still swing her sword as a Rowdy."

Lackland's eyes twinkled as he said, "In fact, your fame as the intrepid lady hero has leant your father a bit of a cachet that he would not have had otherwise. It is considered to be quite gallant to be able to claim friendship with your father and thereby be thought to rub elbows with the famous Lady Mags."

His face turned serious. "But as to my travels - once the weather improves after Yuletide, Slippery Jack and I are going down south to settle up the debt for Davey and Percy." There was steel in his voice and a cold light in his eyes as he spoke of his plans. "If all goes as planned, though nothing is ever sure, Henri will be down in the Bekenberg Pass securing the border with Lanqueshire and diverting attention from us. All eyes will be on him, and that is when we will do what must be done. Henri is going to use this tragedy to settle the situation down there once and for all."

"When you speak like that, I see the man who is the Arms-Master of Waldeyn, Lackland; and I pity your enemies. Henri is fortunate to have you. I am glad for the babies that you will do this."

They both looked over at the two women that cradled dark-haired babies, both of whose fathers could only have been one man; an obvious thing now that the truth had been told. They were the image of Davey; black curls, deep blue eyes with dark curling lashes and perfect little faces. Their mothers were deep in conversation with Jack, and though the ladies were crying, they seemed happy about what he had been telling them. Lackland and Mags watched as Jack reached his arms about them both and hugged them consolingly, promising that their boys would have the knowledge that their father had been avenged.

Seeing the babes that looked so much like Davey, Mags suddenly hoped that Jules still had her looks, so that he would not be so obviously Lackland's son.

As if reading her mind, Lackland said off handedly, "I am quite amazed at how much your brother looks like you must have looked at his age, though he is quite as tall as your father already, and will be much taller when he has his full growth. He too, has your father's red hair and your aunt tells me that he is the very image of his father as a youth. He will be quite the lad, I am sure."

Mags smiled, and nodded with relief. Lackland was too well known at court, and if it had been otherwise someone would have put two and two together.

Mags said, also in an offhand manner, "I am relieved that you will be at court this fall. Many of the young men in Henri's court will be much better knights because you will have taught them the art. You will keep them on the right path."

The doors swung open and Huw and Beau entered, making a beeline for their table. Lackland stood up and clasped hands with Beau, who once again immediately felt unsure of himself in the presence of the Great Knight. Everyone knew him to be the love of Lady Mags' life, and he didn't know what to say, exactly. He was younger, only twenty-seven. 'The Beau' had joined the Rowdies two years after Lackland had left, but he had always known Lackland as a great hero; the hero that had rescued him from a grisly death as a young lad.

Soon, Lackland had him relaxed and laughing, as he told the true story of how he and Slippery Jack had rescued him so long ago. "That sounds much worse than the way Huw tells it," Beau said, laughing at the mental picture that Lackland had painted for him. When handsome, golden Beau laughed Lackland could see what attracted Mags to him, and felt a kinship with him. His laugh held so much joy and love of life that all who heard it had to smile. The four of them laughed and chatted, finding comfort in the stories that each of them had to tell about Davey and Percy.

Soon, young Brand was helping his father close up the common room, and Lackland went off to stay with Huw for the night.

As they sat at Huw's lonely table, in his lonely house, Lackland could see that Huw had not changed a thing since Lucy had died.

Huw noticed him looking around, and said, "I have a woman who cleans for me, but I won't let her change a thing. I am not ready for that yet."

"Well, are you feeling like making a trip south come spring?" asked Lackland with a look in his eye that Huw recognized. "Jack and I will need a guide who knows the long valley, and you need to get away from this for a while." He gestured around the room where everything had Lucy's touch written all over it. "It could be that the trouble you were running from seventeen years ago has settled down and you are not known there any longer."

"If you are meddling in politics, I might be interested," replied Huw after a moment's consideration. "I confess that I have been feeling like seeing the Old Country for a week or two now, myself. I would dearly love to murder a certain grand duke; quite as much as I once wanted to murder his uncle." His bleak eyes spoke volumes, reflecting the depth of his despair and anger.

"We will come back and get you then, when we go south, after the Yuletide," replied Lackland. "Mickey said he would watch your place while you are gone."

Huw grimaced. "I'll bet he did. He'd best not change a thing or I will kill him."

Lackland had no doubt of that. The look on Huw's face told him all he needed to know as to the depth of Huw's mourning.

After a long moment of silence, Lackland spoke again. "We will need supplies, so this should cover it," said Lackland as he put a small purse full of gold on the table. "Jack and I talked to Billy, and he is agreeable to our plan. We aren't going to return to the Rowdies because we still have much to do for Henri on the border and can't leave him until those tasks are complete. So, instead of joining back up, we are hiring you and one other to be selected later. Billy has the gold now, since I had it along with me anyway."

After a moment of contemplating, Huw said, "I think that in the meantime, I am going to use my contacts and find out what I can about who would want to kill an unknown merc like our own God's Gift using a ritual assassination, like that which Johnny and Fred described. There has to be a larger reason for such an expensive murder."

"There is, Jack told me so; but I can't say for sure until I know it for a fact." Lackland sighed morosely. "I suspect though, that this will affect Waldeyn's troubles in the long valley much more deeply than one would think that the murder of a mere merc would. The clan war down there is boiling again; what with the young Weyllyn Duchess Gwenevere about to be married to young Prince Harry. That is sure to ruffle the feathers on not a few of your Black Crows; since it will cement the crown's claim on the long valley once and for all. Harry and Gwenevere will be living in the Eynier at the old family home, ruling the long valley on behalf of the crown, handling the local peoples' crown petitions, providing crown justice in the valley.

"Henri sees it as a way for them to get the training they will need to assume the reins when he has passed on. Also, it gets an Eynier Princess back in charge of Eynier; thus gutting the Grand Duke Grefyn's most salient argument in his bid to break away from Waldeyn."

"I advised Henri to do just that when he was through here last year, and he wanted my take on the situation with The Crow. I am glad to hear that Gwenevere is going to marry Prince Harry. It is the best way to bring peace to that poor valley." Huw thought about what Lackland had just told him, and then said, "I will look into Davey's name. Leweyllyn is the most common name in the northern end of the valley. That is a clue, but I can't figure out how it fits, unless... what did Johnny say they were calling him?" A stunned look came into his eyes. "My God! He couldn't be!" Abruptly, Huw changed the subject. "I believe that I will need Jack on my spying mission. And Lackland, don't worry, I will make the arrangements with Tom Stanton for the supplies."

Lackland yawned and apologized, then Huw stood up, saying it was long past time for bed. As he showed Lackland to the little guest room he said, "We will expect you back here after the Yuletide. We will be ready to go on this end of things, I promise."

*

Lackland's visit to House Portiers had gone as he had expected. He had barely arrived and his mother had begun lamenting that he had never found a bride.

There was, of course, a lavish formal dinner party for the Yuletide 'celebrating his return to the family hearth'. In reality, his brother was using every inch of Lackland's fame and prominence at court to further himself in the eyes of his cronies; all of whom wished nothing more than to be seen as a dear friend of Sir Julian Lackland, the Great Knight of the Realm.

His old uncle, Uncle Evelyr, had cornered him at dinner regarding his lack of a wife. Speaking from far down the table, he had loudly wanted to know if the problem was a 'lad-loving-the-lads-sort-of-thing'. Stating that he was sure that is perfectly fine nowadays, almost respectable.

"I am so relieved that you approve, Uncle!" Lackland had replied equally loudly with a wicked glint in his eye, causing his Uncle to choke on his wine. As Lackland's nephew pounded the old man on the back, Lackland had added merrily, "I will bring my lad home with me next year. Your approval means the world to us!"

Forks had dropped all down the table and his sister-in-law had fainted. Lackland's mother Isabelle and his young nephew Melvin had both laughed quite merrily at the consternation in Evelyr's red face and his brother had said pompously, "*We* are not that modern here, Julian. *We* have an image to maintain."

"Well, I don't. I can do as I like and to hell with my image. Besides, everyone knows that I am in love with one woman, and if she won't marry me then I will never marry, end of story." Lackland had beamed a brilliant smile around the table, receiving many shocked and weak smiles in return.

"We don't approve of those sorts of jokes, Julian," said Morty stuffily.

"Oh, stuff it Morty," replied Lackland, releasing the full brunt of his pent up irritation. "People who ask personal questions at dinner parties should be content with whatever answer they get."

It had taken Lackland all of two minutes to realize that his brother Mortimer was still a pretentious ass; and Morty's wife, Letitia, was still unbelievably silly, desperately hanging on to her fading beauty in a frantic sort of way. Despite her limited intellect, Lackland had always liked her because she meant well. Daily, she begged to hear that she looked as young as ever. Ever the gentleman, daily he obliged; treating Letitia with the courtliness with which the Knights in her favorite romantic tales always treated the fairest of ladies.

But his nephew, Melvin, had been rather a surprise. He was refreshingly simple and honest, considering the poisonous environment he was growing up in. He had learned all that he could, as quickly as he could, from Lackland, knowing that his uncle was only there on a brief visit.

Mel was desperately looking forward to going to Castleton and having some real adventures. With the prejudice of youth, Mel was barely able to tolerate the posturing of his father and abhorred the social-climbing that was his father's only joy in life; an attitude which had immediately endeared him to Lackland.

Thus, Lackland had passed a tolerable Yuletide. He prepared to leave once again, at the first week of January. Though the roads were mushy with the winter rains, he was eager to get on with his grim mission.

Lackland had not spoken of the fact that he and Davey had been lovers for a very brief time, during the time that Mags had turned cold to him; although he was aware that the others had known of it at the time, since they did not bother to hide it. It was part of his personal code of honor that Lackland never discussed his lovers with anyone. It was not out of shame that he was reticent in these matters; Lackland had a very wide view of sexual morality. It was his natural discretion and innate sense of politeness that made him reluctant to discuss it. He believed that what was between two people should be only between them, and should not be the topic of casual conversation.

But he did take the deaths of Davey and Percy personally. He had cared deeply about Percy, as much as he had about Davey. They were old friends with a long history, and Percy had forgiven him when he and Lackland had been able to talk it out. Percy knew that Mags was his true love, and that Lackland had been heartsick over the trouble he had caused between Davey and Percy. That had been ten years before, and Davey had been faithful to Percy after that, with the sole exception of his arrangement with Babs and Annie. His heart had belonged to Percy.

As he took leave of his Lady Mother, Julian told her that he thought Melvin would do well at court. She rolled her eyes, and said that Mortimer had just announced that he was angling to get Melvin married to Princess Rose.

Lackland laughed, and said that as far as he knew, the girl was betrothed to the Earl of Bunder's son. Morty would have to look elsewhere to advance the bloodline.

"I wish you had stayed here and done your duty," she said irritably. "I can barely stand Morty's posturing and pratting about. Of course, he is not going to marry that boy to a princess, that is ridiculous, but I have to listen to it day and night. At least Melvin looks like you and my side of the family, instead of Morty and your father's family. At least he has some looks to bring to the bargaining table. Morty is squandering the family's fortune with his pathetic attempt to make Portiers into an Earldom."

"I have no duty here, Mother; it is all Morty's duty, and he is not disposed to be charitable about it; he made that clear long ago." Though his face remained pleasant, his voice held a note of steel as Julian answered his mother, causing her eyes to widen fractionally. "I refuse to help Morty out the slightest bit, though I am more than rich enough to do so," replied Lackland firmly. "I won't put up with his noise, and he knows it. Besides, once Morty is gone, I will make sure Melvin has all the gold he will need to keep the doors open here, don't worry. If it looks like Morty is going to lose the place, of course I will save his arse, but he will have to dance to my tune if that should happen. He will be polite and conciliatory about it, though!" Julian's face had a look that made her mother shiver. It was, she thought, the look he must have when he dealt with a particularly nasty nest of beasts.

He put his arm about his mother's shoulders, and hugged her close, smiling his warm, charming smile that was his trademark. "Don't forget that I will have Melvin for my own for the next five years! I will have his attention for four hours out of every day, and I will make sure that he understands how to properly maintain his estates by staying involved with him. I will insure that the rest of the time, he is learning more than toadying for favor. Our Melvin doesn't need a princess to be the finest Knight in the realm. Besides, there are plenty of fine young ladies of good breeding out there for him, who will be much more to his taste. Rose is quite taken with her betrothed, so I hear!"

"Mel will fall in love like you did, Julian." Isabela's voice was sharp and she knew it but she couldn't change the way she felt. "Everyone but your uncle knows you are pining for Margaret De Leon."

"Well, some things can't be helped, Mother. I just live my life as best as I can and get on with things," he replied cheerfully. "I have been fortunate enough to be able to make my own fortune, and if some other things haven't worked out as well as I would have wished, well that is what it must be. I am richer than even Morty could dream of, and I have earned every piece of gold that I own. I am content with how I live my life. Melvin will greatly benefit from my good fortune."

"Are you content spending half of every year at Bunder's House De Leon? Why would you do such a thing if his daughter won't marry you?" She was pushing forward into dangerous territory now and Julian was dancing on thin ice. Deciding that pressing his own attack was his only choice he said, "The Earl is a good old thing, and I do love his daughter. I would be his son-in-law, if she would just agree to marry me. Besides, he needs me. Since I have no land of my own and if I was his son-in-law, in truth, I would be there with him, so what is the difference?"

Lackland felt that he had her confused and off balance, so it was a good time to kiss her cheek and leave. "Edward is far better to me than my own father ever was. So I find it no ordeal to help him with managing his estates when I am not at court, until his son comes of age to help him."

"Jules," she said as he bent to kiss his mother's cheek. Startled, he looked sharply at her, for a moment thinking that she had somehow guessed, but it was just her old nickname for him, and he relaxed.

"I might not see you again, my dear," Isabela De Portiers looked at the wall instead of her son. "I am dying."

"Why do you say this now, instead of a month ago," Julian asked, feeling stunned. "Why? What is it, Mother?" He knelt before her, and took her cool hand between his and looked into the blue eyes that were so much like his own, if only he knew it.

"It is breast cancer, Jules. The priestess cannot cure it, but she does ease the pain. It is one of those things one can do nothing about, and polite society does not talk about." She exhaled heavily, and said, "I don't know why I have not told anyone. I haven't told Morty either, and I probably won't until I have no choice. It is personal," she said sardonically. "It is my death and I want it on my terms."

"I can understand that," he told her, holding her cool hand to his cheek. "I would feel the same way."

"You are a lot more like me than you know, my Julian. We think alike." Isabela smiled and pressed a package into his hands, a heavy wooden box wrapped in a silk scarf. It was the scarf he had given her for Yuletide his first year at court; an eager boy of twelve so pleased to be able to give his mother a silken scarf from Vyennes. She had worn it often, pleased with both the gift and the giver.

He began unwrapping the box, but she stopped him. "There is a letter. Look at it when you get back to Billy's Revenge and pick up your friends." Lackland was startled again, and she laughed. "Where else would you be going but to avenge your friends? The St John's are expecting it; and it is what I would do. Just stay safe, my darling," she kissed his stunned cheek. "I want you to live to see your son married to Henri's daughter." And with that she swept out of the room.

Lackland stood in shock for a moment, staring at the package in his hand. Then he strode up to his rooms and picked up his gear, placing the package safely in his saddle bag.

He stopped by the class room where Melvin was suffering the administering of a lesson in the language of Lanqueshire. It was a lovely, liquid language called Lanque that was similar to the common tongue of Waldeyn, but different in many ways. "I am off now, nephew," he told the boy, speaking in perfect Lanque. "Study hard and I will see you when you get to court in the fall. I will be working with all of you young courtiers, as the King's Master at Arms. In the meantime, study hard. I will be supervising your education and testing your skills in every aspect of the knightly arts, of which the ability to speak Lanque is one. You must be able to speak the languages of all our neighbors, Lanque, Lournesque, Vyennesk; all of them; even Fornost!"Switching to Waldeynier he said, "One never knows where the king will send you, and you must be ready!" He winked at the surprised tutor.

"Uncle! How will I survive without you? It is absolute Hell here, with only father for entertainment," replied Melvin, standing and feeling rather proud of himself for having managed to use a curse word in an appropriate and defensible manner. At the age of eleven he stood on the verge of manhood, and the next five years would be the making of him; of that Lackland was certain.

Melvin's stance, and the way he held his head, reminded Lackland of another boy; one with burnished mahogany hair and warm brown eyes so like his 'sister's' eyes. They were the same height, and had such similar mannerisms that for a moment Lackland was overwhelmed by his longing for Jules. *'They are so obviously blood-related,'* thought Lackland. *'Maybe no one will notice. Maybe it is my guilt that makes me see this.'*

"If you would do something for me I would appreciate it," replied Lackland, seriously. "I want you to spend one hour each day reading to your grandmother." At Melvin's stubborn look, Lackland handed him a well-worn book, saying "This is her very favorite book. I read it to her for one hour every day until I went to court at your age, and I have read it to her every day since I have been back. She is dreadfully lonely, Mel. You must take up this task."

Melvin looked at the book with the contempt that only youth can bring to such a venture, and then did a double take. "This... this is her *favorite* book?" he asked incredulously, looking at his Uncle's serious blue eyes.

"It is. It would please her no end if you would read for just one hour each day," Lackland smiled. "You will find that your grandmother is an amazing woman."

Clasping Melvin's shoulder, one warrior to another, he turned and left the classroom, leaving his nephew holding a somewhat battered copy of 'The Merrye Adventyures of Sir Roderick Smythe – A Tale of Wyne, Womyn and Song'.

Melvin looked at his tutor. In perfect Lanque he said, "I have to go now. My grandmother is waiting for me to read her a story," and he left the classroom, heading straight to his grandmother's suite of rooms.

With some trepidation, he knocked on her door. When the serving-woman opened the door, Mel bowed and said, "I wish to see my grandmother, if she is having visitors."

Melvin would forever be grateful that his uncle had pushed him to read to his grandmother, as she passed away the following summer. He had read to her every day for more than one hour, starting again at the beginning when they came to the end of the wonderful book. Over the course of those months, he had discovered that inside of his frail old grandmother was a merry girl who had always craved adventure as much as he did.

*

Huw was waiting for Lackland when he rode into Limpwater the next afternoon, leading two pack ponies heavily laden with all his worldly possessions. He had emptied his rooms of his old treasures; Lackland would never again call House De Portiers home. Huw stood at his gate with a rake in his hand, and said "Jack rode in this morning. He is already at Billy's getting settled in, so I will just meet you there later."

Lackland looked at the little cottage. The soil was freshly tended around the apple tree, and the crocuses were poking up their green shoots there. Huw saw where Lackland was looking, and said, "I have planted forget-me-not seeds there just this morning. She will not lack for flowers this year, my Lucy Blue Eyes won't."

After a moment, Lackland said, "What a pair we are, Huw." Sighing, he looked toward Billy's and said, "I will meet you there then. Maybe Billy has a room for me."

"He does, and always will. You know that," said Huw. "But he knows why you won't come back permanently. She loves you, but she will never leave the trade. You know it, I know it and Beau knows it."

As Lackland rode into the courtyard in front of the stables, he felt disoriented, like he had come home, and yet, he knew he had not. Handing Strider and the ponies off to Betty, he walked over to the smithy. "I will be back to get my luggage, I just need to talk to Gertie first!"

Standing in the warmth of the smithy, Lackland spoke to Gertie about commissioning a pair of shields, one for Jules and one for Melvin with their respective family coat-of-arms on each of them. She was, as always, more than happy to help Lackland. "Lady Mags has commissioned helms for these same two young courtiers," Gertie told him with her eyes twinkling. "She values these two lads as much as you do, Lackland. I will have them for you by the time you are to go to court, I promise!"

After he had spoken to Gertie, Lackland lugged his baggage up to the room that Billy had ready for him, noting that he was now in the room that that had been Lucy Blue Eyes' room so long ago. Unpacking his bags, he soon had everything put away. His poetry books filled the shelf, and on the mantle were several small silver-framed portraits: Jules, Mags, Melvin and his mother all smiled back at him. Several delicate figurines that he had bought in Vyennes made the room his.

"Now it feels like home," he said as he surveyed his pictures and their beloved faces. With that done, he sat at the table by the window and opened the box his mother had given him; finding a small fortune in jewelry, much of which he recognized and much that he had never seen her wear.

"These are for your son, to give his bride when he is married," she had written. "They were my mother's; she was a St Clair, and as you know, she was sister to Henri's paternal grandmother. I have made my will, and registered it with the local crown ministry. The ministry has charge of that which I have set aside for Melvin, and is aware of my reasons for such an arrangement. It will be for you to manage as Executor of my personal estate. Mortimer shall not squander his son's entire inheritance!

"Eight years ago, De Leon and Jules visited me while Morty was at court pretending to be a knight, and while the rest of you were off fighting a war. Edward and I talked and we have agreed that this is only right. Young Jules understands the situation, and is content to keep the truth close to his heart. They have visited me twice every year since then, when Morty is away. De Leon writes me regularly, keeping me informed as to all that is going on in the lives of both of my charming boys who reside at House De Leon. I am so very proud of you, and what you have accomplished with young Jules, who is so much like our Melvin. They are both very like you were at their age.

"Forgive me for hounding you so visibly about your marital status. It is necessary, as you well know, that your brother remain as ignorant as he is..."

As he read the letter, his eyes filled with tears. It was a long while before Lackland could go down to the common-room.

*

It was quiet in the common-room. There were few Rowdies hanging about; those who had just returned were mainly up in their own rooms or in the bath-house. Lackland saw that Bess was looking a bit harried and took Annie's baby, little Devyn off her hands. He sat in the corner, rocking the boy to sleep, while he waited for Huw and Jack to join him at his table.

The only Rowdies there were Huw, Beau and Brand, along with a young Lady Rowdy named Bold Lora Saunders. She was rather hard-eyed, and somewhat less refined than the Ladies that they usually had, but then she was the first Lady to join up in two years. Huw was playing his harp, and the sounds of it lulled Lackland into a sort of dreamlike state. Brand was occupied with helping his father bring up a keg, and Beau read a book in the other corner.

Lora was merry enough and seemed like a good enough sort, but she would never have been accepted if Mags had been there when she had applied to Billy just before Yuletide. She had made few close friends in the month she had been with them. Lackland remembered her father quite well; he had been a likeable man, though he had never been very clever.

Bold Lora was sixteen and was certainly legally old enough for the work, but she laughed a little too raucously, talked a little too loudly and disdained needlework which the other Ladies all enjoyed. She had little in common with the other Ladies, whom she rather openly despised. She was over bold in her way toward men, and her taste in clothing was nowhere near as refined as that of the other ladies. She flaunted her charms, rather cheaply, instead of the elegant way of the women of Limpwater. Lora always behaved as if she had something to prove. It grated on the older Gentlemen Rowdies who had to travel with her, and fend off her heavy-handed advances.

Annie Fitz had bluntly told her, on more than one occasion, that her manners were quite lacking; and that if she continued to lower the tone of the Ladies, she would be out on her ear. "WE are Ladies. We get the job done, but we are ladies. It doesn't matter whether you are high or low, who you sleep with or what your accent is. None of that matters. Your demeanor is what matters; you will behave like a lady, or you will be gone."

During the four wakes he had attended during this last year, Lackland hadn't really noticed the fact that most of the old crowd had moved on because all the old faces had been there; the right voices, and the right laughter, all except for the honored dead, whose passing had left a gaping wound in the life of Billy's Revenge.

He realized now that he didn't really know any of these newer Rowdies, though he had played with most all of them on his knee as babies.

Young Brand and Bennie Smith were nearly eighteen and well established in the trade. It seemed like only yesterday, he had returned to teach them the skills that they would need to know. Though, now that he thought about it, it had been three years since that summer.

Still, they were men now; proven and hardened by two years in the saddle. It surprised him to think that so many years had passed since he first came to this room looking for adventure; when the room still smelled of fresh cut pine. *"I'm thirty-six now. I came here when I was no older than they are now, but sometimes I wonder if I was ever as young as they are."* His thoughts were gloomy, but he couldn't escape them. Holding the sleeping baby seemed to help a little, and he took comfort from the clean smell of Devyn's baby-hair.

As the evening passed, Bess reclaimed Devyn. Bennie Smith and Babs returned from their job and it began to be a merrier place. Bennie, Gertie's oldest boy, was quite infatuated with Bold Lora Saunders. She appeared to like him well enough, but loudly declared she was married to her sword, while looking at Lackland with hot-eyed glances. Lackland sighed heavily, on seeing the interplay between them, determined to stay out of that triangle. He wanted no ill feelings with Bennie in that regard, and the girl was not to his taste at all.

Lora was the daughter of Tom Saunders, a merc that Billy would never have in the Rowdies because of his long association with Bloody Ball-less Bryan. Tom had gone to the Badgers down in Wister when Bloody Bryan ran afoul of Lucy's knife. He had died in the saddle some two years previously, when the caravan he had been guarding to Vyennes was ambushed.

As he sat in the familiar room that seemed so full of strangers, Huw and Billy sat down with him. His sense of not belonging vanished; it was almost like he had never left.

Almost, but not quite.

"I have been off the road for a while now. Teaching arms isn't the same as fighting for real," Lackland was saying as Jack joined them. "I have been fighting with the King, and carrying a shield, so I don't know if I am up to the sort of nasty fighting we do here anymore."

"I think that you and Jack will get back into the feel of it as soon as you are back on the road, Lackland. You haven't been out of it for too long." Billy sighed as he too sat down. "You have no idea how hard it is to get good help, no thanks to your efforts on the king's behalf. I suspect that in ten years, Billy's Revenge will be a wayside inn, catering to the travelers, and the Rowdies will be a memory. I had hoped that Brand would have more of a business to come to, but there it is. The good ones are going off to help your cousin fight the Lanques, because they all want to be like you, Sir Julian Lackland De Portiers. The young ones worship you. Most of ones that are left are not worth a damn."

"They are only in it for the money or the fame," supplied Babs, glancing out the corner of her eye at Bold Lora. "*Some*," she said meaningfully, "want an epic tale of their exploits told at every wayside inn on the trade-road if they rescue a cat from a tree." She shifted her son Donal to her other shoulder, but he continued fussing, chewing fretfully on his little hand.

"Well, there are still a few of us who will do the bad jobs," replied Lackland stoutly. "I haven't turned down a request for help yet, and I hope I never do."

Taking Babs' fussy son, putting him over his beefy shoulder and expertly burping him, Billy said, "Well, this job you are off on now… it is likely to be a bad job. We are keeping it close, just those of us who have to know."

Lackland raised his eyebrow at Billy's son Brand who still sat with the other young Rowdies, with a questioning look.

Billy shook his head. "Even Brand thinks you are back here to teach arms and take a few jobs here and there for old times' sake and out of boredom; the same as you have always done. So far as they know, you three and Beau are taking a long job, traveling to Vyennes with some ice-wine from Bekenberg for the next two months. Jack will tell you what he found out over the Yuletide. Beau knows what you are riding into, and he volunteered anyway. He begged to go, actually. This is going to either get you all killed or get you an earldom, Lackland." Babs retrieved the sleeping Donal from Billy's damp shoulder and Billy sat back, raising his hand and said, "I heard a tale from John Caskman over in Dervy. It seems there was this traveling friar…"

Brand promptly got up, went behind the bar, and came over to his father's raised hand and put a foamy mug of ale in it. Everyone at Billy's table was laughing over the tale, and Huw had begun another involving a lady and her footman.

Once he had moved off, Huw finished his joke and the laughter died away. Billy leaned forward, saying, "If you do manage to get ours back for Davey and Percy, you will gut the opposition to Henri's claim in the long valley. It turns out that our Davey was a lot more than a pretty face and a fancy sword. Our Davey was born the Duke Dayved Weyllyn of Imrysdock. His father had been murdered a month before his birth. It was a fairly minor peerage when he was a child, but by the time he walked away from it and came up here, he was a very prominent person in the Eynier Valley. And while he was off up here, paying absolutely no attention to his family and their troubles, little did he know that with each year he was growing ever closer to being the heir to his uncle, the Grand Duke Allyn Weyllyn, despite his efforts to the contrary. Jack will tell you."

Lackland's eyebrows had both risen nearly into his hairline. "But I know exactly what the name Dayved Weyllyn means! In the eyes of Eynier, he was as royal as Henri Dragoran. He was to be the head of his clan, but he abdicated and vanished. I know his sister very well!" His whisper drew nods from Huw and Jack. "And all the time he was here… under our noses!" He sat back in shock, saying, "Our Davey… who would have guessed that such a humble, beautiful man was so famous a person."

Jack began speaking softly so as to not draw attention to what he was saying. "Huw figured it out. Apparently, Leweyllyn means 'of clan Weyllyn'; just as De Portiers means 'of Portiers', and could mean anything high or low. But our God's Gift *was* Weyllyn. He was Weyllyn, the way Henri Dragoran *is* Waldeyn.

"As you know, Lackland, his abdication and disappearance was much discussed. With the passing of the years, many had thought him dead, until a chance encounter two years ago with his cousin in Castleton proved he still existed. Still, he had made it clear to his cousin that he was not going back; that he would not leave Percy, which he would have had to do. They would have made him marry for the clan, you see. They don't approve of lads like him at all down there. So he had given his cousin a letter once again renouncing his claim in favor of his sister and her children, and as far as Davey was concerned, that was that."

Still in shock, Lackland shook his head slowly, saying, "He always claimed to be just a farmer's son. With his heavy Eynier accent, you couldn't tell what his family background was, and you know that it would have meant nothing anyway here in the Rowdies. Many are of high birth, even our Percy was the younger son of Lord Alban St. John. Percy and I were close friends during our youth in the old days at court. No one cares where you came from here, which is why Percy and Davey came here, I would wager. They could just live like normal people."

"Weyllyn still follows our Henri, but clan Grefyn wants their power. Grefyn began murdering Weyllyn off in earnest for the last two years," Jack's serious words were delivered as if he was talking over old times, as they were supposedly doing.

"All of the misery of the last twelve years in the long valley has been an orchestrated power grab by the Grand Duke Amstyce Grefyn. It was not a grass-roots movement of the people who have suffered for it, despite his strident claim to the contrary. Clan Grefyn has been making their move to break away and reestablish the kingdom of Eyn, with themselves as the new Kings of Eyn. They have been long in planning this, too. Henri will lose his seaport of Ludwellyn if that happens. The last twelve years of fighting the Lanques off down there will have all been in vain, because the day that happens, the inconceivably stupid Grand Duke will have handed Eyn to Lanqueshire."

Lackland was silent, his anger rising close to the surface at the thought of all the lives that had been lost in trying to preserve the Eynier Valley, now being thrown away by a traitor in their midst. He was speechless at the thought that the very traitor who had ordered Davey murdered so brutally, had seven years before, held a grand ball to celebrate their victory in the war against Lanqueshire; slapping Lackland on the shoulder and toasting him, referring to him as 'friend' and 'comrade in the great war'. Grefyn's 'assistance' in the war had been nothing but lip service and useless argument over strategy. His troops had never materialized when they were promised, and he had sent word that they were 'mired in snow and unable to move'.

"I am well acquainted with him. He is a cretin." Suddenly, he felt the full force of his own white-hot rage. "He has dared to reach too high. I will kill him myself," murmured Lackland, speaking in low tones that did not disguise his rage. His blue eyes were as cold as winter as the full knowledge of what Amstyce Grefyn had been up to sank in. "I should have killed him when he failed Henri at Bekenberg Pass. He nearly cost us the war then. I should have killed him then."

The others were stunned at his uncharacteristic show of anger. They looked at each other warily and tried to give him a moment to compose himself. He immediately did, burying his anger under his usual veneer of mindless pleasantry.

Hiding his surprise, at the depth of feeling evidenced by Lackland's comments, Jack sipped his mug of ale, before he continued. "And now the best part is this: the weaselly Grand Duke Grefyn is completely unfit to rule. He has all of the finer qualities of a Lournesque highwayman, without the conscience or flair for style. He can barely sign his own name. His dearest friend and close confidante, 'Lord' Gwartney has a very slight foreign accent, as if he originated in Lanqueshire. For the last three years, Gwartney has handled all of Grefyn's affairs, and it is he who guides him in his quest to 'return to Royal Eyn that which is theirs'."

Huw spoke up for the first time. "The reason that an incompetent, brutal cretin like Amstyce Grefyn has been able to cause so much grief and misery, to Clan Weyllyn and the people of the long valley, is that Gwartney and the Lanques are secretly supporting him, using him to undermine and weaken southern Waldeyn. They have seen the opportunity there, to finally win their war and they aim to take it." He looked around the room, but no one else was paying attention to them, instead the lads were listening to some tale Lora was spinning, though both Beau and Brand appeared to be rather bored.

"All of Eynier had been searching for our Davey for years, none more so than Grefyn. When at last they found him and realized that you were a friend of his, Gwartney of Lanqueshire sent his own unique assassins after our Davey. They were disguised as Eynier rebels in order to bring Henri's wrath down on the Eynier through you and Percy, Lackland. They thought, that by making it look like an inter-clan murder of a 'lad with a stigma', your righteous anger would fall on Weyllyn, as the representatives of Eyn; and that you would bring Henri down on the Duchess. They fear you, Lackland. You have sent them back over the passes three times, and they don't see any other way to win this.

"They should fear me," replied Lackland with that steely-eyed look. "I will settle this once and for all. There will be no mercy for the high Grefyn or Gwartney."

"They have nearly decimated the high clan of Weyllyn. There is only the sixteen year old Duchess Gwen who is to marry Prince Harry in two weeks, and two young Dukes left of the true bloodline. They are our Davey's niece and nephews. His sister, the Grand Duchess Madewyn is their mother and guardian."

"I know her very well; very well indeed. What of their safety?" Lackland was aghast at the bloodletting that had been unleashed in an already unbelievably bloody conflict. "How are they being protected?"

"Henri has taken them to his court at Castleton Keep for safe keeping," said Jack. "He has just arrived in Castleton with them. Young Harry is quite agreeable to the whole thing, having fallen madly in love with the Duchess Gwen when he first laid eyes on her. She is a sweet thing, with a backbone of steel. She will make a fine Queen when the time comes. She would make a fine Lady Rowdy! In the meantime, Henri wished me to tell you that her brothers will be under your tutelage, along with the rest of the young nobility when you return to court this fall."

"Now what Henri wants you to do," said Billy, handing a small pouch of gold back to Lackland, "Is to remove Gwartney, Amstyce Grefyn and any of his heirs who are involved with Gwartney, then point the finger directly and visibly at Lanqueshire. Then you are detached to help me out a bit with training the newer lot here over the summer, before you return to Castleton and get on with training his next generation of knights."

Lackland looked at the pouch of gold that he had given Billy two months previously. "I suppose that I can be a Rowdy again for a while, until September, anyway. I have missed the old place; and I confess I have been somewhat bored."

"So, we will leave at the end of this week," said Huw. "The road should be firmed up pretty well by then from the recent melt, and anyway, Gertie has to get the horses reshod in the Southern style. Though we are well known, we want to avoid notice, so we will be traveling in disguise, and speaking the dialect. Your hair is too light, so Annie Fitz is going to color it dark. She will show you how to keep it that way until the job is done."

Billy leaned back and called, "Beau! Come here and tell Lackland that joke you told me about the farmer's daughter!" Smiling the smile that elevated him to beyond handsome, Beau came over to sit with them. "Golden Beau here is getting lovely dark tresses too, Lackland, so don't feel special."

Lackland laughed, as Billy knew he would.

"I hope you are going to bring your famous bow, Lackland," said Beau. "I have a hankering to learn the art myself. It would be good to have some standoff capability at times."

"Of course! Tomorrow we can begin your training in that!" replied Lackland, feeling an unaccustomed sense of joy. His own extraordinary smile creased his face. "You are the first Rowdy to ask to learn the art of archery. We will cut the bow and begin your training immediately in the morning!"

They sat happily discussing weaponry and techniques for killing some of the stranger beasts that still roamed the wilds, until Billy closed the common room and they regretfully went their separate ways.

*

The next day, Mags returned from her job along with Little Fred, Johnny Malone, George 'One Shot' Finch and a Lady named Belle Tanner, eldest daughter of Belinda the shoemaker and Tom the tanner. Like all the rest of the younger rowdies, Belle had taken up the trade that her parents had loved so much, having been raised on Huw's romantic tales of their exploits. She was a lady of about twenty-two and had been a Rowdy for five years or so.

She had no lad at this time, and with things being what they were with Mags and Beau, Lackland had found himself to be quite attracted to her. She had smiled at him with her dark eyes and burnished mahogany hair, so like someone else's hair. Indeed, she was enough like Lady Mags that they could have been sisters.

Surprisingly only to him, he found that he enjoyed her company much more than he had thought he would enjoy a woman's company again. She was witty and well able to hold her own, in either a swordfight or a conversation, and was just his sort of a lady.

Of course, he tried to keep it casual, letting her know from the outset that when he returned from his long-job he was only going to be there temporarily through the summer. Adding that yes, he really was and would always be in love with Mags.

Belle was fine with all of that; she had no desire to settle down yet either, unless she could still swing her sword. They spent their evenings playing stones with Beau and Mags or dancing to Huw's harp. Their nights were spent in each other's company during the week that the four men were gearing up for their long job.

Sometimes in the evenings, Beau and Huw would sing duets; Golden Beau had a beautiful tenor that soared when he sang with Huw. Once, Huw had wanted to train him as a bard, but Beau was only interested in singing for pleasure. He had wanted to be a Rowdy, and save people's lives and property, since his own life had been saved as a ten year old boy. His one ambition had been to follow in the great Lackland's footsteps. However, as the son of the village baker, his best chance of that was by joining the Rowdies.

Bold Lora Saunders took a dim view of the relationship that had developed between Belle and Lackland. She saw herself as a very desirable woman with the reputation of having had many notable lovers. She had aimed to add Sir Julian Lackland to that list from the moment she had heard he was returning to the Rowdies.

Indeed, she had dogged him and followed his every move since the first night he had returned, turning up at every corner with an open invitation to her bed. That very first night, Lackland had been quite clear with her that he had no intention of taking her up on that. She was not the sort of woman he wanted to spend the summer with, and he felt that she was still far too young for him, even if she had been to his taste.

One night, she slipped into Lackland's room not an hour after he had left Belle. Lackland had woken to find her naked self sliding into bed with him, with a rather surprising, at least to her, result.

First of all, Lackland was a man who had always slept lightly, and he was, as were most of the other Rowdies, a dangerous man to surprise. She had suddenly found herself with a knife at her throat, and then, once Lackland realized who it was and what was happening, he had gotten out of the bed and said, "I am sorry, Lady, but I will not dally with you. You have an understanding with Bennie Smith, and that is something I will not get involved in. It makes for trouble on the road. I have an understanding with Belle Tanner. I am thirty-five, and am older than your father whom I knew well, and respected. Please, return to your bed and we will forget that this happened."

Instead of leaving, she had lain there in his bed, smiling challengingly at him. So, he had then done the only honorable thing he could think of, and went to Babs and Annie's room to stay the rest of the night. He fled down the hall in his nakedness, carrying his clothes in front of him.

He had knocked on their door, and Babs had let him in with a surprised look on her face. It had turned to anger, as he stood naked and shivering, telling her what had driven him out of his room. They had genteelly made room for him in their bed and giggled, telling him that in the old days he would have been running from the frying pan into the fire by coming to them for 'safety'.

He laughed. "In the old days, I would have been up to it!"

"Your arse is still a wonderful thing to look at, dear," Babs told him, eyeing him appreciatively as he pulled on his drawers. "The years have been very kind to you!"

The three of them had talked about the changes that had come to them all for a while longer, and then gone to sleep.

Needless to say, the two ladies had taken a dim view of it. The next morning, Bold Lora Saunders was gone, quietly and with no fuss. "A man should not be considered as fair game; to be just a trophy about your neck," they had told her. "If it is wrong to force a woman, then it is wrong to force a man."

Thus it was, that on the fourth morning of the week, Bold Lora found herself and all her gear riding out to Bekenberg, to perhaps join up with the Ravens if they would allow it. "They have fewer scruples than we do here, so perhaps you will do well there," Annie had told her crisply.

No mention of why she had left was made, and Bennie got over her leaving so suddenly, by promptly falling in love with Anna Tailor. She had chosen that week to join the Rowdies and 'go out and do some good in the world'.

While the horses were being reshod and the last of their supplies were being gathered, Lackland and Beau had gone out and found the perfect yew for Beau's longbow. They then began looking for the good shafts and flint for the arrowheads, since being able to knap your own arrowheads was integral to the craft.

Gertie's apprentice made Beau ten good iron arrowheads for his shafts, but they were quite expensive. Like Lackland, he would be quite careful of them, using the flint ones for practice.

After that, Lackland had shown him the proper construction of the bow, taught him how to string it and how to keep the string dry. Then they had taken the longbows out and practiced. Beau had been born with the gift apparently, because he was surprisingly quick in learning the skill.

During the week that they spent waiting while Tom Stanton was getting them geared up and Gertie was getting their horses re-shod, Lackland and Beau spent long hours together in the paddock practicing. During which time, Beau developed quickly as an archer. The two men had found that they truly enjoyed each other's company immensely, and had quickly become inseparable; causing Belle and Mags to each feel private moments of jealousy.

Neither lady would admit to it, nor did they discuss it with each other, but both feared that the two men would find all that they needed in each other's company while on their long journey. *'What will I do if Beau leaves me for Lackland?'* Mags asked herself that question as the two blonde men strolled past the window of the common-room, laughing as merrily as she had ever seen either of them to be in anyone's company. They were completely light-hearted and relaxed.

*

The four tubs were full in the men's side of the bathhouse. "I must admit that I now know why you are the strongest man in Waldeyn, Lackland," Beau said as they soaked sore muscles in hot tubs of bubbly water at the end of the third day of his training. "I don't think my muscles have ever been this sore, not even from lugging sacks of flour for my father at the bakery."

"You will get use to it," Lackland had assured him. "I am sometimes away from it for a long period of time, and have to get back into the right mind for it, and I too feel it sorely."

"I have never understood how you all can shoot those things so accurately, Lackland," said Johnny Malone from his tub. "You scared me to death when you killed that bastard that was sneaking up on me in Feinberg that time. You were clean across the clearing and he was right behind me!"

"I practice a lot, and I seem to have a good eye for it still," Lackland replied. "It is important to be skilled in as many weapons as you can be, since you never know what the situation will present you with at any given time."

"When your eyesight starts to go, it is best to give it up," added One-Shot George from his tub. "I'm no good with the bow anymore, but I dare any bastard to run themselves onto my sword any day!" Everyone laughed, as not two weeks before a desperate highwayman had accidentally run himself up George's sword, in his effort to escape Beau.

"That is how George got his name, Beau," Lackland said merrily, "He shot one bolt at these two Lanque highwaymen who were attempting to flee in the dark with the goods. Our camp was ambushed by a group of six and it went clean through the first one and nailed the second though the heart! There were only the three of us guarding Dolman the wine merchant; me, George, and Alan Le Clerk. Alan and I didn't have time to string our bows, but we cut four of them down before old Dolman could even get out of his bedroll! Then, George nailed the two others with one shot, which was one of the finer moments I have seen as a bowman!"

"Sadly, my eyesight has suffered, and now if I wish to shoot someone I must ask Lackland where to point my

Bow!" Everyone laughed again, and Johnny began a story about how he and George, Davey and Percy had ambushed a pair of thieves that had been laying in wait to ambush them on the caravan route to Fornost. "George snuck up and shot the bastard in the arse," said Johnny laughing. "I would bet he never sat in a tree waiting to ambush anyone again!"

"Yes, he did come down out the tree rather quickly," laughed George. "He finally yanked the arrow out of his arse, and the last I heard of him, was his cursing as he tried to find his horse. Of course, Davey had stolen both of their nags."

*

Early in the afternoon of a cold, clear Monday, Lackland and Beau sat in the courtyard while Annie Fitz colored their blonde tresses black. Rowdies often went disguised for various reasons; each job had its requirements.

Annie showed them what to do each week to keep it black, and made sure that they had enough little packets of the dye to maintain their disguise for six weeks, if it should take that long. Lackland fervently hoped it would not, a sentiment echoed by Slippery Jack who was not looking forward to leaving Merry Kat and the children alone in Castleton for that long.

"Each day that passes is another day that can bring trouble down on you. I have to get home to my Merry Kat and our boys; already I miss their racket, Lackland," he said in an uncharacteristic fit of homesickness. "If I find myself working out of Limpwater too often, we will have to move back here."

The next morning, Julian Lackland, Huw the Bard, Beau Baker and Slippery Jack Hodges rode south, purportedly on a trip to guard a shipment of fine wines from Somber Flats to Bekenberg and from there to Vyennes.

Chapter 6 - The Murder of Crows

As they rode out of Limpwater, the four men began to feel that lightness of heart that they always felt when going out on a particularly nasty job. Huw began singing a ditty and Beau joined in, singing a sweet harmony. Soon, they were all merrily singing Huw's bawdiest ballads. Before they knew it, they had passed Somber Flats and were on their way south toward Bekenberg.

Somewhere beyond Somber Flats, Slippery Jack began feeling that they were being watched, and the feeling did not go away as they progressed. Finally, as they made camp on the third night, he said to Lackland in a low whisper, "Someone is following us. I haven't seen them, but they are there."

"I know. Beau mentioned it too," replied Lackland. "We will just pretend like we don't know and see what happens." He and Beau had been riding with their bows strung, but they would have to dismount to use them. They had been looking for good material for smaller bows and arrows, and would be working on those at night.

"It won't happen until we get down to the long valley," predicted Jack. "It isn't good, whatever it is."

After four long days and three short nights on the road, they entered the rather gloomy town of Bekenberg, and promptly found the inn known as the Broken Wheel. Long ago, it had been a decent enough place, but it was not a patch on Billy's Revenge, as far as the food, cleanliness and quality of the furnishings went. Still, the baths were good, being hot-springs, and the privies were kept clean enough.

They deliberately did not go to the Raven's Nest and check in with them, though it was far and away the better place. They wished to simply blend in with the rest of the travelers heading south. Sara, leader of the Ravens, would know that they had been through town anyway; and would know that it was on business, since two of her Ravens stood quietly at the bar looking over each merc and merchant that passed through Bekenberg.

Lackland had surreptitiously given the two watchers a signal that told them everything Sara needed to know, as the four sat down to a bowl of something being billed as stew. They had found a spot in a corner of the common room and pretty much kept to themselves. The room was full of lower class merchants and mercs that were guarding the merchants on the road south. However, there was not the atmosphere of camaraderie that characterized most such places.

It was not surprising that Jack had the feeling that they were being watched by more than just the two Ravens, but no matter where he looked, he couldn't see who it was; and in truth, they *were* being observed by every merc there in just the same way that they were observing everyone else.

The town of Bekenberg was too close to the border with Lanqueshire, for the mercs halting in that low place to relax their guard. Only ten leagues to the west lay the Bekenberg Pass and the official border and entry post; located at the entrance to the only pass that was open year round through the Claith Mountains. Trouble was simply not welcome in their town and mercs that were between jobs were often trouble.

The four Rowdies had been offered one room to share, but after seeing the bed, they had opted to camp just outside of town. The room had looked suspiciously like it could be bedbug-infested. Even those who slept on the floor in their own bedrolls would be eaten alive.

At dawn, they were back on the road, and heading for the village of Clythe which guarded the narrow pass into the Eynier Valley, also known as the Long Valley. The south fork of the Limpwater River flowed to the sea through this pass.

In truth it was a very long, wide valley: almost two hundred leagues of verdant farmland dotted with tiny villages stretched from Clythe to Ludwellyn. The mountains to the east were the border, with the country of Vyennes and the mountains to the west forming the border between the long valley and the small seafaring country of Lanqueshire. The Eynier Valley formed a wedge to the sea between them.

Two-hundred years previously, the Eynier Valley had been a country beset with troubles. Two generations of weak kings had made it into a very desirable opportunity for the pirate kings of Lanqueshire. Their own country of Lanqueshire had little farmland, being mostly mountainous. The common people of Lanqueshire were very poor; often they were victimized by the pirates who ruled them.

The various 'kings' of Lanqueshire were really just the more powerful pirates, preying on the ships of Lournes and Waldeyn, as they plied the seas on their way to Vyennes and the east. Any man could claim to be the king and many did. The small country had been completely embroiled in a bloody civil war for so long that no one could remember peace.

While the old country of Wald had actually bordered on Vyennes, the land route was a long journey through steep, treacherous mountains that were impassable for six months out of the year. To sail there cut the journey in half, even if they sailed out of Waldport, the northern seaport on the Western Sea, only one days ride northwest of Castleton.

Unfortunately, they had to sail south past Lanqueshire to sail to Vyennes if they sailed out of Waldport. It was a definite problem; to sail north was impossible most of the year because of the frozen seas and bitter weather the rest of the time. And to sail south meant that there was always a chance that the Lanques would be 'having trouble with pirates, so sorry'; and half of the time ships and crews did not arrive at their destination. Thus, before the joining of Eyn to Wald, the caravans to Vyennes had been the primary means of trade for the five months of the year that the mountains were passable.

When King Aelfrid Dragoran of Wald married Queen Merewyn Weyllyn of Eyn, they joined the two countries under one crown, Waldeyn, which had preserved the Eynier way of life and had also given Wald a southern seaport.

They had been at war off and on with Lanqueshire ever since. Both of the far-northern countries of Fornost and Lournes were eager to support Waldeyn in their fight against the Lanques, as was the eastern country of Vyennes since their treaties with Waldeyn allowed them to travel the central north-south trade road freely, as long as they hired Waldeynier Mercenary Guards for their protection. They shipped their goods into and out of the port of Ludwellyn which greatly increased the commerce in both Waldeyn and Vyennes.

On the second day out of Bekenberg, the Rowdies rode into Clythe. It was a small village, with an inn that served the traveling merchants and their guards, and little else. "You won't find anyone who can claim to be a bard here in the Eynier," Huw told them sadly. "The old Grefyn purged the valley of Bards, arresting and murdering them for 'treason'. Bards told the truth, you see; so he had to eliminate them. My friends helped me escape to the north. I may be the last fully trained Bard of Eynier still alive in Waldeyn. What you will find though, is that the people still make their music, and it is unlike anything you have ever heard. My soul has missed the valley more than you will ever know."

The Green Man was a neat and clean place, as Lackland and Jack well remembered from other journeys down in the Eynier Valley. They found that the old man who had run the place had died, and it was now run by his niece; a lady, by the name of Sinean, who was apparently an old friend of Huw's from his youth in Ludwellyn. She had only one room for them as she was full up, but there were two beds and she brought up two cots for them.

Sinean was overjoyed to see Huw; although she was shocked and terribly concerned at the grief and desolation that was now an integral part of Huw's somber countenance. Huw had been surprised to see her that far north; but introduced his friends, using the names Joules, Bo and Jacky, which were all good Eynier versions of their real names.

"I thought you would be still saving the world down in Ludwellyn," Huw said, obviously pleased to see an old friend; a smile lighting his sad face. "You regularly vowed to never leave the road until Grefyn was naught but ash, as I recall; valiant lass that you are."

"Things come along that change a person's view, Huw. But, my uncle died two years ago and left me the Green Man. So, I brought the crew up here with me and we have stayed busy enough here in Clythe," she had replied, with a somewhat anxious cast to her face. "We must talk privately, Huw, and hear each other's news."

While nothing of import was openly discussed in the common room, Huw had spent the evening in Sinean's company, as apparently he had often done in the old days before he left the long valley under a cloud. Her son had cast a surprised and then worried glance at them as they went up the stairs, Huw looking uncomfortable and unsure of himself.

"Huw is still thinking only about Lucy," said Lackland, speaking in Eynier as they settled into a corner; they would only speak the local dialect from here on out. "He is too deep for his own good, sometimes."

"How he has changed," remarked Beau sadly. "How we have all changed, Joules; even you, though I am at fault for that, I think."

Lackland clasped Beau's shoulder. "No, Beau; that does not lie between us. I set her free ten years ago, and I meant it. I love her that much, and I am content with the way things are. She needs you; she can't bear to be alone and you are the best man in the Rowdies; indeed, you are the best man that I know. I feel better knowing that she is with you."

Beau looked searchingly into Julian's eyes and saw that Julian had told him the truth. "You are too good for your own peace, sometimes, Joules. I know what keeps you at House De Leon, and why you left the road; she told me all of it. Nevertheless, I feel caught between the two of you, in a way that I can't explain."

"This is just the way it is. It affects nothing between you and me. I trust you more than any man alive." Lackland's assurance eased Beau's guilt somewhat;

though it would never completely go away until Mags married Julian which would never happen.

Jack took that moment to return from the privy, and soon they were discussing the small, inconsequential things of the day, as the room began to fill up.

While Huw was up in Sinean's rooms, the other three sat in the common room quietly playing a game of stones. Sinean's son Culyn served them excellently brewed ale, and a superior stew. Culyn was a fine lad of about eighteen years of age who was quietly making a name for himself in Clythe, as both a musician and a merc. The room was crowded with folks going north and some few others who were going south.

"Where are you lads off to, then?" he asked companionably as he brought them a second round of ale. On arriving, they had exchanged the usual signals so Culyn knew they were Rowdies, and had guessed who Lackland was despite the dark hair. He didn't know the others, though his mother apparently knew one of them well enough to invite him upstairs. They were fitting in well; no one would guess they were from up north. He thought that they must be doing something of interest, and decided to give them a friendly heads up.

"Ludwellyn," replied Jack. "We are to meet Murfee's ship and see to it that he makes it to Castleton with all his merchandise, since we were already down here on a run to Vyennes." Lackland and Beau both admired his flawless Eynier accent. It was as thick as Huw's.

"Well, the weather still hasn't cleared much, so you might want to watch yourselves, especially at night," he said with a casual glance about the room, as if he were discussing nothing of great import.

Immediately, Jack's ears pricked up, though he didn't show it. "So the weather has been that bad, then. From which quarter does it blow? That will decide how we set camp."

"Ah, well... as you might imagine it comes in off the sea from the land to the west and blows through Ludwellyn. It can be very rough going as you head toward the sea right now. I would also watch the wind that blows over the pass west of Bekenberg on your way back north. The weather up there has been fierce this year."

"Well, that is good to know," agreed Jack. "It is true that the weather can be brutal down here."

"Many have lost their lives in the storms that have battered us these last years," Culyn's deep blue eyes held a fleeting bleakness as he made that sad comment, but his cheerful, professional smile remained in place. "I expect that will pass too; all things pass in time."

"Under the light of the sun, all things will pass," replied Jack, easily answering the Eynier proverb. The speech of the Eynier was littered with such; it had been an endearing thing about Davey. Huw was not so given to spouting proverbs as Davey had been, but still all the Rowdies knew the Eynier proverbs by heart from having been around the two of them for so many years.

Then Culyn looked at the three of them and asked, "Is your friend a good man? That is my mother he has befriended."

Lackland replied with his good Eynier accent, "Huw is a good man, and true. It seems they were young together, and have much to catch up on. Some of Huw's news will be distressing and not to be bandied about the common room."

"Ah," Culyn said. "He seems a poignant man. His face is full of sorrow."

"He lost his wife and unborn child, along with several others very dear to him, just this last year and may never recover," said Beau. "It was a terrible year at home, with four wakes. We feel that he will never stop grieving for her; she was the love of his life."

"I have heard that some men do not survive such tragedy," Culyn said, sympathy for Huw clear in his honest blue eyes. "They take it to heart, and cannot let go of the beauty of the dream. But I can see he has good friends to help him through his hard times."

As the evening progressed, the men of Clythe gathered in the common room and made their own music. One or another of them pulling flutes or viols out to play and each fellow was applauded by his mates. Then, as if by common consent, they all began to play as well as any troupe of bards Lackland had heard at court.

Culyn played a harp, the likes of which the Rowdies had never seen. The men of Clythe were wonderful musicians. With Beau's clear tenor rising sweetly above in the harmonies, it was very wonderful. Jack, Lackland and the other men with no instruments danced to the pounding of the bodhran, unable to stay still with the thrill of the music firing their blood. They danced until near on ten o'clock, when it was time to close the common room.

If Huw had been there it would have been the best evening they had had since leaving Billy's Revenge.

Later, as they went up to their room, Lackland kept wondering where he had seen Culyn before; a thing that nagged at him. After an hour or so, Huw came into their room and found Lackland lying awake and reading, unable to sleep. As Lackland looked at Huw, in the light of the candle, he realized why Culyn looked so familiar.

Huw had a stunned look about him, and wasn't disposed to conversation.

Lackland understood that feeling, and respected his privacy; if Huw did not mention it, he would not mention it either. He blew the candle out and now that the thing that had occupied his mind was settled, he promptly fell asleep.

Huw Owyn lay wide awake. His whole life had just turned upside down.

The next morning, they had gathered in the empty common room, ready to go south but they weren't leaving just yet. Huw was talking to Sinean quietly in the corner behind the bar. Lackland and Beau had stepped over to the hearth to give them some privacy.

"I think it is for the best, Huw. Let him decide." Sinean's voice carried. Huw's voice, as he replied, was muffled. Then they could hear Sinean saying, "You need a guide, and this way, he will know what he wants to do. It is hard for him here, with the stigma. There he would have a future." Huw replied something low again, and she said, "Ask Lackland, then. See what he says."

Lackland, Beau and Jack looked at each other, somehow not surprised that she knew who Lackland was, despite their black hair color. They looked at Huw as he reluctantly walked over to them. His expression was that of a man torn.

"What is it, Huw? Is it Culyn?" Lackland's question took Huw by surprise. "This changes things for us. We do need a guide, but has she told him what you are to him?"

"Lackland... I only found out last night. How did you... never mind," said Huw. "She told him after the music was done. We talked for a few minutes and then we went to our beds to think about things."

Beau and Jack looked from Lackland to Huw with surprise, and absorbed the information they had just heard. "Well, how I missed that I don't know, except that everyone has black hair, blue eyes and sings like an angel in this place," muttered Jack. "That boy could only be your son, Huw. He is the image of you the day you walked into Billy's Revenge and began playing your lute."

"What do you want to do, Huw?" Beau's gentle question was echoed by Lackland.

"I want to get to know him, more than anything! He is the son that I thought I would never have," said Huw. "But this is a nasty job. I don't want to involve him in a blood feud with the Black Grefyns, which is what we are involved in here. And they are black; blacker than anything you can imagine."

"He seems to me to be quite an able man," replied Lackland. "If he is willing, we could use his help." Jack and Beau both nodded their heads. "Why do you feel so reluctant?"

"If it goes awry and I lose Culyn over murdering the Crows, I would never forgive myself," said Huw, his turmoil and conflict apparent on his face. "I have lost my Lucy Blue Eyes, my bright treasure. So many deaths this year, Lackland; so many graves! I fear I would go like Percy if I were to lose Culyn, now that I have found him." Huw's bleak eyes met Lackland's supportive eyes. "I understand Percy now; I know why he went that way. There are some sorrows that kill you, but forget to tell your body that you are dead."

"Let me just do this, Father. We will both be better for it. I have wondered my whole life," said Culyn, his voice so like Huw's as he walked over to them. He was wearing mail, and carrying saddle bags. His sword was in a well-worn scabbard, and he walked as if he was well acquainted with it. "We didn't have my childhood to share. Let's have the time that we have, and be grateful for it."

"This is a bad job, Culyn. We have come on a two-fold mission to collect for our honored dead," he said. "We have come to collect for two wee babes of Dayved Weyllyn, who are our children now." Culyn's eyes widened. "Yes, Culyn," said Huw. "We are collecting from high Grefyn. This is not a good job. There will be blood spilled; a river of it. In the process of settling up for Davey, we will be carrying out a task for Lackland's highly placed cousin. If we are discovered, we will not be treated well, nor will we survive the hospitality of Grefyn."

"All the more reason for me to come along then," said Culyn, smiling Huw's old smile; the one that had charmed women high and low, but with his own particular honesty. "Let me just say that I have skills that go beyond playing my harp and pouring ale." He sighed and looked away, and then he said, "I also have a grudge against Grefyn, though I do not have the right to collect for my dead, as these things go. It lies festering there anyway."

"What is your grudge?" asked Jack warily. "We are not interested in going too far afield in the completion of our task. That will get us killed, and I for one am not ready to leave this world." His wry glance at Huw and easy smile received an answering one from Culyn. All eyes had inadvertently turned toward Huw; to see his reaction to Jack's words.

"I have a reason to live too, now," muttered Huw, feeling keenly the scrutiny of his fellows, "And more reason than ever to protect what is mine, if I can." This last was delivered to Culyn, rather gruffly.

"It is not my right to bear this particular grudge against the Crow, any more than any other man who loves Eynier and hates to see the destruction and murder that they wreak upon us has the right to bear him a grudge. Yet, mine is personal, and cuts me deeply. Sit down in the corner here, I will tell you." They all sat down, and Culyn began his tale. "There was a town some ten leagues to the south of here, Maury."

"Any tale that begins with 'There was a town' is bound to be a sad tale, I think," said Huw as Culyn fell silent, lost in his dark memory. "I remember Maury well. I grew up there."

"Then I suspect I do have a right to justice in this matter. It is a sad tale, father," he said. "Did you have family there?"

"No longer; my mother died when I was your age. I was all she had of family." Huw shook his head, saying, "But I fear I have heard what you are going to say; and it is bad, what I have heard."

Looking at Lackland and Jack, Culyn explained, "Maury was a famous weavers' town, and was home to the girl I once thought to marry. The Weyllyns had the town on the Maab River, with the Grefyns locked out of the cloth trade. The river powered the water wheels that in turn powered the great looms upon which the cloth that made Maury famous was woven.

"The Weyllyns are good to the people, and do not tax them harshly. The Grefyns have a grudge against the Weyllyns that goes back generations, and the higher you go in the clan, the worse the grudge is; until at the top there is only hate and the desire to crush Weyllyn, with room for nothing else.

"Grefyn had come twice to demand that Maury town turn to him and aid him in his effort to 'restore the crown to royal Eyn' by taking it from the Weyllyns and Wald. They sent him away unsatisfied, saying that all that would do is leave the valley open for the Lanques to plunder. Anyone with eyes to see can see that.

"Maury was built as a weaver's town. It was situated in a perfect place for the looms to be powered by the water wheels: the Maab River rarely freezes over, and is fairly constant in its depth and speed, and the looms were seldom idle. The cloth they turned out was famous all over the continent.

"One bright Thursday morning two summers ago, they were all occupied at their looms, and various other tasks; just as they should be. As they worked, a large band of 'masked highwaymen' came into town, creeping through the shadows and moving in stealth. Fanning out, they crept to every factory, shop and house. They nailed shut the doors and windows and set fire to the town, cutting down any who tried to escape the flames." He saw their shocked faces, full of compassion for the people of Maury.

"Grefyn put it about that the people of the long valley had risen against Weyllyn in that town, and murdered the Weyllyn traitors in their midst. All knew it to be a lie, but it was one more way to divide us, to make us weaker.

"Carynne and I were young and not yet betrothed. We had met at the May-Day Faire only that spring. I had begun courting her, in keeping with the concerns of her father, visiting her on Sundays afternoons and sitting in their garden under the watchful eye of her grandmother. We were only sixteen, and while I had a stigma that her father did not look kindly upon, he had begun to find favor in me and my prospects. I do not know if we ever would have been betrothed. Our love was new; a possibility only, though I had hopes," Culyn finished his tale, looking at his father with earnest blue eyes that were old beyond his years, "So you see I have no proper right, as our people see it to collect for the dead; but I do bear Grefyn a grudge. If I can help you with your task, it will ease my own grief somewhat."

The others were silent, watching the byplay between the two men who looked so alike; one man who was old and sad beyond his years, and the other man so young and so wise beyond his years. "It may be that aiding us in our task will provide some consolation to you," replied Huw after listening to his son's tale. "We must eliminate the rats from the granary, and we will be doing this by starting at the top."

"So, let me be your guide in this extermination. I know where they do business. I have had some success in other ventures of this nature and know just the way to accomplish this thing." Culyn's sincerity shone in his countenance as he urged his father to agree to allow him to join. "Besides, if I were to die today, I would die happier than I have been in my life. I know now that you would have claimed me, had you been given the opportunity; but you know how mother is. She doesn't do things any way but her own."

"I aim to rectify that today," Huw said firmly. "I will go to the chapel now, this moment; and re-register your birth today. You are Culyn Owyn, son of Huw the Bard, and all shall know that. Today you receive your true name!"

*

They rode the long trade road, camping alongside it, getting to know each other well and finding Culyn to be the perfect Rowdy in the process. The first time they were attacked by highwaymen Culyn acquitted himself well, as Lackland had suspected he might.

The Highwaymen were not of Eynier, but spoke with rough Lanque accents. It was not even a contest. They buried the dead in a large cairn, and continued on.

Over the next week, that charade was repeated twice more before they reached the end of their journey.

One week after leaving Clythe, they arrived in the port city of Ludwellyn. It was a city that was twice as large as Castleton, and was crammed to bursting with people. They went to an area of town that Lackland was not known in; the poorest and most crowded section right on the docks. They made straight for the inn that Culyn directed them to.

The inn, called 'The Sailor's Rest', was full to overflowing, but Culyn persuaded the innkeeper to move out the current tenant and rent to them a particular room that he wanted on the second floor; one room for the five of them. "I'll do it because you are Sinean's boy, scamp! What you are up to, I don't ask. You have that look about you."

"Hello Waite," said Huw's voice, as he came up behind Culyn. "Remember me?"

"Well... Huw Owyn, The Golden Throat; the maiden's dream come true! Ah, lad; what has happened that has left such a melancholy mark upon you?" Sharp blue eyes under a thatch of white hair surveyed Huw sadly. "You left here so long ago, vowing never to return. The bastards that caused all that grief are long gone, lad; but we hear tales of you and your golden voice." and shaking his head Waite looked at Culyn and then at Huw and did a double take. "I don't know why I never saw it before. It can only be you that is this lad's true father."

"I am," Huw replied proudly. "He is Culyn Owyn, as he should have always been."

"Now I know for sure that you must be here on business, or your father would not be here. He has made a name for himself elsewhere. But I must stay out of it, right? What I don't know can't hurt you, if you know what I mean," said Waite, as he bumbled about getting the cots for their room. "I am glad to have made your acquaintances, Joules, Jacky, and Bo." Waite shook hands all around. "It is good to have Sinean's lads down here on business. She runs a tight ship; I won't have to worry about you lads fighting in the tap-room!"

Though it was tight, they managed. The stables were decent enough, but there were no proper baths and only an outdoor privy in the tiny courtyard that the inn was built around. However, there was plenty of water for washing in a jug on the wash-stand. Best of all, they were fortunate in that a tall spruce tree stood outside their window which faced the alley, allowing them to come and go as they wished in the dark. "The tree is why I pressured Waite to give us this room," Culyn told them as they stowed their possessions, as neatly as was possible. "That is our private way in and out."

Ludwellyn was the port town where all of the great families had their main residences, to enable them to remain close to their commerce. Lackland had originally planned to go straight to the Duchess of Weyllyn's residence where they would have been received exceedingly warmly, even though she was away up north for her daughter's wedding. She had been quite fond of him when he had been down there with Henri Dragoran stamping out piracy.

Instead, they were crammed into the rough room down by the docks, but they agreed that it was a better arrangement. They would draw no attention and would not be associated with the Duchess or the crown, and thereby accidentally incriminate her.

The mood of the laborers on the docks and the merchants in the market was confused and angry. Fierce verbal disagreements resulted in many a beating, as words failed to convince and fists took over the conversation.

A notice had been posted that Crown Prince Harry Dragoran and his new bride, Princess Gwenevere of Weyllyn would be taking up residence at House Dragoran within the month. The common people of the southern Eynier Valley were ecstatic to know that Eynier would rule Waldeyn as equals, and that their future king and queen would soon live among them.

Violence had erupted as Grefyn fought desperately to counter that joy; using their weapons of lies and their endless supply of armed bullies to gain the people's sympathy, to little avail. Still they pressed their claims, despite their rejection by the citizens of the long valley.

House Dragoran was located two days ride south of Clythe, and was nothing more than an average northern Baron's estate, rather reminiscent of House Portiers actually; but it was the hereditary home of Queen Merewyn and as such, it was sacred to Eynier. The kings and queens of Waldeyn had always summered there until Henri's father's time. The old pile of stone was small and shabby but the rose gardens were famous all over the continent.

Henri's mother, Queen Katryn, had declared it unfit for human habitation and refused to go there for any reason. She had been a princess of Vyennes and was used to living in much nicer surroundings. She never forgave her father for marrying her off to 'an uncivilized barbarian' like Herrold of Waldeyn. Henri always stayed at House Dragoran when he was in the long valley, and now the Crown Prince and Princess would be living there.

The Duke Amstyce Grefyn scathingly referred to it as a 'mud-hut'. Indeed, compared to his palace on the hill overlooking the harbor in Ludwellyn, it was rather small and shabby.

When the mayor of Longcham asked if they would build a palace in the style of the other notable families in the Eynier Valley, Prince Harry had looked quite surprised and said, "I don't see why we should; it is already much finer than most other peoples' homes, and the roof is still good." He had paused and thought about it for a moment and then said with a self deprecating smile, "Well, a few new slates and it will be fine again. We should probably expand the stables, though. We have a lot of family who will be visiting."

The people loved Prince Harry for that, calling him 'Our Harry'.

But there were naysayers: those strident voices whose cries of derision left a sour sound in the ears of most all who heard them. They were few, but long and loud in their declaiming of their dissatisfaction with 'Wald's get'; loudly postulating that the Weyllyns were black traitors for 'selling Eyn to Wald for a shiny crown'.

It was a dangerous time to be in Ludwellyn, and folks feared for their safety. The women and children stayed behind their locked doors, and even the men did not go out except that they had to earn the family's living. Many a fight erupted on the docks, with the naysayers and rabble-rousers often being beaten within an inch of their lives. The people were tired of the conflict, and just wanted it to end. The street corners were dangerous places to linger at for any length of time.

The companions noticed that the naysayers were most often people of a slightly different accent, whose origins were unclear. The fact that they were supported and employed by the Grand-Duke Grefyn frequently became apparent upon further examination of their daily rituals. These beggars and drunks came in on Grefyn cargo ships, and quickly dispersed into the crowds. They then turned up on street corners trying to rouse the rabble against Weyllyn and Henri. As long as they were successful, they received a daily wage from the Grefyn paymaster.

Most of his gold was similar to that of Waldeyn but had been minted in Lanqueshire. Still, it was legal tender since it weighed the same as gold minted in Vyennes, Waldeyn or Lournes. In the interest of trade, all gold was acceptable in Ludwellyn, where it was traded for Waldeynier Crowns at the exchequer's office down on the piers. The crown clerk at the exchequer told Lackland that they had been flooded with 'Bones', as Lanque golds were called. The pirates' golds had a ship on one side and a pair of crossed oars on the other. It had been said that that they may as well have stamped a skull-and-crossbones on it, and the name had stuck.

Once they were known by the community to be in the pay of Grefyn, they were no longer of any use as rabble-rousers and so they were cut off from Grefyn's payroll. Once unemployed, the foreigners quickly reverted to their old ways of thievery and other violent crimes; the only employment they had ever had in Lanqueshire. For the last year, there had been a crime wave of monumental proportions in Ludwellyn and it had been slowly moving north in the form of highwaymen and gangs of thieves.

Of course, Grefyn loudly blamed the crime-wave on weakness of rule by the Grand Duchess Madewyn Weyllyn.

Many people were heard to scathingly tell the rabble-rousers that if a rat drowned in a rain barrel they would blame it on Madewyn Weyllyn.

Culyn arranged for gainful employment for the Rowdies; and so it was that in the guise of street sweepers Huw, Lackland and Jack secretly watched the palaces of the Grand Duke Grefyn and other notables of that family. Culyn and Beau worked as stevedores, listening to the gossip and picking up much information that was useful.

At the end of two weeks, they had gathered enough information that they knew exactly what they were going to do, and how they were going to do it. They were at the point where they would have to make their move, or go home unsatisfied.

On the morning of the day that they were to implement their plan, Lackland wrote a note to Henri's local spymaster detailing what they had discovered;

recommending that he search each Grefyn ship for Lanques disguised as Eynier.

"The neighbor is ridding their own yard of vermin by boxing them up and sending them to our house in the guise of crows from the sea. The proof of his complicity stands on the corner, loudly voicing their derisive caws with a foreign accent, and his foreign gold lines their pockets. The Crow who nests in our tree eagerly accepts them, thinking that their raucous cries advance his own cause. He does not seem to realize that the neighboring family is manipulating him and will crush him with the rest of us, as if he were the merest of insects. I have heard that the health of all of the birds in question is precarious; many are not likely to survive the week. Any who do not wish to suffer from the plague must keep to their own homes. Inspect his counting house; you will find it full of Bones."

He had signed it with his own name and sealed it with his own signet ring. Disguised as a common laborer, Jack had then taken the letter to the Weyllyn's dockside paymaster's office and asked to speak to a certain man. He had been quickly and quietly shown into an office where he had spoken with this man for several long minutes, after which he had been shown out through a different door. Within half an hour, a detachment of armed soldiers poured out of the crown armory and marched to the docks where they began boarding Grefyn ships that were still in port, seizing and 'deporting' Lanque infiltrators, by knocking them on the head and tossing them unconscious into the harbor. If they woke up on hitting the water and tried to swim to shore, the archers filled them with arrows.

The local citizenry in the southern end of the valley, fed up with 'the troubles' soon took up the same hobby.

In what seemed to be no time at all, it became a sad fact that anyone who could even possibly be of Lanqueshire was in danger of 'taking the long swim home'. Unfortunately by evening, many innocents were caught up in that particular nastiness as the desire to rid the long valley of the influence of the hated Lanques raged in the streets.

That same night, Grefyns began dying all over Ludwellyn; ten in seven different houses. The first to die was one Lord Gwartney. He had somehow garroted himself in his sleep. Though his front and back doors had been well guarded, the alley and the stepped chimneys had provided the entry into his bedroom, and the way out.

When he strangled Gwartney, Lackland had felt nothing, not even the satisfaction that he had avenged Davey and Percy.

"I somehow thought it would ease the pain, to be rid of the creature that ordered such a horrific thing done to our Davey," he told Beau, who nodded sympathetically. "It just makes me feel soiled, instead."

"It gives new meaning to the words 'a murder of crows'," Huw said with satisfaction as he crept in the window before dawn that first morning. The five had been out all night taking payment in blood for both the Rowdies losses and the burning of the village of Maury. For Huw, it had been cathartic; he was taking payment for the Bards of Eynier.

At breakfast that morning, Waite advised them to keep to the inn, as Grefyn was apparently suffering from 'the plague', and it was likely to spread into the community. Out of deference to the good innkeeper's suggestion, they did not leave their room by the front door, being conspicuously present under his roof while the streets were full of rioters. Indeed, two of them stood guard at his door around the clock with cudgels keeping the rioters outside and protecting his premises. They rotated the guard duty, and Waite was grateful to them for saving his windows and his livelihood.

And it was truly a plague of sorts that Grefyn was suffering. Lackland and Beau would be going out the next evening, while Huw, Culyn and Jack kept the innkeeper thinking they were all still languishing under his roof.

Over the next three days, an interesting thing began to happen in Ludwellyn, and indeed all over the long valley. It seemed that once Grefyns began turning up murdered, other people began to find happiness in that sport. Within days, Crows were being found dead all over the southern end of the valley; so many, in fact, that the murders could not be laid at the feet of one faction. Some were garroted, or smothered in their beds; some were set upon and murdered by common criminals as they went to the shipping office; guards and all. Several prominent Grefyns were found with their throats cut; their own guards having turned on them in anger for the losses that their families now suffered on their behalf.

On the fourth night of the riots, Lackland and Beau had found themselves trapped on a once minor duke's balcony, hiding and eavesdropping from behind the lush potted plants while a group of angry men with the accent of Lanqueshire dealt out rough justice. The rough men were distressed that they had been brought there to a foreign country and then abandoned when they had lost their usefulness. On the run and hunted, they had returned to Ludwellyn hoping to make an escape back to their homeland on a Grefyn ship.

Unfortunately, what few Grefyn ships that were in port had been seized by the crown. The Lanques had been summarily denied passage on any ship, with the constable's men beating them nearly to death before they were run out of town. Having barely escaped with their lives, the pirates were going to have to make the trek over one of the high passes, which would remain impassable until May at the earliest or try to make their way north to the Bekenberg Pass. Desperate and furious at their treatment, they had invaded the poor duke's villa. Holding Duke William Gronwy and his terrified family hostage, they had demanded payment to support them on their trip home.

Though he had given them every bit of gold in the house, they had wrought their revenge anyway. After the poor duke had been torn asunder and his whole family down to the children had met with equally gruesome fates, the gang had then left his home a shambles, looting everything of value and much that had no value.

Only when the raiders had finally gone did the two climb down from the balcony. They returned to their room at the Sailor's Rest, slipping fearfully through the dark and the shadows, and giving a wide berth to the knots of rioters in the streets.

"We have started something terrible," said Lackland, feeling the horror of the sight of the Duke's babies and their mothers, mutilated beyond all recognition. He knew the fault was somehow his as they slipped though the dark and deadly streets, hiding in the shadows. "The poor children are suffering for it now." He stopped in the shadows of the dust-bins and garbage of the alley. Shaking and trembling, he could not go on. Sobbing, he choked out, "How could I ever have thought that this massacre would ease my grief? It was my duty to protect those poor babies and I failed them, Beau! I failed them."

Beau simply shook his head, putting his arms around Julian's shoulders, trying to find something to say that would help Lackland, but failing miserably. "You did not cause this, Julian. Even you could have done nothing once the scale was tipped in this direction; the weight of the anger that the Grefyn's have stirred up is too great. There will be worse ahead, but you did not cause this! The guilty fathers have brought this massacre upon their own children, God help us all."

At last, Lackland was able to get himself under control, but the horror of the slaughtered children never left him. Finally, he was able to continue sneaking through the dark to the tree that served as their private entrance to their room. Beau said nothing of Lackland's breakdown to the others. *'He is a fragile man who always believes that right will triumph; and the world is just not that way.'*

With each day that passed, the Grefyns were diminished. Fingers began to point at a dissolute young Earl by the name of Lyn Pyndrys; a dissipated man with a nasty reputation. Pyndrys had suddenly risen to the high station of Heir to the Grefyn Duchy, through the deaths of seventeen of his more prominent relatives and all their children and grandchildren. Although his good fortune had been through no action of his own, he had thought that it was to his advantage to imply by vigorous denial that he was the mastermind behind a power-grab. Pyndrys was suddenly seen as a man to be reckoned with, and his close association with Lanqueshire was much discussed.

However, the good Grand Duke Amstyce had also heard those rumors, and decided that there was a threat to his own health posed there. In retaliation for the death of Gwartney, whom he had loved 'like a brother', he took an immediate dislike to his new heir, eliminating the upstart Earl Pyndrys of Grefyn, and his entire branch of the family down to the babies as retribution for daring to reach so high. His bold announcement of the Earl's punishment took Ludwellyn by surprise.

The Grand Duke Grefyn was known to be ruthless but this action had bordered upon hysteria. It had shaken an entire community who had grown rather blasé about things up to that point.

The five conspirators were shocked at the retribution that their actions had brought down on Pyndrys, especially the babies. "This just proves that The Crow is consumed by evil," Huw had told Lackland, his eyes gleaming with more than simple anger. "I would not have done such to the babes, no matter if they would grow up to be Crows. He has eliminated his entire bloodline in his rage; all that are left are fourth and fifth cousins twice removed, and they can't flee to Henri's protection fast enough. What sort of man murders his own blood wholesale?"

Now the deaths of Earl Lyn Pyndrys' children also began to weigh on Julian's conscience, a nearly crushing weight. He pretended that nothing was wrong, but his dreams were nothing pleasant to mention, visions of slaughtered babies haunting even dreams that had begun in a pleasant way. Still, he managed to continue carrying out the tasks that Henri had set before them.

At the end of the Rowdies' fourth week in the long valley, the few remaining members of clan Grefyn with any claim to nobility were suffering from extreme paranoia and a panic-stricken desire to go north to demonstrate their loyalty to the crown. The long simmering troubles had erupted in a small stampede of nobles, formerly known as Grefyns, out of the Eynier Valley. Many now called upon their long disdained Weyllyn roots, claiming to be Leweyllyn now; and of no particular clan within the Duchy of Weyllyn.

During the first week of the slaughter in the long valley, Grefyn ships began disappearing on the high seas; and it was said that the Pirates of Lanqueshire had been owed a debt of money by Grefyn, and that his ships had been forfeit. Of course, Lanqueshire denied that any such thing had happened.

Not two days after the sensational murder of his nephew's family, the Grand Duke Grefyn was found dead at the age of thirty-four, having 'eaten something that disagreed with him'. That had been rather a surprise to Lackland and Beau, since they had actually planned to slit his throat that night. They had crept over the roofs and in through the third floor study window only to find the Grand Duke laying contorted on the floor by his desk, frozen in a twisted, agonized pose and dead for several hours at least. They had looked around his study, disturbing nothing.

"Who of his close circle would poison him?" Beau wondered, as they stared down at the cold body of the Grand Duke. On his desk lay the letter he had been writing in Lanque; a desperate plea for assistance.

"He looks as if he has been unwell for a long while, even though the murderer at last resorted to poison," Lackland answered, looking at the emaciated man with a critical eye. "But we know that he is the most hated man in the Eynier Valley. It is clear that he was completely the puppet, and Gwartney the puppet master, pulling the strings for Lanqueshire."

*

The others were waiting for them with the horses just outside of town. They had each solemnly bade Waite goodbye earlier in the day. He had understood, though he wished that they would remain. The streets were now quiet; the King's men were patrolling them in aid of the constable's men and protecting the citizens of Ludwellyn. It was definitely time to leave; they had run out of hair dye for Beau and Lackland, and within days the two would begin to show their fair-hair again.

With the last task completed through no effort of their own, they had begun the two-day's journey north to meet King Henri's entourage at House Dragoran for Harry and Gwen's official installation as the first Prince and Princess of Eynier. After their second bath in a frigid creek, both Lackland and Beau were back to their usual 'golden-haired splendor' as Jack sarcastically pointed out. "Ah Jacky, you know you love to look at them, so why fight it?" Culyn had needled him. "Enjoy the view, hair that color is rare indeed here in the long valley!"

As the Grand Duke had left no living heirs, and Black Grefyn was no more; his lands and properties would now revert back to the crown; going to Princess Gwenevere and her brothers in particular. Their children would inherit them; a decision which made the common people of the Eynier Valley happy. They could clearly see that it had not been a grab for land on Henri's part, but was simply the result of stupidity on the part of the Grand Duke Grefyn and his complete corruption by Gwartney of Lanqueshire.

The Duchy of Greff was summarily dissolved, now being known by the greater name that encompassed the valley as a whole; they were now simply Eynier. Small pockets of stubborn resistance still remained, but sadly, they too were dealt rough justice by their neighbors who were fed up with 'the troubles'. The few who were still harboring grudges were forced to remain silent.

One day after the five arrived at House Dragoran, King Henri and his royal entourage arrived to see his son and daughter-in law properly settled. During the ensuing week of celebrations, the king knighted both Beau and Culyn.

On being told of his son's impending knighthood, Huw had sent a message to Sinean. She had immediately come down to Dragoran to see her son knighted, arriving just in time. She had agreed to ride back to Clythe with them, saying, "I am going to flaunt this turn of events all over Clythe, Culyn. You have long suffered for my folly in not telling Huw about you when I could have done so anytime; and now they will just have to shut it, won't they." Her merry smile had lightened his heart.

The tale was told that the honors were a reward for their services in the Bekenberg Pass. Many feuds that had long festered in the valley were settled amicably during the ceremonies that marked young Harry and Gwenevere's official entrance into the world of ruling a country.

Sir Beau Baker and Sir Culyn Owyn both were surprised and deeply honored to be accorded such esteem from their king. Huw and Jack had graciously declined the honors, explaining to Henri that too many new honors would draw unpleasant attention from any Crow sympathizers still hiding within the population, and eliminate their usefulness to him. Lackland's recommendation had been, "Let these two young men be thought of as being part of Harry's court, and not as being connected to our presence here with you."

"Lackland, you always give me good advice. I warn you though, I will deal with you later," Henri had said. "You have become less sunny of late, my cousin. That sort of work is not for you, is it?"

"No, Henri; I much would prefer to face a man in the open and defeat him in fair combat," replied Lackland wryly. "This has poisoned my soul somehow. But it had to be done, that much I do know. It is just that so many innocents were caught up in this, and I couldn't save them."

"I will only tell you that the Grefyns received the same sort of treatment that they had meted out for the last two Grand Dukes' reigns. Think of the Bards, Julian, and the weavers of Maudy town," replied Henri, clasping Julian's shoulder. "You care about people too much for your own good, but that is what makes you who you are!"

Several days after the knighting ceremony, Lackland, Huw, Jack, Beau and Culyn found themselves in Clythe. They spent their last two nights at Sinean's Green Man, making music and dancing all the night long with the men and women of Clythe. When Huw and Culyn played together, the entire crowd were on their feet clapping and whistling their approval at the end of their set. Many a man tearfully said to Huw that they had thought that they would never hear the great tales told by a trained Bard, and thanked him for his tales over and over.

Culyn, somewhat tearfully, hugged his mother as he left her, saying that he thought he would be gone for a long while. "I don't think that the long valley is my true home any longer."

Tenderly holding Sinean and kissing her cheek, Huw assured her, "We will both of us return at Yuletide. I will not let the distance separate you from our son permanently."

Soon, the merry tale of Culyn Owyn and how he found his father, joined the Rowdies and came home a king's knight was a staple tale in the taverns of the long valley, though the tale that was told placed him at Bekenberg Pass saving the King from highwaymen.

Chapter 7 - The Rowdies and the Firedrake

The five Rowdies had left Clythe, and now they traveled up the trade road to Bekenberg. On the morning of the second day out of Clythe, they came upon an overturned wagon; refugees from the recent troubles in the south from the look of things. Everything of value had been stolen and the dead had been either dragged off or scavenged. The white bones of a single horse gave mute testimony to the violence of the attack. There were few travelers on this stretch of road, and from the look of things, it had been a week or so since the attack.

Culyn came across several strange tracks, which he had shown to Jack. "I have never seen anything like these. What makes a track this big, and with only three toes?" The tracks had Slippery Jack quite upset.

"Of course! This is just wonderful," said Jack, miserably. "It is a firedrake." He remounted his horse, and looked suspiciously at Lackland who was dismounting and rooting around in his gear. "What are you doing? Get back on your horse and let's get out of here."

Lackland replied, "Now Jack, we can't really leave it here, nesting by the trade road. Henri will be returning this way, with his family."

He was humming.

In Jack's experience, that happy little hum meant that Lackland was going to be a hero. Smiling the contented smile that he always smiled when things were about to get messy, Lackland looked expectantly at Jack.

"Well?" He stood with one eyebrow raised, as if Jack was lagging behind on the way to a tea party.

"Henri has a bloody army with him, Lackland." Jack looked at him, aghast. "We are much less able to take care of it than those fine, brave men who, by the way, are carrying bespelled shields and are *paid* to rout impertinent firedrakes that may bother the king." He dismounted again, looking at the tracks. "Let's go home before it finds us. These are far too fresh for my liking."

"Ah... you worry too much, Jacky-lad," Lackland replied in Eynier with his innocent smile, "This will be good, clean fun! We have been skulking around doing murder in the dark for too long. It has poisoned my soul. I need to do something good and necessary that I am not ashamed to admit to doing. I am not cut out to be an assassin. This will clean some of the blood off my hands."

"I agree, Lackland," said Beau with a smile that perfectly matched Lackland's, in both its perfection and its innocent enthusiasm for Lackland's mad plan. "This is more the sort of thing that makes me happy, too. Though I do see the sense in what we just did down south, I hated the way we had to do it."

Jack spoke up again, with his dark eyes flashing in irritation, "But you two are damned good at skulking, once you get past your silly, unnecessary scruples. This, though; this sort of thing is not fun for me! Skulking around in the dark is much more the way Slippery Jack does business, you know that," and as he spoke, he mounted up again. "Less chance of being eaten by some bloody creature with teeth the length of a man's hand, and breath that sets your clothes afire."

Beau was merrily checking his weapons, and stringing his bow as was Lackland, their smiles lighting up their faces. "I will play at bowling with it, Lackland; and then you and I will both shoot it full of arrows."

Lackland nodded, saying, "They will most likely have no effect on the beast, but these new arrowheads from Gertie's forge are very sharp. We should definitely test them out."

Culyn said, "What about Jack? He seems to be unhappy at the notion of dealing with this creature." He looked from Lackland to Beau; both men were visibly happier than he had ever seen them.

"Oh, don't worry about Jack. He is just like any other creature of the dark. The poor old thing is just a bit crotchety at being suddenly thrust into the light of day, instead of hanging about in the warm, comforting dark!" Beau's good mood was contagious; he was a man preparing to do a task that he enjoyed.

"This will be fun! He will get into the swing of it soon enough. Once he sees us having fun, he will perk right up," Lackland's comment was obviously part of a lifelong difference of opinion between dear friends in how to approach certain tasks. "When the going gets rough, he will be right with you; never fear. Jack always has your back, no one better."

Beau's sunny disposition had returned in force, as had Lackland's at the thought of fighting a real fight instead of sneaking around and killing in the dark. He also hummed a happy song as he loosened his sword in its scabbard, and settled his armor. Huw recognized Beau's little ditty as 'The Firedrake in the Kitchen', a country melody that everyone knew and sang. Soon Lackland and Beau were merrily singing the chorus.

"Oh Lord, Huw, I knew it! Look who is just as bad as Lackbrains," muttered Jack to Huw, who also was not really too thrilled at stopping to rout a firedrake. "Those two deserve each other, God help the rest of us."

Culyn and Huw both shrugged at that assessment.

Culyn said to Lackland, "I have never fought one of these creatures, so this will be different. What are they, some sort of a dragon?" There was a peculiar sort of eagerness in his eyes.

"They are like dragons and yet they aren't," replied Lackland cheerfully. "They are smaller, quicker and stupider. They have a second breath that is a weapon, and they are a wee bit temperamental. They don't fly, but they can run faster than a horse, and they have those strange little arms with the claws at the ends. Something about their breath catches fire when they breathe it at you, so what you have to do is stop them up so that they can't breathe the fire-breath. I think Beau's solution to that little problem is quite elegant. I will definitely be using it myself the next time I have to take one on alone."

Rolling his eyes, Huw said in the tones of a man who had heard it all, "Don't get carried away by the enthusiasm of the idiots, Culyn. These things are bloody dangerous. You have to stay away from their breath, whatever you do or you will be well roasted." He raised his sleeve so that his son could see his scarred arm. "I personally prefer to sing about those two fools over there routing the damned things."

Slippery Jack had been wracking his brains for a way to get out of fighting the beast, and finally he had hit on one that sounded helpful. "You know, Lackland... the area in front of the den is likely to be rather cramped. Huw and I will just stay out of your way, unless you lads look like you are in trouble, right Huw?" Jack looked at Huw, who nodded most agreeably, smiling as innocently as a child. "After all, you are really the professional in these sorts of matters and we would just be in your way."

"Good idea, Jacky," Lackland replied, oblivious to Jack's manipulation of the situation. "They do tend to nest in rather tight places, and the beast is going to be thrashing about somewhat. The three of us should be able to handle it." Then Lackland said to Beau, "Once you have plugged him up, we will swarm him, and try to get the head off quickly. Agreed?"

Beau and Culyn nodded enthusiastically and began to follow Lackland. "Be sure to stay nimble; they tend to be snappish," he said over his shoulder to Culyn.

The trail led to a lake; then wound along the edge, where it turned sharply into the entrance of a cave that appeared to be the den of a carnivorous beast. Many bones, of both horses and humans littered the outside of it. Tying the horses up where they would not be able to see the beast or the fight, they followed the trail to the cave entrance.

Great piles of shit randomly dotted the landscape outside the den. "This is just wonderful, Lackland. You always manage to find low paying jobs that involve shit, or stench, or... did I say shit?" said Jack from across the clearing, hanging back with Huw.

"I knew you would get into the swing of things, Jack," Lackland replied, smiling his charming best and winking at him. Bravely (or idiotically, depending on the point of view) standing in front of the cave Lackland shouted, "Hey! Firedrake! Come on out and play!"

Huw whispered urgently, "Don't piss it off, Lackland. This is more than stupid enough, without pissing it off."

There was a strange, dry rustling sound in the cave, and as they watched, a huge shadow filled the entrance. The beast lingered just inside its cave, curious as to what was happening out in the clearing.

"Sometimes they are a wee bit coy, and you have to woo them out," said Beau helpfully to Culyn. "This one isn't really too hungry. We'll need to tease it out."

Beau looked about in the debris and picked up a round stone and bowled it at the entrance. A huge, scaly triangular head on a long, sinuous neck darted out and snapped at the stone, swallowing it faster than anything Culyn had ever seen; disappearing back into the cave. The drake made a strange gagging sound, followed by a burp.

"They can't resist snapping at anything that moves quickly. It seems to be a reflex of some sort," Beau told Culyn, grinning. "Human skulls work for this if you can't find a good round stone, but they have to be big ones. There usually are plenty of good skulls around a drake's lair."

The odor of burning sulfur filled the air.

"I need a bigger stone," said Beau as he poked around the edge of the lake. "That one went all the way down, I think."

"Ooh... that is going to constipate the poor beast," said Lackland sadly. "Oh well, it can't be helped."

Jack and Huw looked at each other incredulously. "He's mental," muttered Jack. Huw fervently agreed with him.

"How about one this size?" asked Culyn handing Beau a small round boulder.

"Perfect!" said Beau. Once again he bowled it at the cave entrance.

Once again the Drake snapped it up. This time it gagged, unable to get the boulder up or down his long throat.

The distressed drake staggered out of his cave, a round bulge in the middle of its long neck. Lackland immediately fired off an arrow, which bounced off its scaly chest. Beau fired an arrow just as Lackland fired a second arrow, and again they bounced off the huge chest.

The drake's head swung back and forth, and he made strange gagging noises as he tried to either swallow the boulder, or cough it up.

"Ah well," said Lackland as he abandoned his bow. "I was sure that would work, but... oh, well." Drawing his sword, he ran, yelling at the drake and began hacking at it, with Beau and Culyn right on his heels. Hacking and slashing, they attempted to hamstring the beast, while dodging its snapping maw and whipping tail.

The three men kept slipping in the piles of shit that were randomly dropped in the clearing, but somehow they managed to stay upright most of the time.

With a lucky blow, Lackland sliced half of the whipping tail off. That was when the beast really began thrashing about, with blood splattering about and really making their footing slippery. Strange choking sounds erupted from the beast but its cries were somewhat stifled by the stone stuck in its throat.

At last, Beau cut the hamstring in one huge leg and they had the beast somewhat down. However, the snapping jaws continued to dart and snap at them as they now hacked at the whipping, sinuous neck and huge head full of sharp knifelike teeth the length of a man's hand. The short little arms with the vicious claws were surprisingly fast as they lashed out in an attempt to slash the attackers, and the stump of the tail had become a vicious and deadly club.

Blows rained randomly down upon the beast as they dodged the snapping jaws and slashing claws, trying to hack off its head. Most of the blows glanced off the heavily scaled skin, although they were beginning to tire the beast.

Thinking he might have a way to keep the creature's head occupied, Culyn tossed a large branch, one thicker than his arm toward the drake's head and the beast deftly caught it, and with splinters flying he crushed one end of it in his terrible jaws, and then tossing it the way a bird does a fish, he caught it in an effort to swallow it. It caught at a bad angle, jamming the poor beast's jaws open.

Pawing at his face with his little hands rather like a dog trying to dislodge a sticky bun from its mouth, the drake momentarily paused in whipping its head about long enough for the three to finally decapitate it. They stood looking at the great head, and then at each other.

"You have something on your shirt, Sir Culyn," said Lackland, smiling broadly as he took in the look of his companions.

"You have something on your boot, Sir Julian," replied Culyn grinning widely. "And Sir Beau has it in his hair."

Huw and Jack stood across the small clearing leaning on their swords, laughing uncontrollably. "Well, you three seemed to have that under control so we decided to just let you get on with it. We will just see to the horses," said Jack, once he could speak. "And you had better bathe before you come near the horses. The smell of dragon shit makes them nervous."

Walking back to where the horses were tethered, Huw and Jack once again began laughing hysterically.

"And don't forget your bows. They are sticking out of that pile of shit by the stump!" called Huw back over his shoulder. His guffaws echoed across the lake.

Lackland, Beau and Culyn looked at each other, all of them grinning merrily. They were covered in blood and shit. "Well then," said Lackland. "I suppose a quick bath in the pond would be a good idea. I should have warned you, it is messy work."

"But it *was* fun," said Beau, with a huge grin. "You have to admit, Culyn; it was a lot more fun than other things we have done lately."

Culyn laughed gleefully, saying, "That really was rather exhilarating! Too bad there was only one!"

After searching the den, they found no valuables, which struck Beau and Lackland as rather odd. "These things usually keep a pile of shiny objects that their victims may have had on them. This one has been nesting here for a while, and should have a pile of belt-buckles and buttons and such as that, at the very least," said Beau, mystified. "It has no pile of sparklies. This is the first one I have ever seen with no sparklies whatsoever."

"Well, maybe the folks that the poor thing had for meals lately have not been very well off," replied Lackland. "It could be that while it was away from home someone has robbed it, too. That is a common pastime for some highwaymen, although that is quite a dangerous way to steal a living. They would have to be very desperate." Beau and Culyn nodded in agreement.

"Well, I feel good that I have finally seen a firedrake," ventured Culyn as he looked around the fetid den. "This was a pretty good morning, all in all."

Laughing and joking, they retrieved their bows and quivers, and the arrows that had fallen by the way. Then they walked back down the trail away from the mucky area in front of the den. Once they reached the shore of the pond they stripped, washing their clothes and armor and weaponry before jumping into the rather frigid water.

"Oh! This is damned cold," groaned Lackland as he submerged himself. "It is better than stinking, though. At least I think it is." He grabbed a handful of sand and vigorously scrubbed himself and his hair.

"Yes, it is that" replied Culyn, doing the same; his teeth chattering. "But my nuts are shriveled up to my ears."

"It will be better than stinking, and you do get used to it after a few minutes," said Beau, as he ducked his head under the water. "It is the middle of April, but I could swear there is ice in this pond."

As they paddled about in the cold lake, Lackland said, "It is too bad that we have to kill these poor things. They are such amazing creatures. It is just that they tend to eat people, and we really can't allow that."

"They are growing rarer with each year that passes," agreed Beau. "Someday, there won't be any firedrakes, or waterdemons. I suppose even dragons will be gone. I think the world will be a less wonderful place when that happens."

"Well, there will still be whales in the sea, if you wish to see a wondrous creature," said Culyn. "I recall the first time I saw one. You can't imagine how astonishing they are. They look somewhat like a fish, much bigger than that fire-drake. The one I saw was longer than our ship! Their eyes have something fantastic behind them that I think is intelligence. I could swear they have a soul! They look right into you and somehow they know that you are a person, and there is a kind of knowledge to them. In Vyennes, it is considered murder to kill one."

He paddled over to Lackland and Beau who lay on their backs, floating in the chilly water looking up at the blue sky. "The Lanques kill them to get oil for their lamps, and many other goods that are made from their bodies. Being surrounded by the mountains the way they are, they have few resources and must look to the sea for everything. I have heard that they eat them, but I can't believe that even the Lanques would stoop so low."

Rather quickly, they were shivering too much to continue their swim, and so they gathered their possessions and jogged to where the wagon had been overturned. Huw and Jack had a roaring fire going, and had made camp. They had then gone off to gather more firewood. The three frigid heroes spread their damp clothes and armor out to dry, and quickly put on their clean change of clothing, warming themselves by the fire.

Wrapped in his cloak for warmth, Beau stretched out on his bedroll and told Culyn, "Too bad Lackland couldn't bring his cooking gear on this trip. His cooking is quite wonderful when he has the chance to do it right."

"Thank you, Beau. It is just that I have a great love of eating and since I find myself traveling and cooking for myself so much, I have developed certain skills with fresh caught game." Lackland turned his back to the fire, hoping to warm his frozen backside. "Huw is quite an amazing cook too. We will eat well tonight." They all looked at the pheasants roasting on the spit over the fire. "I am quite looking forward to eating. I seem to have worked off my breakfast."

"Killing a fire-drake is a lot of work, I must say." Culyn yawned. "Where have they gotten off to, I wonder?"

At that minute, Jack and Huw returned from gathering wood. "Jack thinks we are being watched," said Huw conversationally as he stacked the wood near the fire. The others showed no sign that he had said anything out of the ordinary.

Beau turned on his side and leaned his golden head on one hand, leafing through a book of poetry that he had purchased in Ludwellyn. "Another beast?"

"If it is a beast, the beast is riding a horse shod in the style of northern Waldeyn," said Jack, poking at the fire with a long stick, and adding a log.

"Someone camped for a very long time not too far from here," Huw said. "There is a lean-to for a horse and a larger lean-to for a person there. It is impossible to tell how long they have been gone. They knew what they were doing; their tracks have been well covered, so Jack couldn't say if it is our watcher from before or not."

"We will post a guard tonight," said Lackland. "They may be friendly, or they may not be. I too, felt that we were being watched when we were through this area the last time."

Though they posted a sentry all night long, there was no trouble and no sign of whoever had been watching them.

*

The next morning found them riding toward Bekenberg, where they would arrive in the early afternoon.

The ambush came just after mid morning. Lackland vaulted from Strider's back with his sword flashing, as had Beau and Culyn. The highwaymen had quickly fallen, being no match for them.

While they dealt with the highwaymen, Huw and Jack had collected their horses, and stayed out of the way. Their particular skills did not run to melee battles, being more of the assassin variety.

Soon there were six dead highwaymen lined up along the road. After looking closely at their clothing, Huw and Culyn both agreed that they were Lanques. "Their clothes are like those of Eynier, but they are new, and much like the clothes the rabble-rousers in Ludwellyn were wearing."

Jack rode up with six horses, some shod in Lanqueshire, and some in southern Waldeyn.

"Well, we know now who was watching us," said Beau as they built a cairn over the dead men. "And this stretch of road is safer now."

Though he nodded and agreed with Beau, Jack had a nagging suspicion that their watcher was still out there, but decided that he was just being paranoid. *'A firedrake and then highwaymen, one after another; of course, I am paranoid,'* he thought as he tried to settle his mind, but it wouldn't stay settled. "It is just that the last few weeks have made me quite nervous," he finally said out loud.

"Jack, you were born nervous," replied Lackland, laughing merrily at Jack's discomfort, "And your skittish nature has saved us many a time. We will stay alert, because if you are nervous there is a reason to worry."

"Well, we have some horses to trade in Bekenberg," said Huw. "That will give us our cover story. We are down here routing highwaymen that we have tracked for King Henri."

The others agreed that story should be their cover, since without the hair-dye, they were traveling without disguises now. Except for Culyn, they were all quite well known in Bekenberg. "Yes, I think it is best that we travel openly as Rowdies, now," agreed Lackland.

"We are in Raven country once we enter Bekenberg, Culyn. They work the eastern trade routes, guarding caravans and the like. What we will do with these horses is hand three of them off to the Ravens, and then if a Rowdy who is working down here is in need of a mount through accident or, god forbid, theft, a horse will be found for him or her. We have long had that arrangement with them," Huw explained how things work. "The other three we will take back to Limpwater for a similar arrangement."

At mid afternoon, they rode into Bekenberg, and continuing straight on through the gloomy town, they went to the inn known as the Raven's Nest. It was located on the outskirts of town on the Vyennes trade road. There they met with the ostler for the Ravens, a large red-bearded man named Erik. "I see you have been keeping busy, Lackland," he said jovially as they dismounted. "We will be happy enough to take these off your hands."

After a bit more small talk, they continued on into the common room, where they were obliged to sit and gossip with the captain of the Ravens, Sara Murtrey. She was a woman of Lackland's age who was as big as Billy Nine-fingers. Her biceps were easily as big as his from moving kegs of ale.

"Thank you for the new ponies; we will definitely find a use for them." She placed a mug under the tap and deftly filled it. "It was a bad year for the Rowdies, so we have heard," she said, putting a foamy mug of ale in front of each of them, "I heard about God's Gift and Longstride; what a tragedy. We were sad to hear of all your troubles. We will all of us miss our Lucy Blue Eyes," She looked at Huw, whose eyes had filled with tears at the mention of Lucy; and then she looked at Culyn, and then said, "But at least you still have some family, Huw. Is this man your son?"

"Yes he is," said Huw with a smile lighting his normally rather gloomy features. "Culyn Owyn, meet Sara Murtrey, as fine a sword as you will ever want at your side in any melee. And she cooks like an angel!"

"We love to hear your father on occasion in the common room," she told Culyn. "Are you as gifted a songbird as he is?"

"I would say that I love the music as much as he does," replied Culyn with his charming smile, eyeing her the same way that Huw had always eyed the ladies, before his losses had taken the joy of living from him. "Though, I have never made my way with it as my father does."

"Well, I hope you will play for us tonight; you must stay here. I have the room, so please do stay with us." She beamed at them all. "I have a good stew and fresh bread for supper tonight, and jam tarts for sweets afterward!"

Then she looked pensively at her mug, and said, "I must tell you something Lackland, a wee bit of a heads up." Lackland looked interested. Sara continued, saying, "A former Lady of the Rowdies, Lora Saunders applied for membership with us at the beginning of February. We sent her out on two jobs, but while she was good enough with her weapons, she was really not suitable for what we need; I think you know why. So we sent her on to Wister. They are always hard up for help, and she could have done well there, had she been of a mind to."

Warily Lackland said, "Go on. We are acquainted with her."

"She didn't work out well there either," said Sara. "She has a grudge against you, Lackland; for what, I don't know. She blames you for her unemployment from the Rowdies and I feel sure that she means you harm. The last I heard, she was heading west to Galwye, to join up with the Wolves. Her father had been one of the Wolves, if you remember. Well, when Bloody Bryan got involved with the witch from Lournes and pissed off the king, they ended up taking what was left of their crew to Galwye. They are doing well there, with none of the troubles that they had when Ball-less Bryan ran them." She smiled as she said that. "Lora did not arrive there, according to my sister Ella who is married to Tom Watts, their ostler. No one has seen her or heard from her for near-on two months."

"She could be dead. There was a firedrake not two days south of here. We took care of that little matter," replied Lackland. "I would be sad to hear that, she was young and showed promise. She could have done well, had she not been so over bold."

"She was a bitch, Julian." Beau's blunt assessment of Lora Saunders was echoed by Huw, Jack and Sara. "You are too generous to her. She was loud as to her intention to add you to her list of 'famous lovers' that she claimed to have had. You were to be another notch on her belt."

"Well, I don't wish to speak ill of her. She was far too young, and not my sort of a lady at all, but I tried to be polite." Lackland's face was red. "I don't wish to gossip about her."

"You are far too gentlemanly," replied Beau hotly. "She threw herself at every man in the Rowdies. She was like a terrier with a rat in its teeth; she wouldn't stop hounding them until they finally gave in and gave her what she wanted, just to get her to leave them alone. I had to throw her out into the hallway naked one night when Mags was out on a job, and toss her robe out after her! You are apparently the only Rowdy to escape her, other than Huw. When you went to Belle, it made her quite angry. She was surprised and more than a little offended that you would ignore her for Belle."

Huw said softly, "I confess that I was surprised that she left so abruptly. She is the sort who never gives up, so leaving the Rowdies was out of character for her. I have wondered at that." Huw looked at him for some sort of an answer, but Lackland did not meet his eyes. Instead, he looked at his mug, and said nothing. His face was giving nothing away.

Huw and Jack looked at each other, nodding faintly as they saw confirmation in his demeanor of what had happened.

"Well, she was run out of the Rowdies, because she got up Annie Fitz's nose one time too many," said Jack, finally. "She seemed to believe that she was the most desirable woman in the trade, and sex with any man that she desired was her right and her due, instead of the privilege between equals that it is. She had the nerve to tell me that a man can't cry rape, because everyone knows they want it all the time, like rutting beasts." He had been quite offended by her remark, and it was evident in his voice. "That comment got her tossed out of my room. Twice. I am married and I take that seriously; but she would not listen. I had to be harsh with her."

Lackland looked at him sharply, but said nothing.

"But as to what got her fired from the Rowdies: it was a private matter, and I didn't get involved. Annie was quite done with her shenanigans, and made her pack it up and leave, then and there," Jack said, carefully ignoring Lackland. "My room is next door to Annie and Babs, so yes, I did hear exactly what happened during the night, but I won't comment. It is between them."

"Well, she could be dead, if no one has heard from her for so long," said Lackland again; desperate to get them off the subject of why Lora had left the Rowdies. "I doubt she could have handled the Fire-drake if she had run afoul of it. It is hard to survive the gaining of experience with them when you have no one at your back."

"I would not be surprised if she had decided to go on down to Lanqueshire, and try to find work there," said Sara. "She was over bold, and refused to learn to be more circumspect; she is just their sort of woman. She made my lads nervous, and pissed off my ladies. I won't have that. I like to keep the lads happy and feeling secure and I won't allow cat-fights."

As the rest of the Ravens began to fill the common room, the Rowdies were greeted by old friends. All were happy to see them and glad to meet the newest Rowdy. Huw and Culyn brought out their instruments and proceeded to regale them with the music of Eynier, and a merry evening was had by all. Culyn was last seen following a lovely Raven up the stairs, laughing with her over some jest she had made.

"What ever happened to Fair Ellen?" Lackland asked Sara as she closed up the common room. Beau stood at the bar, nursing his ale. Huw and Jack had gone up not long after Culyn. The three of them were talking as she finished wiping down the bar.

"Oh you know; she's married to the silk merchant, Lynnis. She just popped out her fourth," replied Sara, sighing. "Somehow, they all go that way eventually."

"Mags won't, nor will Babs and Annie Fitz. They will never leave the trade. Ah, well," sighed Lackland, "She was a merry lass."

"Feeling lonely, Lackland?" Sara's question took him by surprise. "I've a big bed, should you wish for companionship. What fun we had when you were down this way with the King during the troubles!"

"Now that you mention it, I do recall that your bed was quite large enough for two," said Lackland with a smile.

"Two or three," she said, winking at Beau who choked on his ale. Then looking at Julian to see what his reaction was. "I am a woman who has a very large heart to go with my large bed."
Lackland just shrugged, with his trademark smile. "Two or three," he agreed, his eyes sparkling as he sipped his ale and grinned at Beau's shocked expression. "It is a capacious bed, Beau."

Chapter 8 - Lackland and The Witch of the Woods

They rode out at dawn, leading the three horses that they were taking back with them. As they rode, they were once again laughing; this time about a silly but imaginative ditty that Huw had come up with at the expense of Lackland and Beau's dignity. It involved his own take on their escapades of the previous night in Sara's very capacious bed. Apparently, though her bed was large, the walls were thin; and Sara had been quite enthusiastic in her appreciation of the moment.

The two laughed, somewhat sheepishly and rode merrily along, everyone knowing the long journey was nearly over. Soon they were discussing their homesickness.

"God help me, I even miss Mickey's fussing," said Huw. "He drives me mad, with trying to keep me from 'sinking into a decline' as he does, despite the fact that he is the one who needs worrying about."

"Well, since John passed away, he has no other chicks in his nest to worry over," replied Lackland with a twinkle in his eye. "He is a very maternal man, don't you know."

Everyone laughed, and Culyn said, "I look forward to meeting this paragon of mother-hood!"

"He drives me mad," repeated Huw. "But he is a good soul, and for all that he is near on seventy, he is in amazingly good shape."

By evening, they had found a nice enough grove of oak along the road to camp in and they settled in for the night. Lackland roasted the brace of quail that Culyn brought in, along with some wintered-over potatoes that they had bought in Bekenberg. It was a merry meal, and afterwards, they listened as Huw told the Epic Romance of Aelfrid and Merewyn. Though they all knew it well, they loved to hear it the way Huw told it.

"I love a good romance that ends happily," commented Lackland as he bedded down for the night. He yawned and was soon sleeping like a baby. The others stayed up for a while, but soon they too went to their bedrolls.

*

Lackland awoke in the dead of the night to a sword at his throat.

"Get up, Lackland. Drop the knife." The voice was low, but familiar and hard as nails. "Drop it." She was dressed in men's clothes, but it was Lora Saunders.

Lackland laid down the knife that had sprung to his hand. The sword stayed at his throat.

"You and I have unfinished business," Lora's voice hissed at him. "Keep it quiet, or I will slit your throat now and be done with it. Get up. You are going for a midnight stroll."

Slowly, Lackland rose from his bedroll. He reached for his breeches, and slipped them on, jamming his feet into his boots, with her sword at his throat all the while.

Shifting her sword to his back, she said, "Now walk a while with me." The point of her sword drew blood each time she prodded him gently with it.

He found himself stumbling along in the dark, with her sword at his back. Periodically he felt the stab of the sword's point as he stumbled or paused in his footing, unsure of the way in the dark. "This way," she shoved him down a faint trail. They walked for some time, until two rough lean-tos loomed in the dark. One housed her horse.

"I followed you from the lake to the Raven's Nest. Then I figured out every place where you would likely stop on your way back to Limpwater. You men are so predictable," her voice was harsh as she mocked him. "You picked the perfect place to camp from my point of view."

"Now, take off your clothes," prodding him again with her sword. Several large spots of blood had appeared on his shirt during the walk in the dark.

"You know, this is not going to make it easy to satisfy you," said Lackland wryly as he complied. "I don't work well under pressure." Indeed, as he stood shivering in the cold of the late April night it was evident that he was not aroused in any way by her style of seduction. "Perhaps a small fire would warm things up a bit."

"Yes, and alert your lover that you are here," she smirked. "I will warm you well enough myself, so don't worry."

"My lover? I have no lover right now," Lackland said, mystified as to what she could be referring to. "I have had no lover since March. Well, except for Sara last night, but that was just for fun."

His breath hissed as her sword sliced him neatly across the chest. "I think you had better get used to working under pressure, you bastard. You aren't leaving this place alive unless you do. Now lay down there," she pointed at a rumpled bedroll. Her saddle was at the head of it, as was usual; however there were several other saddles there along with a sack full of lumpy objects.

That struck him as odd, but he was in pain and too confused to think about it.

Numbly, Lackland did as she told him to do.

She stood watching him. "I saw you and Beau playing in the lake with that southerner after you killed my firedrake. Do you and Beau talk about Mags when you are riding each other? Do you think she knows that you and Beau are lovers? Do you both ride her at the same time like you two did Sara the Fat Whore last night? I watched the whole thing through the window. I was on the porch roof."

Lackland just stared at her, at a loss for words.

She began undressing, keeping her sword on him at all times. "I saw how you and Beau couldn't keep your eyes off each other when you were swimming. You could barely keep from touching each other; I rather expected you to have a threesome with the new lad right then and there, bonding over the corpse of my poor firedrake. Traynor was mine, you know; and you killed him." She stepped out of her breeches.

"Your firedrake? You named him after your father's horse? How does a person own a thing like that?" Lackland was completely mystified by her behavior now.

"I fed him, and he protected me from highwaymen," she said. A cold light filled her eyes.

"You fed him? You mean you hunted for him?" Lackland couldn't believe what he was hearing. "You brought him meat? Deer and such?"

"Yes, in a way; you could say that I brought him meat. I brought highwaymen to him. They all thought they were going to lay with me and then go on their merry way. When I was done with them, I led them to the lake and he fed on them and their horses." she said matter-of-factly. "You took that away from me, too." Her sword flashed and a long line of blood appeared on Lackland's belly, deep but not gutting him. "I have been waiting here for you lot to return since the end of February. I followed you for a while when you went south. I knew I would get you sometime."

Shocked at what she had told him and in pain from where she had cut him, Lackland had no words; he was so nonplussed by her revelations. "God in heaven... you have gone over the edge, Lora." He was just beginning to understand the serious predicament that he was in. "You have gone mad."

She just laughed a harsh laugh and said, "You have no idea, Lackland." She was nearly done undressing when he knocked her legs out from under her, and the sword flew out of her hand. "Bastard!" she shouted as they struggled for the sword. Lackland finally got control of her, holding her down, but she held a knife at his throat, her eyes glittering.

She moved suggestively beneath him, spreading her legs, and wrapping them around his thighs. "Go ahead. Stick it in me. You know you want to." He let go of her and rolled onto his back. She rolled with him, her face only inches from his, her knife under his ear. "You are a right bastard, Lackland. You lay with everyone else and refuse to lay with me."

Her knife flashed in the moonlight; a line of blood appeared across his throat, and several more slices made blood trickle across his chest. His breath hissed as thin lines of blood appeared on his thighs horribly close to his manhood, and then the knife was back under his left ear, drawing blood. He was now bleeding profusely, and beginning to feel the pain in all his slashes quite keenly. But more than anything else, he was terrified that she would castrate him. *"I don't want to go like Bloody Bryan,"* he thought frantically as he tried to grab her arms.

"This will not do," she said with a mad grin. "Why are you still struggling? I thought you would try something like that so I placed this sharp little sticker where I would be able to reach it."

Holding her knife under his ear, she reached into her saddlebag with her free hand and came out with a length of rope that was looped at one end with a slip knot. "I can tie you up if that is what you really like." Lora grabbed his right arm and slipped the loop over it one-handed, tying his wrist to the sapling that made part of her lean-to. "I have had a lot of practice at this. I knew you would need to be tied up at some point. You lads always do."

Her knife stayed at his throat the whole time, and her eyes glittered madly. "If you are really good to me, I will leave the rest of you free, so that you can treat me like a woman should be treated."

She pointed the knife between his legs. "Now get that up, and make love to me. You owe it to me. I can't get work anywhere because of you." Her voice was hoarse with rage. "You owe it to me. Make love to me and tell me that I am the best woman you ever had, or I will be the last woman you will ever have."

"What makes you think I have caused you to not be able to get work," he asked her, as first she moved to lie on top of him, and then she straddled him holding the knife at his throat. Lackland's wounds burned and stung as she lay on him, tearing them open. "I have never spoken to anyone about what passed between us, other than Annie and Babs. They have told no one. They respect me too much to tell my secrets." The pressure of her on his slashed thighs was hard to bear.

"I have been run out of every crew that I have been with, since that night, you bastard. You left me alone in your bed like I was dirt and jumped straight into bed with those two old hags. You had the strength to do the two of them, but none to spare for me! I have nowhere to go, I have no home. I have no one! I have nothing and no one, thanks to you," she hissed. Lackland flinched as she drew blood across his throat again. "Annie said I tried to rape you. Men can't be raped, everyone knows that. That was a lie! You can't rape a man! Men are in rut all the time! They want it all the time!"

"You don't have to do this, you know," Lackland said sadly. "I will give you what you want." He tried to get more comfortable, but he was in agony, and laying on a rock or a root or something; with the cuts on his back tearing open each time he moved. "Let me get more comfortable, there is a stone that is killing my back." Finally, he was sitting up, leaning against her saddle; feeling a little more comfortable with a little slack in the rope that tied his right wrist to the tree. With her remaining straddled across his lap and the knife at his throat, it had been interesting and painful to say the least, getting into the better position. Lora had made it as difficult as she could, while smiling that mad smirk all the while, her knife at his throat.

"You want me to be your lover tonight. Alright, I will do as well as I can. Do not expect much from me though." Lackland tried to sound conciliatory. "I am sure that I can make you happy."

"And you will stay with me," she said fiercely. "You will stay with me and we will go down to

Lanqueshire and get work there." She wrapped her legs around his waist, leaning her head against his bloody chest and holding the knife under his arm. "Promise me that you won't try to escape! Promise me!" Lackland was silent, unwilling to make that promise. "I know you won't break a promise. You are far too noble!" She drew blood under his right arm this time.

"I will do as you say," Lackland finally said. He knew that he was bleeding heavily, and felt a weakness coming over him as the pain and the near-freezing cold of the mid-April night began to take their toll on him. *'I must owe her something... I could have done something long ago to change her life...'* Lackland's mind was clouded and fuzzy; he couldn't think well. Finally he agreed, "I won't try to escape. I promise."

"Promise that you will stay with me forever, and never leave me alone," Lora's voice was almost like a child's voice, lost and afraid.

Lackland nodded, unwillingly. "I will do as you say, but this is cold and loveless. Where is the romance in this, Lora? There is not even any friendship between us, only your pain and suffering and my debt of friendship to your father."

She had not heard him; she had only heard him agree to her wishes. Lora hugged him, and kissed his unwilling mouth joyfully. "I knew that if I could just get you alone you would understand! We will go down to Lanqueshire; no one knows us there. We can hire on to a crew of mercs down there, and we will be together. Think of it: Bold Lora Saunders and Julian Lackland, together and living happily ever after! We will be famous!"

Lora laid her head on his bloody chest with her knife at his ribs, and he unwillingly put his free arm around her, deciding to just get on with it, and at least perhaps get some warmth in the chill of the night. *'It won't matter. I will bleed to death before I leave here, I think,'* he thought, feeling almost hopeful at that thought. Nothing seemed real to him; he was light-headed and trembling with cold.

"I love you Julian, and I am going to make you so happy; you will see!" She set the knife down beside them and leaned back reaching between his legs to fondle him, still astride his knees. As she did so, a bolt from Beau's bow transfixed her, piercing her heart.

Lora clutched her chest where the arrow had protruded through from her back. Gasping for breath she tried to stand but fell forward onto Lackland's chest, and his free arm went around her, cradling her, his eyes wide with shock. Behind an oak some fifty feet away, stood Beau nocking another arrow. He lowered his bow as he saw that she had collapsed.

"You promised…" her eyes were the eyes of lonely, scared child as they glazed over. Julian just held her with his one arm, dazed by the turn of events. Beau lifted the dead girl off of Julian, and his eyes widened as he took in the bloody wounds crisscrossing Julian's chest, stomach, his throat and his thighs. Fresh blood welled from countless cuts and slashes as the pressure of her body was taken off of him. Beau's breath hissed as he saw what she had done to his throat.

"Oh God, Julian, you are a bloody mess." His breath hissed as he took in the bloody gashes that covered Julian. "God in heaven; what am I supposed to do about this?" Worriedly, Beau checked him over then cut his arm free. "Julian… what has she done to you?" Blood covered his legs and loins; in the dark, it was impossible for Beau to see exactly what had been done to him. "You will bleed to death." He was tearing his shirt into strips to bind Lackland's wounds, wrapping his throat, and trying to cover the deep wounds as best as he could. "I have to get you back to camp; then we can see what needs to be stitched up."

Lackland had no words to tell Beau what he was feeling just at that moment. A ragged sob escaped him, and wordlessly, he clung to Beau as a drowning man might cling to a rock.

"Julian? Are you all in one piece?" Beau waited until Lackland was able to get himself under control.

"I am cut; she did cut me, but not too badly, and not anywhere important. She had plans for that part of me but wanted it in one piece, I guess," Lackland finally said, wiping his eyes with the back of his hand. Then looking at Lora, said grimly, "Oh god, Beau; I held this child on my knee when she was a babe. She was the sweetest little thing; all dark curls and big eyes. I don't know what went wrong, that she should have come to this end. Her mother died young, and Tom never left the trade, so she was left alone a lot, and then he died. She was trying to find some way to feel loved. I don't know why she chose me."

"I think we are going to have to stitch you up before we can go anywhere," Beau told him, worry making his voice rough. "It's a good thing we still have some of that brandy your royal cousin gave us. You look like you need a good swallow or two of it. You are in shock."

Lackland tried to put his clothes back on over his bloody bandages but Beau ended up having to dress him as well as he could. With his teeth chattering Lackland told Beau most of what had happened, but did not tell him what Lora had said about the two of them. "But in a way, I did owe her something," he finished. "It was because of me that she got sent away from the Rowdies."

Wrapping Lora's cloak about them both, Beau put his arms about Julian, hoping to get him warm. "You owed her nothing. She tried to rape you then and she was raping you tonight," replied Beau, angrily, briskly rubbing Julian's arms to get the circulation going. "She would have killed you, you know. She had to know you would never have left with her."

"I promised her," Julian said, miserably. "She knew that I would not break my promise." Tears ran down his face. "She made me promise."

"Oh Julian, in some ways you are the most innocent man. You always believe the best about people. People are never as good as you think they are." Shaking his head and holding him close, Beau said fiercely, "We need to get your wounds fixed up and get you warmed. You will die of a chill from this nights work, I am afraid."

Beau stood up and offered Lackland his hand to pull him to his feet, but he ended up having to lift Lackland up. Once on his feet, he was able to walk, though he was feeling quite dizzy.

"I heard what Lora said to you about you and me." Beau said as Julian tried to get his balance.

Julian froze, standing dizzily trying to pull his thoughts together and then said, "She was not right in her head, Beau. I don't want what she said to turn you away from me. She was spying on us with Sara."

"I know. I heard her, and she was somewhat right about some things," Beau laughed that low laugh he was famous for, and placed Julian's arms around him. "Hold on to me so that you don't fall. Let's walk now. We will talk seriously later, I promise. There are some things we have to talk about," Beau said as he once again wrapped the cloak about them both, and started walking to their camp. "She was nuts, Joules. We never have once discussed Mags, although I do eyeball your arse regularly, and I did have a lovely view of it last night, bad boys that we are! It is one of the finer arses I have ever seen."

Julian laughed, weakly. "People keep telling me that." He was unsure if it was relief or loss of blood that made him feel so dizzy.

In the end, Beau had to half carry Lackland back to the camp. Jack and Huw did the best that they could to clean his wounds while Culyn stitched him up. Culyn was surprisingly gentle at cleaning and suturing the deep cuts on his thighs and his belly, and the brandy helped Lackland, both as an antiseptic and to ease his pain. Beau forced him to drink several good tots of it, hoping that it would settle Lackland's nerves. The other three were so shocked at his appearance that they could hardly speak.

After they had finally gotten him to sleep, Jack guarded him while Huw, Beau and Culyn buried Lora and brought her horse, her saddle and her stash of saddles and loot back to their camp. She had all the trinkets that should have been found in the firedrake's den. Lora's horse was happy enough to be picketed with the others, as the mare had not liked her solitary life, and had not liked the firedrake at all.

Then, the four of them talked over the events of the night until dawn, shocked and quite disturbed that she had stolen Julian out from under their noses while they slept.

Beau had heard her whispering to Lackland, and opening one eye he had seen her with the sword at his throat. He had pulled on his breeches and shirt, stuffed his feet into his boots and had followed them, staying far enough behind so that she had not heard him.

Beau described how he had had to wait to shoot her until she laid down the knife and leaned away from Lackland. He feared that the bolt would go through her and pierce Lackland too, or that she would kill him, with her knife continually at his throat or at his ribs. It was good that he had waited, since his bolt had protruded through her chest and would have impaled Lackland. But his unhappiness at having to watch what Lora did to Lackland was quite evident.

"I knew she was threatening him, but I couldn't see exactly what she was doing in the dark," he said, his face full of misery. "He almost had her. He knocked her feet out from under her and got rid of the sword but she had that knife stashed, and that is when she really started cutting on him. She had this whole thing well planned."

Huw was enraged. He was ready to dig her up to kill her again. Culyn watched in amazement as his quiet father paced back and forth, describing in detail the hell he would love to put Lora through. His passion and anger brought him to life; a sad echo of the man he had been before, and it touched Culyn deeply to see his father so livid. Jack and Beau were glad to see this side of Huw again; it meant that he was finally recovering.

Once Huw had calmed down somewhat, they discussed the loot that she had accumulated while she had been lurking near the trade road. Beau told them what he had heard her say to Lackland as to where she had gotten it.

When Beau told them that she had called the firedrake 'hers' and had named it Traynor, feeding it with hapless highwaymen whom she had seduced, Jack was speechless.

"Traynor – that was Tom Saunders' horse! She named it after her father's horse," Jack's shock and disbelief were quite evident as they discussed how a good, sweet child could have come to such an end. Eventually though, they settled down and got some rest, before they left that place.

It was evident that Lackland needed to be seen by a healer, the sooner the better.

Lackland's wounds made it difficult for him to ride, and soon it was clear that he was not healing well. As he began to be feverish and incoherent, they tied him to his saddle. Each of them took turns holding the reins and leading his horse, and they finally did get to Limpwater. On the fifteenth day of April, they rode into the courtyard behind Billy's Revenge, with Lackland tied onto his saddle, delirious and raving.

He was tended to by a priestess from the chapel infirmary, Sister Leona. She used her healing Majik on his wounds, removing the infection and healing the many still-open wounds. Then, she turned to healing him of the pneumonia that he had developed.

Once he was at last sleeping peacefully, she told Beau and Mags that Lackland would survive his ordeal. They stayed at his bedside until he woke.

Sister Leona was unable to keep his wounds from scarring him, as he had gone too long on the road before her healing. She praised Culyn's skill at suturing the worst of Lackland's injuries, telling him that those would be the most minor of Lackland's scars.

She also spoke seriously to Beau who hovered over Julian's bedside, "He will bear many scars from this ordeal, and the ones that you can see are the least of his scars. He is in for a long, troubled time of it, but he will recover physically in a few days and be able to work again in a week. He will have his full strength back in about two weeks." She looked at Beau, saying. "You must encourage him to talk, and you must let him talk about whatever is on his mind. It will be a long and difficult time for him, and those who love him."

By the next morning, Lackland had woken up, and was 'sitting up and taking nourishment'. Chicken Mickey had then clucked over him like a mother hen, until Lackland got out of bed just to get away from Mick's mothering. He began going down to the common room to sit alone by the fire and read, taking his book and staring at the fire for long hours.

On the positive side, Billy was overjoyed to have Culyn Owyn to be a Rowdy; Culyn was exactly what he was looking for in a new recruit and was immediately dubbed 'Fair Culyn', as he was easily the most glorious man to join the Rowdies since Davey 'God's Gift' Llewellyn's passing.

Culyn agreed to send a letter to Clythe to see if any more wished to come north. "Though if any do, they will be those like me, with a stigma of some sort. The south is not kind to lads who love other lads, or ladies who wish to swing swords. Any sort of stigma is hard down there. But they will fight the harder for you because of it."

Huw finally made several good ballads out of their adventures, despite the fact that nothing resembled the true events. 'Lackland and the Witch of the Woods' became quite popular, despite having only a tenuous basis in reality as it was told. Lackland had enjoyed it when he heard it, but was confused as to who it was actually about. It told the story of Lackland being seduced by a witch, and then given to her pet firedrake when her glamour wore off. When he came to his senses and tried to escape, Golden Beau and Fair Culyn had came to his rescue; first killing the firedrake and then the witch. It was very dramatic, and made a great romantic tale.

'The Murder of Crows' was also designed to chronicle the events of the demise of clan Grefyn but pointed directly to Earl Lyn Pyndrys, Duke Amstyce Grefyn and Gwartney of Lanqueshire. It was a tale of greed and lust for power in those men who were, in the end, responsible for the slaughter of their own clan.

Several other good ballads came out of their journey; 'Dancing at the Green Man' was acclaimed by all to be one of his best galliards. Beau was rather dismayed by the hysterically bawdy tale, 'Rowdies Bouncing on the Raven's Bed'. Though it named no names, there were only two gentleman Rowdies who were "fair-haired lads with eyes of blue". Many a knowing glance was cast their way while they hooted with laughter and thumped the tables in appreciation. He had turned a slight shade of red and looked out the corner of his eye at Mags, who had greatly enjoyed the tale, smiling broadly at his discomfort and winking at him.

When that tale finally drifted down to the Raven's Nest in Bekenberg, Sara had enjoyed it so much, she had made the musician play it twice.

Despite his healed wounds, Lackland was a changed man, and the difference in him was evident to everyone. He avoided being alone with any woman, especially

Belle and Mags; and the only person he would talk to seriously was Beau, although he maintained a steady banter of nonsense and fluff to cover his depression. Huw and Culyn did their best with him, but they knew that he was going to be a long time getting over what Lora had done to him.

Jack returned to Castleton and his life with Merry Kat, once Lackland was back on his feet. "Don't let it kill you, Joules," he told him, speaking in Eynier, as he sat on his horse in the courtyard. "Don't let what she did destroy you. Kat and Bess know what you are going through. They have been through hell too. You can talk to Bess."

Lackland nodded, unable to look Jack in the eye, but he had smiled and replied, also in Eynier, "Aw Jacky-lad, you are getting to be as bad as Mickey."

Jack had rolled his eyes and ridden off through the rain.

Looking up at the windows that faced the rear of Billy's Revenge, Lackland had the sudden urge to get on his own horse and ride as far and as fast as he could. *'But where would I go? My mind follows me everywhere. I can't escape my own mind.'* Seeing Mickey headed for him, Lackland turned and quickly walked up to his room, shutting the door and locking it.

Chapter 9 - The Rowdies' Picnic

Julian Lackland, Belle Tanner, Huw the Bard and George One-Shot Finch had just returned from riding guard on a shipment of casks from William the Cooper to an apple cider mill in Dervy, a straight-forward day trip. It had not been a bad job at all. As they rode back to Limpwater and Billy's Revenge, they were in fairly high spirits as a group. The exception was Lackland, who was rather quiet, as he had lately become. Still, he smiled and looked as if he were enjoying himself; listening to their quips and laughing at all the right places.

It was Lackland's first job since he had returned from the Eynier Valley gravely injured two weeks previously. Billy was worried that it was too soon for him to be going out, but Lackland had insisted that he go along. His temper had flashed to the surface, as it was wont to do now, and the stress in his voice was evident. "I will go mad if you don't let me get away from Mick. He is mothering me to death! There is no escaping him!"

Billy was not the only one to note that Lackland's temper was unpredictable now. He had been very quiet and reserved with Belle since he had risen from his sickbed. She didn't know what to make of it, so she maintained a professional distance and camaraderie with him. Lackland thought he could see her drifting toward Culyn, but he couldn't seem to muster up the desire to stop her, and in some ways he almost hoped that she would.

Beau and Mags, along with Culyn and three others, were off on a trip to Castleton with a silk merchant, and would be returning any time.

Johnny Malone, Bennie Smith and Young Brand were due back from a long trip with Alan Le Clerk. They were picking up a shipment of goods in Bekenberg for his store in Limpwater, an eight day trip.

Old Alan liked to think he was still a Rowdy, and indeed he was, but he had grown somewhat stout. His sword was a might slower than it had been, though he was still a fighter, never having let his skills completely languish. Alan was fifty-five and no longer used to the road, having been off for nigh-on twenty years. He had readily admitted that he was no longer up to it.

"That is why I hire you lot; I need protection from the bloody Lanque highwaymen and I don't have what it takes any more. My daughters are all mad to join up, you know. Anna is sure that this will be her year to join the Rowdies. Mags has taught her what she will need to know." Alan's pride was evident as he spoke of his daughters.

Billy had decreed that the next day would be a proper day off for every Rowdy who was in town. Well, actually, there was no work currently in the offing, but it had sounded generous when he said it.

As Lackland settled in to soak in his nice bathtub full of steaming hot water, he looked down at his new scars. He had not been the same since that night in the forest with Lora, and he knew it. He had been unable to bring himself to court Belle, and she was hurt by it, but he didn't know what he could do about that. His heart wasn't in it, and it wasn't fair to her. He was going to have to talk to her sometime, but he didn't know what to say.

"Lackland, can we talk?" George was soaking in the other tub. George was the oldest Rowdy still working, being fifty-two. He had been off on a long job with Annie Fitz, young Denis Tailor and Bennie Smith when they brought Lackland home, so he hadn't heard the complete story, although he had heard some of it.

Lackland nodded, resigned to the fact that George was going to meddle where he shouldn't.

"Lackland, we have been friends for a long time." George was the master of stating the obvious.

"Yes, we have," replied Lackland, smiling brightly. "I too have noticed that."

"Look, I know something happened while you were gone. It was something bad; I did hear some of it, but you are doing yourself harm, holding it in like you are. You need to talk to someone." George wanted to talk and help him, but Lackland was not ready for that. George was as bad as Mickey. "You were so quiet today you might as well not have been there."

"But I *was* there today, George. I had your back, just like always. I simply felt rather quiet, that is all," Lackland was feeling rather irritated at this point.

"I know you had my back; of course I know that. I wouldn't doubt that for a minute," George sighed. "It is just that you are as silent as Huw, and as jumpy as Mickey. That is not like you at all. I am just concerned, that is all."

"I am sorry, but you are right. I am jumpy and I am not in the mood to talk. And when *he* decides that I need to talk, Beau and I talk. Huw and Culyn know what happened. Ask them." Lackland said, as he abruptly got out of the tub. "I will be fine, you will see. It is just that I was sick with wound fever, and you know that affects you for a while afterward, so… thank you anyway for caring, George. I am just not really in the right mood to talk about it."

As he dried himself off, George got a good look at the myriad red scars that now crisscrossed Lackland's chest and throat; the long ropy scars on his belly and the smaller scars under his ears that his hair usually hid. His thighs were a scarred mess too. When he turned his back, George clearly saw the scars where he had been repeatedly prodded with something sharp. "Lackland… Who tortured you like that? Was it the bloody Lanques?" George's voice was shocked and full of angry concern.

"Ask Huw or Beau or Culyn what happened, George; they were there. It is over, and I don't want to talk about it. But thank you for caring." He threw his clothes on and ran out of the bath-house as fast as he could, heading up to his room.

Lackland lay on his bed, unable to rest thanks to George's well meaning concern, and unable to think about anything except how he could have done things differently with Lora. *I could have fought back more. I could have grabbed the knife and turned it on her at any time. Instead, I let her do this to me. Why?* His mind ran in circles, like rats in a cage.

A quiet knock on his door, and Belle's voice asking to come in, got his attention.

Sighing, he got up and opened the door. "I am not really so well right now, Belle. Maybe I tried to do too much too soon. I just need to rest a bit," he said and tried to politely close the door.

She pushed past him and sat on his bed. Patting the bed beside her, she smiled reassuringly at him.

"Ah… I see. You are not taking no for an answer," said Lackland as he closed the door. "Would it make a difference if I said that I am not fit for companionship of an intimate nature?" His charming smile had a slightly crooked quality, as if he were working hard at maintaining it.

"I am not here for that, my dear friend," she said. "Sit here, beside me. I will not pressure you in any way, and I promise I will go downstairs for dinner with my hair un-mussed!"

"That will surely ruin my reputation," he said with an attempt at humor which fell flat as he gingerly sat next to her.

"Julian, something bad happened to you; something that has scarred you in more ways than the obvious. I saw what you looked like when they brought you back. Mickey told me then that someone had cut you up on purpose. I know that I had nothing to do with this, so I know you do not blame me. But I care for you," she said. "We only had a week together before you left. I don't know if I love you or not, but I care a great deal about you. We did have that week and we had an understanding of sorts. You have been avoiding me. Don't cut me out of your life, please. I want to help you."

Lackland was silent. His shoulders shook, and he was simply unable to speak for a few moments. "I don't know how to tell you what happened. You must ask Beau. He will tell you."

"I did," she said simply. "He did tell me what she did to you. Julian, you did nothing wrong. You didn't deserve what happened to you." She reached for his hand. "You are killing yourself with guilt, trying to tell yourself that you could have stopped her."

He looked sharply at her, and then looked away. "It wasn't even the torture that kills my soul. I let her do it to me, don't you see? I let her do this to me because of who she was; because I held her as a baby, and played games with her as a tiny girl. She was Tom Saunders' girl, Belle."

Belle nodded, encouraging him to continue.

"Whenever we stopped over in Galwye on the coast run guarding old Montrose and his apple brandy, we always stayed with the Wolves after they reformed under Dick Jenson at his Rocky Pointe Inn. You know how it is; you play with the children and it's all a family. I know for a fact that I could have done more to stop her. But you see it was my fault that she had gone mad."

"Julian, she was verging on madness before she ever laid eyes on you, if we had only known it then. The signs were there all along; in the way she behaved toward all the men, treating them as if they were naught but her personal stable of stallions and refusing to taking 'no' for an answer," Belle said. "Maybe you could have stopped her, but you had an attachment to her. You knew and liked her father, and you kept thinking that it was all going to go away and she would be normal and let you go, if you were just polite and nice to her."

He began to relax a bit, speaking almost to himself. "Yes! You do understand! I did think exactly that! I was sure that she would decide that she had scared me enough and let me go. But after she told me about luring highwaymen for the firedrake to feed on, I knew she had been taken by a madness of some sort. I did fight back then, but she had a knife hidden. It was that which gave me most of these." He raised his shirt. "They aren't the worst. You should see what she did to my legs. But I am glad she cut me, in a peculiar way."

"Julian, why?" Belle was stunned to hear him say that. "Why did you deserve that punishment?"

"Because, Belle. Because I rejected her, and then the world rejected her; believe me, I have thought about this long and hard. I think I finally know why she went so badly astray. When she came here she had nothing; her mother died when she was only a babe. She was pushed from one place to another while her father worked, not really wanted by anyone but Tom. He was paying them well to keep her so they kept her, but didn't love her the way Bess does the babes here. She was always hoping he would come back to stay, but he never did. And then her father died and she had no one. She just wanted to be important to someone. She thought that if she was famous, that would fill the emptiness."

Belle started to speak, but Lackland said, "No, listen to me. What band of mercs is more famous than the Rowdies? Of course she decided to become a Rowdy. But her clumsy attempts at gaining fame failed and she was sent away from here. She couldn't keep a job because of her instability; and then, the only friend she had was a firedrake and of course, I insisted that we kill it. I had taken everything away from her, leaving her with nothing, no one and nowhere to go."

He looked at the window bleakly; not seeing the view. His mind's eye saw dark woods and Lora's mad eyes. "What was even more cruel was that I had not even the slightest idea of what I had done to her. I had dismissed her from my mind as completely as if she didn't exist. Once she was gone from Billy's Revenge, I forgot all about her."

Lackland's eyes turned from whatever inner landscape he had been seeing, and he looked earnestly at her; trying desperately to convey to her what he now understood. "But she did exist, Belle; and she was a human being who had been driven into madness by actions of mine that meant nothing at all to me at the time." He ran his fingers over his throat, feeling the ropy scars. "They remind me to be kind to people. You never know what they might have lost."

For a moment, Belle was stunned, trying to understand the complicated grief that Lackland was suffering from. Finally she spoke. "Will you go with us tomorrow? We have a day off, so we want to picnic by the river, if the weather is as nice as today was. You can be with me, and I will protect you from people asking you questions, with no strings attached." She patted his hand and stood as he reluctantly nodded agreement. He would much rather have stayed in his room while the others went without him and she knew it.

Smiling, Belle said, "You had better come down for supper, or George and Mickey will be up here wanting to know if they should send for the Fat Friar to give you the last rites. Mick swears you should still be in bed, and George is loudly agreeing with him. If they see you with me, they will assume you are back to normal."

"Oh God, not Mick and George together; please not that. Kill me now," He followed her out and down to the common room. They sat with Beau and Mags, and chatted about silly nothings through the meal, and then played a game of stones, which of course, Mags won.

As they went up the stairs to bed, Belle kissed Lackland's inexplicably tensed cheek at his door and to his intense relief she kept on walking to her own room. Feeling confused and worried about feeling so relieved, he lit the lamp to light the room and added more coal to the fire in the fireplace. Lackland could not stand to be in the dark now, and a part of him knew that was not quite right but he felt that if he just learned to live with it, it would get better.

He slept fitfully as he always did now; waking up, off and on all night long, thinking he was still in the forest. Sometimes, he was unable to tell if he was dreaming or not. At one point, he got up and stood in front of his mirror, looking at his scarred reflection. The deep red lines crisscrossing his body and his legs interested him, as if they were on another person's body.

'She didn't cut my manhood, but she might as well have,' he thought to himself as he looked at the lattice of scars. *'I can't bring myself to touch Belle. I don't know what to do about that.'*

Lackland had not been able to sleep through the night without a sleeping potion since Bold Lora Saunders had taken him at swords' point from his bedroll. At some point every night since he was healed, he found himself standing in front of his mirror, staring at his scars and wondering how to get past his problem.

Morning found him downstairs first, sitting before the fire 'reading a book' when Billy Nine-Fingers began stirring about. He jumped as he came upon Lackland sitting in the corner, holding a book and staring into the fire as if seeking answers. "Lord Almighty, Lackland! You gave me a turn," he said. "I have to say I was not expecting to find anyone sitting there."

"Ah… I just felt the urge to read a bit," replied Lackland lamely. "You know how it is."

"Well, no I don't, actually, but if you say so," and with that Billy bustled back to the kitchen where Bess was preparing porridge and starting the days baking. He said to his wife, "This little plan of Lady Mags' had better work. Lackland just near on gave me a heart attack, lurking in the dark by the fire like that, pretending to be reading! If getting him off to the river for a frolic in the reeds with Belle doesn't help him, I don't know what will."

"Billy darling, you don't know what it's like, to go through what he went through. Neither did Julian until it happened to him. No one ever does," Bess worked her dough, and turned it on her floured board. "I know some of what he feels like, and so do several others here. It is different for everyone. Don't be surprised if their plan doesn't work. He is suffering from guilt, which he should not take on himself, but it happens." She gave her dough a good thump. "*You* made me whole again. Lackland just needs time and understanding. He can do his work just fine, so don't worry. It is his personal life that will suffer."

"Well, I loved you the minute I laid eyes on you, my darling, the day you joined the Rowdies when I was only a lad of fifteen. And later, once you saw me as a man, I was fortunate that you would give me the time of day, poor crippled lad that I was," and he pinched her plump bottom as he put his arms around her. "You were so elegant, and dainty. Your quick sword and quicker wit laid me low. I thought I would never be so lucky as to have your kisses, when I was so much younger than you!"

"Crippled lad my arse," replied Bess with a smile that lit up her plump face. "You were never crippled. Your hand was wounded but your wits were as sharp as ever! Besides, I always did like the younger lads! And the five years doesn't seem so much now, does it."

"You are a good woman, Bess. I did it all to make you love me, and it worked. You were the most beautiful Lady the Rowdies ever had and you still are!" Billy hugged her again, as flour puffed in little clouds around them. "I would have done anything to make you want me!"

"Well, get out of my kitchen and let me get on with my work, silly man, or there'll be no food for the picnic today," said Bess, with a fond smile and a kiss for her husband whose embrace had become a bit too confining. "Shoo!"

*

Only Billy Nine-Fingers and Chicken Mickey remained behind to keep the doors to the inn open. Gertie of course, would not leave her work, but Bess took Gertie's young ones as always. Bess was every child's mother while their parents worked, and she loved them all. All of the Rowdies had walked out past the old bolt-hole, where the sounds of the smithy could be heard ringing in the morning.

Sadly, the young teenagers had to attend school despite their fervent wish to the contrary. Limpwater boasted a 'finishing' school that was open for children ages twelve to fifteen to complete their educations. Every family taught their children to read, write letters and do figures so that they would not be cheated; but the school, which was run by former Lady Rowdy Susan De Neves taught them about the wider world around them. She taught them to understand the basic contracts they might enter into and what was fair in such an agreement, and among other things, history and the basics of foreign languages. The school gave them a little polish and a touch of class that other lesser towns could not offer their children.

Susan was the younger daughter of the Baron De Neves of Berneton. She had been a lady whose love of her sword was much like Lady Mags. When Eddie passed away, she had stayed on with Billy for a year, but she retired from the road when she had married Richard Green. They had no children of their own. She had decided that the children of Limpwater should have the benefit of a court education, and so Richard had built her a schoolhouse. Her school was modeled on the education that the nobles gave their children, and every parent in Limpwater took full advantage of the opportunity. Billy's rule regarding the children of Limpwater was that they must complete their education with high marks before they could offer to join the Rowdies. He also insisted that they be at least in the last half of their fifteenth year, because they should be old enough to enter into contracts, marry and leave home.

"The life of a merc is a commitment you don't make lightly," he told his own children. "If you choose to be a merc you will make that decision knowing all your choices."

Bess and Gertie's young children ran on ahead, laughing and chattering, while Annie Fitz and Babs carried their babies. All the younger children were wearing sunbonnets that made their little faces look like flowers. The three older children, who were not old enough to attend the school, wore wide-brimmed straw-hats and trying to behave like proper young Rowdies. It looked like a flock of merry butterflies running down the path, with everyone wearing their summer finery.

For the adults, sun hats also abounded, gaily bedecked with flowers and scarves for the ladies, or for the gentlemen, simple flat brimmed straw hats shading faces that had seen little sun so far that year, with the weather being the way it normally was in the spring.

Soon, they had passed though the hilly field where the cows grazed happily in the sun, and then after walking down the steep path to the lower meadow they arrived at the riverside. Blankets were quickly spread on the grass, as folks staked their claim to the best spots in the shade, and the children ran merrily, tossing several bean-bags amongst themselves.

Though the river was still running high with the spring melt, the meadow was dry from several days of good weather and the shade trees were full of bright green leaves. The day promised to be quite warm; a true harbinger of the long awaited summer.

They lounged for a while in the warmth of the morning, and then the adults, too, began a game of toss-the-beanbags. There was much laughter, as toss-the-beanbag became hide-and-seek, which became a game of tag-you're-it.

At last, exhausted, they sat back down and chatted a while before eating the wonderful picnic lunch that Bess had prepared. After they had eaten, the adults were lulled by full stomachs and the warmth of the day to nap in the shade with the babies and the younger children while the older children ran off exploring.

"Don't go too far," called Bess. "Stay where you can hear us, and we can hear you. And don't go near the river!"

Four heads had earnestly nodded, saying, "Yes, ma'am," before running merrily to see the bird's nest that young Eddie MacNess had found in the crab-apple tree.

Lackland found himself lying on a blanket that Belle had spread under a maple tree near the brush that marked the riverbank. They were somewhat away from everyone else, which he rather enjoyed. He lay looking up at the sky through the leaves, listening to the river and the children playing, unable to sleep, and not at all in the mood to talk.

Belle had drifted off to sleep, and he looked at her peaceful face, feeling a peculiar sadness as he did so. He had the fleeting thought that he would never be able to make love to any woman that he truly cared about again; that he would be forever soiled by the memory of Lora and what she had done to him.

The children's voices grew nearer, and he could hear their conversations. They seemed so merry and happy, and indeed they were. With Bess and Billy taking care of them while their parents worked, they had a loving family and security. Not the sort of life poor Lora had, now that he thought about it.

Young Eddie MacNess had apparently climbed onto a fallen log and was trying to impress little Estelle Smith with his ability to balance on it. Their laughter tugged at Lackland's heartstrings; it was so innocent and free.

He was almost dozing off when he heard Estelle say, "No, Eddie! You'll fall in!" followed by a splash.

Leaping to his feet, he quickly shucked his boots, and then ran to where Estelle was hysterically calling to Eddie to 'grab the branch'.

As he ran, he was met by five year old Mary MacNess, who was terrified that her brother was going to drown. "Lackland!" she screamed when she saw him, "He fell in and the river has taken him!"

Beau was right on Lackland's heels as they ran to the river's bank and dove in. Eddie was clinging to a floating branch and being carried swiftly down the river. While the Limpwater was not an unusually wide river, it was a deep river and it ran exceptionally cold, originating in the high snow-capped mountains to the north. It was running high with the spring melt and though it was a bright, warm day in May, the river was icy, and sucked the breath out of them as they dove into the fast-moving water. The River Limpwater was much colder than the firedrake's lake had been. Ignoring the cold, they pressed on, swimming as fast as they could.

Both Lackland and Beau were strong swimmers, and they soon caught up with the branch, just in time to see the terrified child lose his grip and sink beneath the surface of the river.

The bank was lined with adults running along, following their progress as they were carried down the river. Bess called to her son hysterically, while Mags and Johnny Malone forcibly restrained her from leaping into the river herself. Both Beau and Lackland dove under, searching frantically. Finally Lackland spied him, and grabbing his shirt, he pulled him up to the surface, coughing and choking.

"Don't fight, me, Eddie! Don't fight! Just let me take you to your mother," Lackland said urgently as the boy struggled desperately. "Don't worry, Eddie; I have you safe. It will be fine, you will see." Fighting the cold, he finally got the boy to the bank and into his brother Brand's arms, clinging exhaustedly to the bank.

"Beau! Beau! Where is Beau?" Mags' anguished cry made Lackland turn and look back at the river, where there was no sign of Beau.

Something snapped in Julian's chest. With no further thought he turned and swam out to the branch, seeing something tangled in it.

Shouts of "Beau's gone!", and "Lackland, you fool! You'll die too!" followed Julian as he searched desperately until he found what he was looking for.

Again people ran along the bank, following them, and calling to him as the huge branch traveled downstream with the current of the river. Racing as hard as he could, he swam to the branch and searched until he found the thing that he was looking for; the thing that had caught his eye. There it was, Beau's golden hair tangled in the branches; the thing that should not have been there that had caught Julian's eye. Pulling his knife from its sheath and cutting Beau's hair free, Julian grabbed him, pulling him up, and getting his head out of the water. He didn't hear the cheers and whoops as he struggled to drag Beau to the bank. His lungs burned, and he desperately gripped Beau's shirt with numb fingers, vaguely wondering if he was going to make it after all.

Just as he thought that he was finally done for, he felt Culyn at his side, helping him to swim the last few yards, helping him to bring Beau back.

Johnny Malone and Benny Smith's strong arms pulled Beau out and helped Brand to drag Lackland and Culyn out of the icy river.

"You have to get the water out of his lungs," shouted Huw, running down the bank toward them as they turned Beau over. "Press the water out of his lungs!"

Desperately, Johnny Malone pressed on Beau's back, trying to force the water out of his lungs. "Breathe," Julian urged him as he knelt gasping beside them. "Breathe!"

Suddenly, water poured from Beau's mouth and nose. With a great gasp, Beau at last began to breathe on his own again, laying on his side and coughing, spewing more water out as he struggled to breathe. Johnny held Beau, letting him cough it all up, while Julian clutched his hand, willing Beau to breathe; hardly able to breathe himself. At last, Beau was able to speak, asking about Eddie. "Eddie is safe, lad. You don't need to worry; he is safe," Johnny's rough voice reassured him. Bess quickly wrapped blankets about them, warming Beau and Culyn, who looked at her gratefully and thanked her on Beau's behalf.

Beau struggled to get himself pulled together, trying to get his breath back. His lungs burned, and his stomach kept turning itself inside out, and he couldn't actually see anything.

Lackland knelt next to Beau's shivering body, listening as Beau puked his guts up. He was bewildered and unable to pull his thoughts together; unable to hear anything except Beau's gagging and gasping for breath. Julian shivered, trying to get warm in the sun. All that he could think of was how terribly close he had come to losing Beau. When he felt a blanket being wrapped around him, he looked up and saw Mags; her face full of gratitude, love and myriad other emotions that she had no words for.

Seeing the mute, distraught look on Julian's face she knelt, putting her arms around him, holding Julian close, telling him that she loved him and that it was all fine, everyone was fine.

"Oh, Mags. We almost lost him, Mags, my love!" he said, and he found himself sobbing uncontrollably as she held him. "We almost lost him. I can't lose him."

"Shh, love, shh. It is going to be fine. Everyone is safe, Beau is safe; you are safe." She held Julian as he shivered and sobbed away the grief and guilt of the last few weeks. He clung to her and sobbed until there were no tears left, telling her everything that he had kept pent up: all his hurt and insecurity; what Lora had said and done to him and how terribly responsible he had felt for his own inability to stop her. He told her everything that had been preying on his mind.

Through it all, Mags held him, rocking him and comforting him as only she could do; murmuring reassurance and love all the while.

At last, he was able to recover himself, and as he did so, he realized that Beau held both his hands, tears running down his face. The others had discretely drawn off to give them privacy and Belle stood guard making sure they had the space they needed.

Lackland heard a little voice worriedly ask, "Mama Bess, is Lackland dreadfully hurt?" and then Bess' voice saying, "He was hurt terribly, Estelle, but he will be better now."

Beau sat on the bank wrapped in a blanket, worriedly holding Lackland's shivering hands in his own equally shivering hands, while Belle and Mags fussed over them. "Are you well enough to walk now?" he finally asked Lackland, his voice hoarse from the near fatal encounter with the water. "I feel the urge to sit by the fire and count my blessings."

"I feel an urge to do the same," replied Lackland, with some of his old sparkle returned to his eyes. "I hope I am well enough to walk; I will most likely have to carry you, and you are no light-weight, you muscle bound moron. Who told you to go swimming in May?"

"Moron? Look who's calling me a moron, Lackbrains," replied Beau. "I will most likely have to carry your old bones as usual!" As they walked back to the meadow, bickering back and forth, they each sounded like their old selves, to everyone's relief and great joy. They ended up leaning heavily on each other, and on Culyn and Brand, by the time they arrived back at Billy's Revenge.

"Do you think we should tell Beau what Lackland did to his hair, or should we let him find out on his own?" Culyn's eyes were full of mischief as he looked at Huw, who just shrugged and grinned knowingly.

"He will be finding out soon enough," said Johnny Malone grinning wickedly. "Why should we spoil the day with mentioning something trivial like Beau's amazing new hair style?"

They all snickered; relieved that whatever else had happened, the incident had snapped Lackland out of his melancholy and no one had actually died.

It had been a good day after all.

*

That evening in the common room, the noise was incredible, as most all of Limpwater had descended on Billy's Revenge to celebrate the lives that had been saved that day.

Young Eddie was rapidly growing tired of being grabbed and kissed by random adults and was thinking about hiding, when his harried father gave him a rather nasty job to do in the kitchen. "I need the help, son, if you are up to it. The whole town is here tonight."

"Thank you, Dad," he said with relief. "I would love to scrub the pots for a while." Once faced with the immense pile of pots, he immediately set to work; reveling in the peace and quiet of the kitchen, shining the pots better than he ever had before, not even fussing when he was later sent to bed before the grown-ups had finished their party.

Eddie had been quite taken aback by the way the day had gone so badly, when it shouldn't have. *'At least they knew what to do to make Beau breathe again.'* The thought that Beau had nearly died trying to save him was more than his nine-year-old mind could handle. *'Now I have to be a Rowdy, no matter what; I owe my life to them. I have to somehow repay Lackland. I must always have his back, and be there to save his life, because he saved me.'* Eddie, also now knew, that he had to work very hard to prove that he had deserved to be saved when his accident had nearly cost Golden Beau his life.

Eight-year-old Estelle Smith sat on a stool in the far corner, unnoticed by him, watching as he vigorously scrubbed and polished the kettles. Her mind was occupied with the way things had all gone for the better, just when it had looked so bad. *'When I grow up, I am going to carry a sword and save people, just like Lackland and Fair Culyn do,'* she thought. *'After I marry Eddie, that is. Lackland saved my future husband, and he saved Beau, and then Fair Culyn saved Lackland from the river.'* Nothing could be a more important task than that of saving people that other people loved so much; and since Eddie was going to be a Rowdy anyway, they would surely live happily ever after, saving many people from fates worse than death.

Not surprisingly, Beau had been rather shocked by the way his hair looked when, after his hot bath, he had looked in the mirror to shave and comb his hair. "Good lord, Lackland! Don't take up hair-dressing, whatever you do!" causing the rest of the lads to laugh hysterically. Annie Fitz had trimmed it up and made him look even better than before.

Huw had, of course, immediately made a tale out of it, and after regaling the crowd with 'The Rowdies'

Picnic', he and Culyn soon had the crowd dancing and singing, making the party that had so nearly been a wake into a joyous celebration of life.

*

That night, when he finally made it into his own bed, Billy lay silent for a long while, unable to sleep. He felt his wife's arms go around him, comforting him.

"What is the matter love?" Bess' sleepy voice said near his ear.

"We almost lost our boy Eddie today, along with two of my closest friends and I didn't even know it was happening," he said, feeling mystified that such a thing could happen without his having some sort of knowledge of it. "Our boy was nearly taken by the river, and two good men nearly lost their lives saving him. I was doing the accounts and wondering how we were going to stretch the wintered over potatoes until the new ones are ready while all this was happening. I never even had any inkling that anything was wrong until you all came back. I wasn't there when our boy needed me. I wasn't there and I didn't even know. I should have known!"

"Billy, love, you can't swim! The only ones who can swim are Lackland, Beau and Fair Culyn, and they did what had to be done. They saved our boy, and Culyn surely saved Lackland and Beau, for I don't think Lackland could have made the last few yards without him," she hugged him reassuringly. "You don't have the gift of second-sight, so how would you know? Besides, now that we are low on potatoes, we will simply make noodles; everyone loves noodles and we need to use the flour before it sets weevils anyway."

"How will I be able to send our boys and girls out on a job? I will fear every moment now, wondering if I have sent them to their death." He was silent, staring at the dark. "It will be like my dad; I wouldn't know until it was too late."

Bess was silent for a moment. Billy rarely mentioned the day his dad had gone out on a job and come home tied across his saddle, dead. "Nothing has changed, love. It has always been that way, and it has happened that our loved ones have not come back alive. What *has* changed, is you, Billy-love: you have children that want to take up the trade, and now you are worried for them." Her voice sounded sleepy. "Brand will be fine, just as we were fine. Eddie and the girls will do well when it is their time too, I know it. You worry too much."

"At least Cissy had the sense to marry an apothecary; boring, chinless lad that he is," he muttered. "Letty wants to take up her sword this year as a Rowdy, and I don't have the right to stop her."

"No, you don't. She will be fine, and she will find her way, as they all do. Anyway, Lackland is going to train her and the other youngsters this summer, and the Ladies have been working with her. You can't ask for better than that." She kissed his cheek and said, "Well, since you have me wide awake, I think you should take advantage of your good fortune!"

Billy's eyes gleamed in the dark, as did his smile.

*

Beau lay awake, staring into the darkness. Mags lay next to him, also looking into the dark. There was a space as wide as canyon between them, and the conversation had drifted into dangerous territory.

"You love him, Mags. Why are you not with him? Julian has never stopped loving you, and would have you back with him right now with no recriminations whatsoever, in regard to me." Beau found himself asking the one question he had vowed to himself that he would never ask. "I love you, Mags; but not the way Julian does. You are part of his soul. You want him, not me. You love him the way he loves you."

"I do love him with all my heart, but I can't give him what he wants. I can't leave the trade," she said, sadness coloring her voice. "I am the worst person he could possibly be in love with. I have done him some terrible wrongs, Beau, things no other man would have forgiven me for. You know what I did, and how I lied to him. I would still be doing him wrong, because there is no place for a lady like me in polite society. Men who are good with the sword can be knights, and that is all perfectly fine; everyone loves a Good Knight. Women who are good with the sword are not discussed, though they are no longer considered to be abominations; but there is no place for them at court. I love my life too much to change it. And yes, it does make me terribly sad that I have hurt you both so much."

"Mags," something in the way Beau said her name made her look sharply at him; wondering what he had been holding back that he wanted to tell her now. "I love Julian too. I have to confess to you that he is more than a brother to me, though he doesn't know it yet. I fight better with him, I think better with him. He has part of my soul and I can't live without him." He felt the sudden sharp intake of her breath and laughed that low sexy laugh that had always sent a thrill through her. "I have shocked you. It is not just a lad-loving-the-lads sort of thing; Julian is the only lad I have ever wanted that way. I will be honest with you about this, as you have always been to me. This is so much more than brotherhood, even; it is love like I have never experienced it before,"

Beau said slowly, smiling sadly as her shock turned to confusion. "When Julian goes to court in the fall, I am going with him, unless he tells me to stay behind."

"I rather thought you might. He will have you, never fear. He loves you too; he told me so today on the bank of the river while you were still puking. It is clear to everyone that you two are very close," she replied sadly. "But if anyone ever knew about this sad triangle they would weep. I find it hard to accept that you and Julian can live happily ever after, but I must lose both of you because of my own folly. It should be the three of us together, if life were fair." She paused, hating the sound of her own misery. "I think Culyn will eventually follow you."

"That will break many young hearts here in Limpwater," he said wryly. "But it is true, that with Culyn, we can get much accomplished for his Majesty that other courtiers cannot do." They lay there in the dark, silent and not touching one another, thinking about their peculiar situation.

After a long silent moment, he turned to face her. "You could come with us, Mags. We would make Henri let you be a knight," urged Beau, applying as much pressure on her as he knew how. "You could have everything that you want, and Julian could have you the way he needs you." He found himself begging her, "Please believe me when I say that he needs you, now more than ever, since that bitch cut him up so badly. Julian is never going to be the same, Mags; now he is fragile and broken in some strange way. He will accept Belle for tonight, but he needs you. You are his strength."

"I know; I know this better than anyone! But I would be an oddity at court, and you know why he must go there. He has to be there for Jules, and that is my fault! This whole mess is my fault," Mags sounded as bitter as she felt; helplessly angry at herself for having caused such a situation. "Conversations would stop when I walked into a room, and the other ladies would not wish to be rude to me because of my high birth. But they would have no idea of how to treat me, because of my famous lovers and equally famous sword. I have a place here and the respect of my fellow Rowdies. I am given jobs that fit my abilities and make me work to grow; and no one doubts that I have their back. I am not brave enough to go to court and lose that. No knight would trust me behind him, other than you, Lackland and Culyn. Perhaps Henri would, but no one else."

Beau was silent for a moment, and then he said sadly, "I wish you would change your mind, but I accept that you won't." His sadness was palpable, and it was for Julian as much as it was for himself. Tears stung his eyes as he lay there. "I love you Mags. I really do love you."

"Beau, you nearly died today, and you are not really as well as you pretend to be. Your voice is still raw, and you couldn't sing tonight. Are you feeling well enough for a little comfort?" she asked, her voice soft and vulnerable. "I need to be comforted. I am losing everyone that I love, because I cannot change the way that I am.

Beau gave her his answer in his embrace.

*

Belle traced her finger along Lackland's perfect profile, looking at him in the flickering light of the candle the he had insisted on having. He was a little embarrassed to be wryly admitting that he feared the dark and couldn't fall asleep without it. She found herself committing him to her memory. He was sleeping peacefully; for the first time since his ordeal in the woods, she suspected.

'*I will miss you when you leave me, my beautiful man,*' she thought, looking at him. She was still in awe of the day's events, and stunned by the terrifying knowledge that had come over her during the aftermath while the four of them sat on the river bank and Lackland had purged himself of his grief.

Despite her best efforts to the contrary, she had fallen for Sir Julian Lackland De Portiers. She didn't care that his heart was squarely wedged somewhere between Mags De Leon and Beau Baker. He loved her a little too, and that was good enough for her.

He had allowed her to make love to him tonight; he had consented to her tentative invitation to her room with a vulnerability that was touching. In much the way that he had always been before Lora, Lackland had been the consummate lover; satisfying her completely before taking his own satisfaction, but he was a changed man. He was unsure of himself now, and there was a part of him that he held back, unable to completely give all of himself to her; as if they were only a brief encounter.

To be completely honest with herself, she supposed they were. Nevertheless, she would try to find the good and be glad for what she had with him while she had him, knowing that tomorrow she would wake up alone, and finding that it didn't really bother her.

Chapter 10 - The Long Years

During the summer that followed, Lackland had to leave briefly to attend his mother's funeral, and then he and Beau continued training up the young people of Limpwater, who were all mad to be Rowdies. They used the time for developing the intensive weapons training that they would be taking to court in the fall, giving Billy's young hopefuls the finest training that any group of recruits would ever again have.

In between training and taking small jobs for Billy Nine-Fingers, Lackland and the others made the most of their evenings, and even Billy had to say he couldn't remember a merrier summer.

Despite her father's secret reservations, Letty MacNess proudly became a Lady Rowdy, as did Anna Le Clerk, Alan's youngest daughter. Two young lads and a lady from the Eynier Valley were sent up to Billy's Revenge from The Green Man, with a note from Sinean detailing their abilities and strength of character. Billy was quite pleased, as he now had a full complement for when Lackland and Beau left in the fall.

The new Rowdies were Donald Bevin, Michael Cyncaid and Celia Dymock. All three were happily accepted into the Rowdies, and Culyn was quite pleased to see his old friends. Huw admitted to enjoying hearing the accent of Eynier around him in the evening once again.

Early in the summer, Belle had accepted the fact that Lackland didn't love her, though he was unfailingly kind and cared about her. She had formed an understanding with Culyn, who had at first been worried that he was causing trouble. Lackland had simply been as honest with him as he could be, explaining that he wanted Belle to be happy and he would never be able to love her. "I will always love Mags," he said simply. "No other woman will ever take her place."

He had been happy for Belle, and happy for himself; feeling a certain amount of relief that he would be able to get on with the rest of his life. "Happiness is a rare thing," he had told Belle when she had broken off her relationship with him. "Grab it and hold on to it, and to hell with what anyone says. Besides," he had said, with is eyes twinkling, "The lad is mad for you! You can see it when he looks at you. Be happy, Belle. Don't live your life with regrets!"

Lackland now suffered terribly from nightmares, waking often and still finding himself in front of the mirror. As his relationship with Belle ended and he found himself alone, his nights became tests of his endurance. After being woken by his screams during one particularly bad night, Mags and Beau began to stay with him. One or the other, or both were always there when he woke in the night, strong arms holding him; sheltering him from the terrors that loomed in his mind.

The deaths of Duke Gronwy's and Earl Lyn Pyndrys' babies and children weighed on his conscience, as did every child that had ever died because of his actions in Ludwellyn. These horrors became entangled with the complicated misery of Lora. All of the children, who suffered because of him, rose to accuse him of failing to protect them. In his dreams, he saw them being butchered over and over again; and he was powerless to stop the massacre, because Lora had him tied to a tree, cutting him again and again as punishment.

Though the other Rowdies knew of the arrangement, no one said anything, feeling as always that what other folks did was their own business. Anything that kept Lackland from screaming the house down in the middle of the night was fine by them. Besides, Lackland was better than he had ever been when out on a job; his reflexes were lightning-quick and he was a jolly companion. For some reason, camping on the road was not as hard on him. Perhaps it was because no Rowdy would ever set camp without a standing watch... ever again, no matter how safe they thought they were.

The summer days passed, with good times and good friends enjoying each moment for what it was. Billy's Revenge had never been so merry a place.

Lackland was never going to marry anyone but Mags De Leon, and if he could not have her, he would be content with his arrangement with Beau. Over the summer, he and Beau had made some decisions about their relationship. Though he had never thought he would feel love for anyone the way he did for Mags, Julian had come to terms with their strange triangle. He decided, as he usually did, that he would live his life as well as he could and to hell with convention. "I accept Mags' right to determine her own path in life," he told Beau. "She loves me; she loves us both, but she will never give up the sword for us, never. It would kill her, Beau. I know this well."

Beau, on the other hand, was torn about leaving Mags behind. Their love for Julian was the tie that both bound them together and tore them apart. Beau's loyalty and his obligation to Henri Dragoran made the choice easy for him.

Nevertheless, before he left, Beau begged Mags once again to come with them; still imagining the three of them living together happily ever after.

"I am begging you, Mags! Marry Julian; it would be the same as marrying us both. We three could be together as we want to be and no one would find it odd. You can have us both, Mags, and we would make them let you swing your sword. You could teach the ladies of the court self defense; and train up the young ladies properly. They are all mad for the sword and want to be just like you! You could teach them properly! They could have the opportunities you never had!" For a moment, he thought she would say yes, but in the end she had simply shaken her head sadly.

In spite of the happy camaraderie of the summer, on the tenth day of September, Lackland and Beau rode out of Limpwater, heading north to Castleton, leading a string of five pack-ponies; four carrying all their worldly possessions, and one carrying special gifts for two boys. Gertie had finished their shields, and had also made two good helms for them; the gifts from Lady Mags. As a precaution and to dispel accusations of favoritism, there were equally fine gifts from Gertie's forge for Henri's children that were still at home and the two young Weyllyn dukes there, too.

Culyn wished to spend the year with his father, but promised to come to court the following September.

In much the same way as Sir Julian 'Lackland' De Portiers, Sir Beau Baker was completely committed to serving Henri Dragoran with all his heart. Beau was very proud of the honor that the king had bestowed upon him, a lowly baker's son, when he had made him a Knight of the Realm down in Eynier during the spring. When

Beau left Billy's Revenge with Julian, he was a free man in every way, except one.

He was tied to Julian Lackland with stronger bonds than he had ever thought possible.

When they arrived at court, the seneschal gave them some of the finer rooms in the older wing that were adjoined with a common sitting room and a shared bathroom. He had decided upon meeting Beau and seeing them together, that they were 'very close friends' who would want to be together. The old seneschal was a nonjudgmental sort, who made it his business to see to it that everyone was happy with their living arrangements. He let other folks make their own rules (and their own hypocritical lack thereof) about court morality.

As the court began to trickle into town, Lackland, with Beau assisting him, began training the young nobility in the fine art of warfare. Slippery Jack had emerged from the scenery as he was known to do, and happily went back to work as Henri's spy-master. He appeared, sometimes before breakfast, in their rooms to chat about old times and bring them up to date on the gossip from Limpwater, and then disappearing again.

Lackland's nephew, Sir Melvin De Portiers, had come to court completely prepared, as Lackland had known he would. So had young Lord Jules De Leon come well prepared. Lackland sought them both out, and made sure that they were settling in well, and caught up on all the gossip from over the summer. Both boys were extremely pleased with their gifts and immediately sat down to write thank-you notes to both Lady Mags and Gertie Smith.

If anyone thought it odd that Lackland was so fond of young De Leon, they simply assumed that his well-known, undying love for the young Lord's famous older sister was the root cause. Indeed, the Earl himself was well known to frequently refer to Lackland as 'my son-in-law'.

Before they went to House De Leon that first Yuletide, Beau had warned the old man about what had happened to Julian in the forest that terrible night, writing him a detailed letter. When old De Leon saw the scars on his throat and the invisible scars that now lurked in his once merry eyes, he understood.

Old De Leon was not blind; he had seen a great deal of life. Though they were very discrete about it, he knew full well what the relationship between Julian and Beau had grown into. Julian, Edward felt, would never be the same, and if he could not be with Mags, then he would be with Beau.

He was not put off by it, although it was never mentioned; in his opinion, happiness was a rare commodity and should be enjoyed wherever it was found. He had developed a fondness for Golden Beau too, and thought of him as a son. The two spent every holiday and summer with him and Jules for the next four years, until Jules was officially a man.

De Leon often declared that the four of them were 'a happy family of bachelors muddling along as best we can', and missed them quite keenly when they were at court.

The two boys, Jules and Mel, hit it off right away and quickly became the closest of friends. Melvin De Portiers was often asked to visit House De Leon. Not surprisingly, despite his father's constant pressure, Mel rarely offered to reciprocate. He told his father that "Poor old Bunder can't be left alone with only Uncle Lackland and Sir Beau to care for him during the Yuletide lull, so you know how it is...."

In reality, Melvin would have killed himself before he subjected his good friend to his father's social climbing and excessive airs. Still, Sir Mortimer got a great deal of mileage at snobbish dinner parties out of simply being able to casually drop the sentence, "Our Melvin is off at Bunder again, you know... Old De Leon simply adores the boy. Quite close friends, we all are. My brother is madly in love with his daughter, the famous Lady Mags; quite a romantic tragedy, that tale."

Both boys worked hard and, perhaps because of their sunny natures and natural charm, they became the more popular lads in the court, and the other boys tried to be just like them. Mel and Jules, in turn, modeled themselves slavishly after their arms-master Sir Julian Lackland and his highly skilled assistant Sir Beau Baker. Between the two of them, Lackland and Beau inspired a whole generation of knights to a new standard of duty, compassion and honor in their daily lives and skill on the battlefield. For the first time since his ascent to the throne, Henri had the quality of leadership among the nobility that he had always wanted in his military forces.

"You know, Lackland, I think the lads we have currently hanging about court would take care of any small emergency such as a dragon or kidnapping with absolutely no second thoughts. How refreshing it is, to know that my home and the neighbors are safe when I am gone!"

Henri had never gotten over the fact that Mags De Leon had been obliged to kill the dragon that his, as he referred to them, 'pansy-assed' courtiers, should have taken care of.

As he had promised, at the end of that first year, Sir Culyn Owyn left his father's cottage and came to take his place at court for a year.

Not long after Culyn arrived in Castleton, a situation arose that required Lackland, Beau, Jack and Culyn to use their unique skills. Henri Dragoran had a little trouble with Lournes that he had to settle quietly and with no finger pointing in his direction. It was a task which absented them for several weeks, but they were back in time for the Yuletide break. This time, there were no innocents murdered, though Lackland would much rather have called the bloody idiot out in the snow and killed him in open combat.

Lournes was a small country perched between northern Waldeyn and the Great Northern Sea. With long dark winters and short brilliant summers, the Lournesque were the furriers to the rest of the continent. Their craftsmen also provided many unique, beautifully carved boxes that were in high demand by the nobility. These boxes often had false bottoms and were impossible to open, unless you knew exactly how to do it.

The people of Lournes were an exotic and slightly barbaric people, being an even more clan-based society than the Eynier or Vyennesk. Their shamans were known to use black Majik to control demons and to cast curses upon those who ran afoul of them.

The task took them deep into Lournes, and was in many ways reminiscent of their adventure in Ludwellyn. The trouble involved Prince Maldred, the younger brother of Aethelwyrd, the current king of Lournes. Maldred and his coterie had recently failed in their attempt to assassinate Henri, and were now attempting a coup in Lournes. Henri didn't want to have to deal, with him or his followers, should they happen to succeed and had decided to do the King of Lournes a favor.

"I am mortally sick of watching my back," Henri told Lackland as they walked in the quiet beauty of the queen's private garden. "Maldred despised his sister, but through her, he had a chance of killing me and taking over the throne here. When Morganna over-stepped herself and went to the block, he regretted the loss of his own chance, not his sister's death. I have become used to fending off and killing his clumsy assassins, but I really don't want to have him in charge up there. The people of Lournes do not deserve that. Aethelwyrd is a reasonably good king, and his daughter Attallia will be one of the great queens when she succeeds him; which we must ensure."

"Maldred; I know of him, but I have never met him. He has a nasty reputation among their mercs. They won't work for him," replied Lackland. "He also has the reputation of being rather hard on his followers. My friends up there tell me that his former conspirators are sometimes known to disappear or be found in an untidy state of disembowelment when a plan goes awry."

Several carefully planned deaths among Maldred's more notorious followers, with the evidence pointing directly to the ferret-faced, weaselly brother of the late Former Queen Morganna, resolved the issue neatly; with no one knowing they had ever been there. The rest of the royal family of Lournes had been extremely happy to try and execute him for his crimes, exceedingly promptly. He had been a thorn in their sides for far too long for them to believe his hysterical protestations of innocence.

Aethelwyrd was mortified that a brother of his could have gone to the block shrieking like a small girl. He ordered Maldred's name stricken from the histories, and decreed that his name never be mentioned in his presence again.

Not long after they returned from Lournes, Culyn Owyn at last convinced Belle Tanner to leave the trade and marry him, and their son, whom they named Hugh after his grandfather, was born with the gift of music, as were the rest of their sons, five of them to be exact.

The next ten years passed, during which the marriage of Princess Rose Dragoran to Lord Jules De Leon caused a stir and no small twinge of satisfaction for Lackland and Lady Mags. They met briefly at the festivities, but did not get together as she had (as usual) a new lad with her. He seemed nice enough, but was quite young and in awe of the company he was keeping.

The wedding was quite nice and not really lavish as these things go, but the happy couple was pleased with it and that was what mattered.

Not two months after seeing young Jules married, the old Earl passed away, and young Jules was now the Earl of Bunder. Everyone agreed that he was a sensible young man who had learned well from his father's wise management, and Bunder town prospered under his leadership.

With Jules' marriage, Lackland and Beau had distanced themselves from House De Leon, allowing Jules and Rose to begin their married life without an excess of family interference.

That same summer, Lackland's brother Mortimer passed away suddenly, having choked on a bone in a fowl-pie. Just as Lackland's mother had warned him would happen, Mortimer left the estate, in somewhat of a financial ruin, due to his efforts to impress the lesser nobility. Lackland had been long preparing for such and was well able to shore up the family finances. Once his father's debts were paid off, Melvin was able to keep the estate running smoothly, having learned much from his Uncle Lackland.

That fall, Melvin married Eleanor De Champ, the only daughter of another local baron, whom he and Jules De Leon had rescued from a fate worse than death. She had been kidnapped while on a pilgrimage to Hyola. Her mother had died when she was quite young and her widowed father had never sent her to court, as he was a scholarly sort and didn't worry about things like that. The two had lived in contented isolation until Eleanor had decided to go to Hyola to study. But when Eleanor had been kidnapped, he had applied to the king for help. Lackland and Beau were on a secret trip to Lanqueshire and so Henri had sent the two best knights that he had: Jules and Mel.

The young knights had of course rescued her, saving her from the highwaymen whose intent had been to ransom her back to her father and not lose their heads over the matter. Which is unfortunately, what did indeed happen to them. After he and Jules had, brusquely but efficiently, cut down the men who had held her, Mel had taken one look at her and fallen madly in love. Their marriage was a happy one, producing three children in four years.

Immediately after Melvin and Eleanor were married, Lackland and Beau began undertaking many more tasks in Lanqueshire for Henri and were away from Castleton more often than they were there. They sometimes passed through Limpwater, but never stayed for any length of time. They didn't really see anyone that they knew, as most everyone was out on the road working when they passed through. It was always good to see Huw, Billy and Bess and Gertie anyway.

During those years, Lackland, Jack and Beau managed to get into many difficulties in dealing with the Lanques. Somehow, they always emerged the winners, and with the occasional addition of Culyn to their team, they managed to nearly eliminate the Lanqueshire pirates. The people of Lanqueshire were able to live somewhat more decent lives; not having to fear the abuses and exploitation that they had endured under the pirate-kings.

In an effort to crush the pirates once and for all, King Henri directed Lackland to take the main seaport town of Port Lanque. After a long and bloody battle, Lackland took the town, burning all the ships in the harbor, and giving no quarter. "They do not deserve the mercy that they beg for! How many innocents have died at their hands? How many more will die if these beasts live? No Quarter!"

As he wandered through the streets of the now quiet town, he wondered if he would be treated with mercy when he came to the end. *'Will God say 'No Quarter'' when I knock at the gate of heaven? I have waded neck deep in the blood of the innocent.'* Still, Lackland persevered, doing his duty for the King and trying to make the world a better place.

However, with the demise of the last of the pirate-kings, Lanqueshire had no strong leadership. The country descended into chaos, with many people dying of starvation and disease. Piracy, once again, became seen as a way out of the grinding poverty that Lanqueshire suffered from. The merchants sent a desperate plea for help to Henri. He realized that he had to do something, or he would face the same problems over and over again. Thus, Lackland found himself and Beau posted in Port Lanque helping the local merchants keep the peace, accompanied by several companies of Henri's finest knights.

As usual, Lackland and Beau worked as much to protect the Lanque people whom they had come to love, as much as they worked to protect Henri's interests. They had found the people of Lanqueshire to be, for the most part, simple men and women who just wanted to be left in peace and to be allowed to live their lives as well as they were able. The two knights had many friends among the common people of Lanqueshire and were considered to be clansmen by the many men and women that they helped with no payment asked or taken. In Lanqueshire that counted for more than anything, to be a clansman.

At long last, the neighboring countries of Vyennes, Fornost and Lournes came together to apply pressure to the merchants of Lanqueshire, urging that the merchants of Lanqueshire petition Henri to be made a part of Waldeyn, to insure some sort of stability for their land.

The petition, when it came, was unanimous, and Lanqueshire was immediately accepted as a part of Waldeyn. Along with appointing his very capable daughter Lucy Dragoran, to be the permanent governor, Henri immediately began sending wagon trains of food and seed. The Mother Church sent the Sisters of Anan with their healing Majik and medicines. The Sisters of Anan also began teaching the local people how to farm their rugged land, in the way that they had always done in Fornost. The poorest, most destitute people were given refuge and hope for a better future. The custom of piracy, which had hung on in small pockets throughout the chaos of the previous years, was completely abolished.

With the joining of Lanqueshire to Waldeyn, there was true peace throughout the land for the first time in more than a century. Henri Dragoran, who had ascended the throne as a politically powerless nine-year old, had not only made strong the country of Waldeyn, he had added territory to it without intending to. Despite the inadvertent addition of the troublesome Lanqueshire, Henri loved the Lanque people, and insisted that they were accorded the equal rights of all citizens of Waldeyn. "The people of Lanqueshire are our family as surely as Wald and Eyn are our family; how can we treat them as anything less than equals? We are one people with many voices."

With the peace had come safety on the trade-roads. Young Brand MacNess had married Anna Le Clerk, and like his father, he had been blessed with the ability to spot an opportunity when it came along. Realizing that the lack of work in Limpwater for mercenaries was not going to improve, Brand finally took the Rowdies down to Plimpton in Lanqueshire. There they were now plying the trade with as much style and grace as they had done in Limpwater.

The new Rowdies were now based out of the pleasant inn that Brand and Anna had purchased and revamped, complete with modern plumbing. They named it 'Twin Oaks' after two ancient oaks that stood in the yard. Gertie's second son, Willy Smith, and his wife and children went with him. They were to be their armorers, while Bennie stayed to work his mother's forge. Tom and Betty Stanton went along as their ostler and provisioner. Young Hugh Owyn was the bard who now chronicled the new Rowdies' adventures, insuring them a place in history.

The tiny, desolate village of Plimpton and rundown Twin Oaks Inn were situated at the southern entrance to the Bekenberg Pass. Once Brand had remodeled the inn and established the Rowdies, they began to see a lot of travelers, much the same way as Billy's Revenge had. With the advent of the Rowdies, Plimpton became a place that was much like Limpwater, only with the particular twist that was the lively and robust culture of Lanqueshire.

Brand had left Billy's Revenge knowing that his father was doing quite well as a wayside-inn; making money hand over fist, in fact. His younger brother Eddie had, of course, married Estelle Smith, and they remained there to help Billy, and take over for him when the time came for Billy and Bess to hang up their aprons.

Good King Henri died suddenly when his horse was startled by a nest of firesprites and reared suddenly, throwing him off. He had landed badly, and broken his neck. His grieving widow and children pulled themselves together with Lackland's support. After the royal funeral, there was a wonderful coronation for King Harry and Queen Gwenevere.

The young King Harry built a castle just outside of Bekenberg, near Bekenberg Pass. He had located it there for its central location and proximity to all the far flung regions of Waldeyn. The city of New Bekenberg grew up around the castle, and soon became the seat of government.

King Harry's younger brother, Prince Geoffrey and his family remained in charge of Castleton Keep. Castleton remained the center of trade for the northern trade routes, and the Mother Church kept the Prime

Chapel there, as it was the most established center of learning for the Majik Wielders and Healers. Thus, the court spent a lot of time on the road to and from Castleton Keep and Bekenberg Castle. This benefited Limpwater and Billy's Revenge greatly, as they were the first main stop over on the trade road between the two royal cities.

King Harry bestowed an earldom upon his good friend and kinsman Sir Melvin De Portiers, making him the Earl of Dervy. This included House Portiers and the towns of Dervy, Limpwater and Somber Flats. This would have killed his father with joy had he lived to see the day. Mel now had a rather large and reliable income with which he could properly maintain House Portiers. Of course, he was now obliged to supply and arm a certain number of trained armsmen to the crown, but he had learned from his Uncle Lackland everything that he would need to know about managing his estates, no matter how large or small. Dervy marched along the southern boundary of Bunder, which made Jules and Melvin both quite happy.

After his marriage to Belle Tanner, Sir Culyn Owyn and his father, Huw the Bard, had established a college in Limpwater. Their goal was to teach the Bardic craft as it had been taught in Eynier in the old days of Huw's youth, before the troubles nearly destroyed the craft. The Bards of Limpwater soon became famous and were quite sought after over the whole continent, even in frozen Fornost. Every young musician and storyteller on the continent wanted to train in Limpwater and all were welcome. The city of Limpwater became known as a center of learning, and culture.

Beau and Julian remained closer than ever, following King Harry to Bekenberg Castle. They remained there for the rest of their lives together, when they weren't working as Harry's diplomats to Fornost and Vyennes. After the settling of the Lanqueshire problem, King Harry sent Lackland and Beau to Vyennes as Ambassadors. The two men were glad to have a place to settle down and to live in relative comfort and peace. The climate in Vyennes was mild, and there was a relaxed and peaceful way about the people. The food was exotic, and the people of the court were refined. Of course, the two men were very discrete as to the true nature of their relationship. However, tales of Lackland's unrequited love for Lady Mags had traveled all the way to Costa De Sol, the capital city of Vyennes, and in truth, both men longed for her.

The phrase that most often crossed their lips was, 'If only Mags were here! She would have loved this!'

While they were there, they picked up many gifts for Mel and Jules, shipping them home on the caravans that they once guarded. The carpets and silks were lavish gifts indeed, and the houses De Leon and De Portiers began to look quite rich.

As they walked through the market, they often found themselves drawn to the craftsmen, and their own quarters in the embassy began to be sprinkled with many small souvenirs; fragile glass figurines and beautiful carvings.

The Vyennesk court adored them, and they were often seen dining with the nobility. They were the Queen's Champions whenever there was a tourney. The Arms Masters of Waldeyn did not let their skills slip; indeed, they learned everything they could about the way arms were taught in Vyennes. He and Beau were considered to be the most formidable warriors on the continent, and their advice was regularly sought after in matters of a military nature.

At last, they were recalled to Bekenberg Castle, to train up the new generation of Knights. They were training the sons of the very men they had trained, what seemed like only a few years before. It was with great pride that Lackland and Beau began training young Edward De Leon and young Jules De Portiers. They also saw to it that their sisters were well trained when they demanded to be taught the sword. Though it was still considered to be a sport for women, it was gradually becoming more acceptable for young ladies of the court to be well versed in the martial arts.

Julian's love for Beau was the grounding force in his life. He had never really gotten over the deaths of the Grefyn children, and his part in that tragedy. That, combined with the horror of Lora and the night in the woods. His nights were frequently plagued with nightmares that he was unable to fully wake from.

Without fail, every time he woke terrified and confused, Beau was there; holding him and telling him that he was safe, that everyone was safe.

Beau had never looked back once he and Julian left Billy's Revenge. He had found a life with work that was fulfilling, and his love for Julian had never faltered.

Beau always called him Julian, never Lackland, unless they were in company. As time went on, Julian felt more and more like he was two people living in one head. One person was the man everyone saw as 'Lackland, the Great Knight'; the knight whom everyone saw as a hero and expected great things from and who always delivered.

The other man inside his head was 'Julian, the Broken Knight' whose fragile grip on sanity was made possible by the love and determination of Golden Beau. Julian's peace and contentment was Beau's first thought in the morning and his last thought at night. No matter what, Beau was strong for Julian, who could shoulder the burdens of kings and make the world a safer place to raise children in. However, he had broken under the weight of his own sorrow and guilt for the children he had been unable to save.

Beau was well known to be a contented man, right up to the day he died in Julian's arms, having suffered a heart attack while they were breakfasting in their rooms. Julian could not believe that he was dead. He sat broken and despairing beside his bier, believing that his Golden Beau would wake up and it would all be just a bad dream.

Beau had grown to love both Jules and Melvin, as if they were his own sons. Upon his death, they both benefitted greatly from Beau's largesse. He had out lived his parents, and had no siblings, and of course, he knew full well Julian and Mags' secret. Right after they left Billy's Revenge, upon arriving in Castleton, Beau had made a will making both Jules De Leon and Melvin De Portiers his legal heirs.

Not surprisingly, after Beau's death, Julian sank into a deep depression. Everything reminded him of Beau and underscored his loss. Cracks had immediately begun to show in the mental state of the Great Knight; the first few nights after Beau's death, Julian was found by the servants wandering the halls in the dead of night, frantically looking for Beau; confused and inconsolable.

During the first days in his more lucid moments, Lackland realized what was happening to him, and he knew what he had to do. He had the servants pack up all their possessions; all the many small souvenirs from their travels and the pictures of them together that had been made over the years by the court portraitist and had them sent to House De Portiers. He then retired from court, unable to stand being in the rooms that had been their home for so many years when they weren't on the road.

At Beau's funeral, both Jules and Melvin begged him to come to live at their respective homes. Though he was quite touched by their devotion, he simply could not be around people, and needed to get away to grieve properly. He tried to explain it to them, many times; but he made no sense, even to himself.

Immediately after the funeral, he left Bekenberg Castle looking for something, though he knew not what it was. Lackland bade both Jules and Melvin goodbye, though they were quite worried about him and begged him to stay. Saying that he could not bear to stay, he began an extended journey to nowhere in particular. His wandering path took him all over the continent.

It was apparent that something had snapped in Lackland's wits; there was a hole in his mind, and he was 'not quite right in the head'; but though Lackland knew that he had suffered some sort of mental breakdown, he did not know how to cure the madness. All that he knew was that something important was missing and that he had to find it at all cost.

More than anyone knew, Beau had been the rock that Lackland had clung to. His steadfast love and continual support had brought him stability after the night of terror at Bold Lora's hands, and he had held Julian together when the nightmares were particularly bad. Now, though, there was no one to hold him and shelter him from the demons that lurked in the night. There were no strong arms to rescue him from the unnamable, shadowy horror of his own guilt: guilt for crimes he could not remember committing, though the woman with the mad eyes and the bloody knife punished him for them so he knew that he must have done it. The night always brought the fearsome nightmares from which he could not wake; and the morning brought no release from the panic and dread.

The loss of Beau had broken his mind.

Lost, alone and nameless, Lackland wandered over the countryside endlessly searching for something important; something of value that he had misplaced. Sometimes that which he sought had golden hair, and sometimes it was burnished mahogany, but he was never able to say what he had lost; he only knew it was gone. He was frequently found sleeping in haystacks and lofts, a nameless vagabond who never failed to stop and help even the poorest of persons.

When asked his name, he had no answer other than, "I am Lost. That is who I am, I am Lost." All that he could tell them was that something of great value had been mislaid and he could not rest until he found it, although he had no idea what it was that was missing. "I will know when I see it, be sure of that; I will know it when I see it." His search took him as far to the east as Vyennes, and as far north as Lournes, but though he searched long and hard, he never found what he was looking for.

At last as his wits gradually returned, Lackland found himself in Waldeyn again, near the border with Fornost. He remained at Hyola for several weeks, helping the nuns. Gradually he began to have some remembrance of who he was, but as he began to come to his senses, he also knew that he could not go home to House Portiers or House De Leon in the mental state that he was in.

One of the nuns asked him what he did for a living, and he told her that he helped people who needed helping. "Are you the knight Lackland, sir?"

He had looked confused, but nodded and said, "I may be him. Sometimes I think that I am he."

For the next two years, Julian and his horse wandered the rural roads and villages of Waldeyn, traveling out to Galwye and the wild western seacoast where the odd and dangerous beasts still threatened livestock. Often, he spent the night in barns, helping farmers to be rid of watersprites or firesprites and other troublesome beasts. He never turned down anyone who needed his help, and hundreds of tales and rumors grew up around the elderly wandering knight who never failed to save the day, and never asked for payment.

It was said that he was searching for the one great love of his life, or that his one great love had died. "Either tale is true," he would say if he were asked.

The old knight talked to his horse, and seemed to believe that the horse answered him back, but no one held that against him. He always cared for his horse's welfare, keeping him well shod and well fed. Frequently, folks wondered why he spent all of his money on the horse's wellbeing, and none on his own. He just laughed, and said that his horse took good care of him, so he should return the favor.

Sometimes he wished he had died with Beau, but something drove him to keep on traveling; something that he could not resist. When morning came, the old knight was always gone, looking once again for the elusive thing that he could not identify. He no longer knew what it looked like, but he searched anyway.

The bards began to tell the tales of 'The Lost Knight', a wiry, canny old man whose kind nature and melancholy touched the hearts of everyone who met him. Many who heard those tales wondered if he could possibly be the long lost Great Knight himself: Sir Julian Lackland. Though they often asked him most politely if he were Lackland, he would just smile and shrug; refusing to answer. He knew who he was, but was not ready to go back to his old life.

Lackland himself was unaware that he was thought to be missing, although he knew that he was lost. He had no idea that he had become the source of many tales of kindness and mercy. He only knew that he had to keep traveling, for when he stopped in one place for too long, the nightmares would begin and Golden Beau was not there to rescue him from the terrors that gripped him in the night.

Chapter 11 The Last Good Knight

On a dismal late spring afternoon, Sir Julian Lackland rode into Limpwater. He wondered if anything had changed since he and Golden Beau had left so long ago to be King Henri Dragoran's Arms Masters. As he looked around, he saw that many changes had occurred in the town; some for the better, and some for the worse. He did not even know the town anymore; nothing looked the same.

The town had grown into a city that was far larger than Castleton, and the residents appeared to be quite prosperous. "I knew this place when all that stood here was Billy's Revenge and the smithy," he told his ancient horse, Baron. "My old horse Farroll hated this place, being somewhat of a pansy as he was. He hated the mud, you see."

Baron snorted his opinion of horses that were pansies.

Even Main Street had changed so much that Julian didn't recognize anything, but still he kept plodding toward the center of town where Billy's Revenge had always held pride of place. He plodded along, passing several newer taverns of lesser quality than Billy's Revenge on his way to the center of town.

Nothing was familiar to him. He could not even find Huw's cottage.

Soon, however, he approached the old inn that had been the scene of so many happy mugs of ale, feeling a sense of disappointment.

The ramshackle building now leaned somewhat over the cobbled square; the hastily built foundation had finally given way under one corner. Peeling grey paint that had once been white was framed by equally peeling green paint about the doors and windows. The faded and unreadable sign hung over the steps, swinging in the ever-present wind.

Once the sign had depicted a bloody knife in lurid colors, but like the rest of the inn known as 'Billy's Revenge' it was now peeling and nearly colorless.

An immense new building built completely of stone and easily twice as large as the original rose next to it. There, with a sign in front, proudly proclaiming that 'the new 'Billy's Revenge' would be open soon, with a grand ballroom and modern plumbing in every room'. There was a scaffold around it, and it looked to be nearly complete, at least on the outside.

Once he reached Billy's Revenge, he had regained his bearings and realized that he had come in on the wrong street – the street that Huw had lived on was still there to his right, but it was no longer called Main Street; it had been renamed Rose Lane. "Huw will be around somewhere, if he still lives," Julian told Baron. "He built his college here, and he would never leave his cottage and his Lucy's apple tree. Besides, Culyn and Belle still live here, and so do Annie and Babs. At least they did when Beau was still alive." Somehow, thinking about all the retired Rowdies who might still live in Limpwater comforted him in an odd way.

For a moment he paused, looking at the old inn. The last time Julian had been in the town of Limpwater for any length of time the building had been well kept and the paint had been bright. Of course, Billy Nine-Fingers and plump Bess had been alive too. That had been long ago, when old Henri was still king, and he and Beau had been working much of the time in Lanqueshire. They had stopped in often on their way to and from Castleton.

He thought of the happier times that he had spent there, remembering the summer of the picnic and Golden Beau and beautiful Mags. That had been twenty-five years ago, maybe more; he didn't really know anymore. That was the last year he had spent as a Rowdy, and it had been the year that changed his life. "But I wouldn't have had my life with dear old Beau," he told Baron. "I wouldn't have had all those good years, without all the things that happened that year." Baron tossed his head. He remembered Beau and his old horse Gooseberry. Baron was often lonely, missing the companionship of other horses, but Julian was good to him. *'He just needs to stop living in the past and enjoy the present.'* Unfortunately, Baron's ability to convey his thoughts was rather limited, so his words of horsey wisdom went unsaid.

Patiently, Baron stood still while Julian was lost in his memories; now he smiled as the memory of one golden summer of some thirty five summers before passed before his mind's eye. The summer of the last dragon and Lady Mags and the field of daisies had been the best summer of his life, for Julian Lackland.

Beau had always understood, and loved him anyway. *'I wouldn't have you any other way, Julian,'* he would say. *'I wish our Mags had come along, but you know how she is. I begged her, but she just couldn't do it. She was afraid of going that much against convention, and nothing I could say would change her mind. She could face down a dragon, but the ladies of the court terrified her.'* It had always gratified Julian that Beau had loved Mags too, almost as much as he had loved Julian.

Now Julian was back in Limpwater, hoping to find something to remind him of the happiness he had when he had been a young Rowdy. Then wildly in love with the beautiful Lady Mags, with the future full of endless possibilities stretching in front of him.

He had hoped wrong. The old place was every bit as beat-up and tired as he was; past its last legs, actually. "It's a good thing they are building a new place," Julian told Baron, who flicked his ears in response. "The poor old place is falling down. Look, the foundation is cracked."

He almost decided to head on back down the road to the Powder Keg Public House in Somber Flats, despite the fact that it was a wee bit too hoity-toity for his taste. However, it was another seven leagues worth of riding a tired horse, over ground he had just covered to boot.

But he was there, so he figured he might as well stay. He still thought that he would look up some of the old crowd while he was there.

Actually, whatever was cooking at Billy's Revenge smelled delicious, and his mouth began to water, just thinking about it.

Lackland tied his horse to the railing and walked though the swinging door. He spoke to the familiar looking innkeeper and paid for a room for himself. The old place looked pretty good on the inside; immaculately clean and neat as always.

"Is there an empty stall for my horse?" he asked the innkeeper, who reminded him of someone. Lackland was sure he knew the man, but though he wracked his brain he could not dredge up the name. He knew that the

Rowdies had all gone down to Lanqueshire long ago, but he didn't know who had taken over when Billy passed on.

"It's two coppers for the horse and an extra copper if you want a nice bit of grain for him." The innkeeper showed Julian up to his room. It was the corner room that had been the home of Davey 'God's Gift' Llewellyn and Percy Longstride back in the long ago days, thirty years or more gone. Mags' room had been across the hall. Julian's last room had been one floor up.

"This is fine, thank you," he said, and the innkeeper went back downstairs.

After stowing his kit under the bed and hanging his armor on the stand in the corner, Julian went out and led his horse around to the stable. Speaking to the stable-girl whose name was Bessie, "Give him a bit of grain in his feedbag, if you will. He's worth the extra copper, and he has been foraging much lately."

She nodded, seeing that he was a man who took care of his horse first and himself second.

"Is there a farrier here still? He keeps picking up stones since I had him shod down in Wister," Julian handed her his reins.

"My uncle is the smith here, sir. He will gladly see to your horse. If you would like, I can walk him over there for you, and get his feet seen to today," Bessie offered. "Uncle will send the bill here for you."

"That would be wonderful, if you would do that. Is there still a bath-house here?" Julian was feeling every league of the dusty roads he had traveled, and a nice hot bath would definitely be a treat. Bessie directed him to the men's bath-house, and soon he was sitting neck deep in a copper tub of hot water. The hot water and indoor plumbing had always been the thing that set Billy's Revenge apart from the other inns on the trade road, and it was still a wonderful thing to have at the end of a long day's journey.

Later in the common-room, he sat waiting for the pretty daughter of the inn-keeper to bring him a fine dinner of sliced ham and mashed taters with a salad. As he sat, he sipped a mug of ale, and found that he was unable to avoid thinking about his current problem any longer.

Lackland was tired. He was bone tired and thinking of finally retiring from the business of saving people. Although Jules and Mel would both have insisted that he go to live with one or the other of them, he was not ready to do that. He knew that he should let them know that he was alive and back in his right mind. Still, he would have to find some other accommodation than sleeping under hedges and in barns, and if Huw was alive he would help him figure it out. He knew that he had more than enough money, because he hadn't taken any money from his account at the ministry since Beau had died. It had most likely grown a bit since then, what with his pension being deposited every month. *'I will talk to Huw tomorrow,'* he decided. *'Huw always gave me good advice.'*

Soon Julian found himself standing at the bar, talking to the inn-keeper, who had turned out to be young Eddie. He was the younger son of Old Billy Nine-Fingers, the very boy Julian and Beau had saved from drowning that summer, so many years before. He was married to little Estelle Smith, who had provided him with seven children, one of whom was Bessie the stable-girl. Billy and Bess had passed on some six years previously, Bess just not waking up one morning, and

Billy losing interest in life and following her a month later. "Beau and I were in Vyennes when Bess and Billy passed away, and we didn't hear about it for several months," Julian told him sadly. "We loved your parents. They were our family for so many years."

"It is amazing just how many people say that," replied Eddie, feeling happy to hear that. "They were special people who never turned anyone away. I have always tried to make my dad proud."

"You can be sure that you have done just that," Lackland replied. After a moment of silence, he asked, "Just what does a knight do when he is long past the glory days? I always mean to retire but it never fails, there is always just one more person who needs my help desperately. I always find myself hunting some creature that is bothering their livestock." Julian found himself confiding in Eddie, just as he had always done with Billy. "I can't say no, though I should."

"Well, there just aren't any heroes to handle the small bad jobs anymore, so folks need your services more than ever," Eddie answered truthfully. "Mercenaries are rare up here nowadays; mostly the boys join King Harry's army, and the girls go down to Lanqueshire because they are welcomed in the mercs there. Now that Lanqueshire is part of Waldeyn, they need the mercs there to enforce King Harry's laws. The outlaws are still hiding in the mountains down there, preying on the unwary. We are too well settled up here, so the heroes always go down to the southwest."

"I knew that Brand took the Rowdies down to Lanqueshire. We were in Fornost for a long while and then Vyennes, after Lanqueshire joined Waldeyn," Julian said. He was feeling quite old and realizing just how out of touch he had become. "Now look at you!

You are building a new inn, much finer than this one. Limpwater is quite cosmopolitan, with a concert hall and the Bardic College. Did I see a cathedral as I came in?"

"You did indeed," replied Eddie proudly. "St Robert's Cathedral, named for our old Fat Friar, Robert De Bolt who brought the church to Limpwater. We have several smaller chapels too, and a proper teaching infirmary." Eddie looked at the sad, scarred old man who seemed to be so much at loose ends, and found his quiet despondency to be quite moving. "I heard about Golden Beau. I know that you and he were together for a long time. Your nephew, the Earl of Dervy, is worried about you, and so is the Earl of Bunder. They were through here just last week on their way to Bekenberg Castle for winter court."

"I have missed so much of their lives," Julian replied after a long moment, thinking of Jules and Melvin. "I should be dangling their grandchildren on my knee before a cozy fire, instead of dragging my sorry old horse out in the cold and the rain to save the world. But I just can't do that, Eddie. It is just that my old bones are creaky and it seems to take longer everyday to get the mobility back in my sword-arm."

"You are not the first to feel that way, Sir Julian," said Eddie, an idea beginning to spark in his mind. *'You saved my life once Sir Julian, and finally I have the chance to save yours.'* Smiling innocently, Eddie said, "Why just the other day, Lady Margaret De Leon was saying the same thing. Her problem is that she has grown somewhat stout, as women of that age will. Bennie Smith has had to make her armor a bit more expansive, if you see what I mean."

"Benny has taken over for Gertie? He is just the one to keep the good name her smithy had. But that is costly, buying new armor is, and it is a cost that is hard for a merc to cover. The poor don't really pay all that well, and they are the ones who always need rescuing these days," Julian said, brightening up considerably. "Is Mags still in town?" His blue eyes were far away as he added, "Let me tell you, she was an armful, Eddie. She was a beauty; she was incomparable!" His mind's eye saw the mahogany-haired beauty and her dark, flashing eyes; with the swing of her hips that made his mouth go dry and the lush, full lips that were meant for kissing.

"No, but I expect her to stop in anytime, tonight or tomorrow," Eddie said cheerfully; seeing how well his idea was being received. "She had to go and take care of a nest of watersprites just down the river, but she should be just about done with that. And for all that, she has silver hair and has plumped-out a bit, but Lady Mags is still a looker! She has always kept herself up, our Lady Mags."

"You know Eddie, I think I will stay a few nights, and wait for Mags. I have been thinking of looking up some of the old gang, and I haven't seen her in years," Julian decided. "I don't have anything going on right now, and it's been a mite lonely of late. I wonder if she is still as spirited as she was."

"She doesn't tolerate stupidity well, but her disposition tends to improve after a few mugs of ale," Eddie assured him. "She's still like she always was, only more so. A bit tetchy, you might say."

With a spark of his old self lighting his somber face Julian laughed, saying, "She could best me in a fight even in my glory-days, Eddie. She always said that there was no such thing as a fair fight; only winners and losers. She was a woman who mortally hated losing!"

"Yes, well she is losing her fire for the hero business, sort of like you Sir Julian. Lady Mags has bought a cottage here in town, down the street from old Huw's and is thinking of hanging up her sword." Eddie walked down to the other end of the bar and served a customer a mug of ale, and returned. "She's bone tired and wants to quit. She only goes out on calls now when it is something that interests her. She usually tells them to roust out the King's men to deal with it. Babs and Annie retired a long time ago, but she can't seem to quit. They have a place not too far away. Of course, their boys have gone down to Plimpton with Brand and Anna."

"I think about doing that all the time, Eddie; retiring, I mean." Julian was silent, lost for a moment in his memories. "Do you know I once asked her to marry me?"

"You don't say," Eddie was surprised. "She was never the settling down type, Sir Julian. Of course, I have heard all of Huw's tales of your star-crossed romance, but you and Beau left here together when I was boy. And well, she just seems to be the sort who will die on the road, still swinging her sword in the trade."

"I know it; and I knew it then but...I loved her," Julian said wryly. "I had hopes. We both loved her, Beau and me. She bound us together in some way in the beginning, and then... well if I couldn't have Mags, I had to live the best way I could. Beau understood. He begged her to come with us, but she just couldn't leave the trade." He stood there, looking into his mug of ale as if it would provide him with an answer. Then he said, with a light in his eye, "I will definitely be staying an extra night or two."

"We will be glad to have you, Sir Julian," Eddie replied. "It certainly wouldn't hurt to have an extra hero hanging around town. You never know when you will need one. I think you might be the last Good Knight we will be seeing for a while. The young ones don't want to take on the sort of jobs you folks all did, since the pay is so low. They all want to be clerks or storekeepers. They don't ever think about who will rescue them when they need saving some day. The best ones go south to work for my brother."

"Yes, we are a dying breed, Mags and I," Julian agreed. "I think we are the only ones still plying the trade up here in the north. Everyone else has long since retired, if they didn't die in the saddle."

"You know, there is a sweet little cottage for sale just down the street, if you are thinking of staying more permanently," Eddie said. "It is right next door to Slippery Jack and Merry Kat's place."

"Are they here then? Maybe I will look into that," Julian replied, "I could use a place to call home, and my poor old horse would like to settle-down I think. I would like to try my hand at growing roses one day." After a little more small talk with Eddie, Julian decided to go and sit before the old familiar fire with his mug, feeling something close to hope for the first time in years. He found himself sitting in the Fat Friar's old favorite corner.

'Imagine that,' he thought with a small chuckle, *'A cathedral and sainthood for good old Friar Robert DeBolt. He truly was a good man, despite his fondness for the ale. I wonder what he thinks about being a saint. Is he up there in heaven wearing a halo? No – probably he is sitting at the ale-barrel like he always did in the old days, wondering what the fuss is all about.'* Soon he was napping just like the old Friar always had, dreaming

of a summer that was long past; a summer of blue skies and endless fields of daisies.

Eddie wiped down the bar, and began closing up for the night. It would be good if Sir Julian stayed in town. He debated waking the old boy up, or just letting him kip by the fire in peace. He finally decided to just let the poor old thing be.

Lady Mags was difficult, but she was a good old thing. The two of them could pick and choose their jobs together, and she wouldn't be so lonely. It was a sad thing when the only people willing to do the dirty jobs were too old to be doing them.

The doors opened, and Lady Mags walked in. "Am I too late for an ale, Eddie? Gah! I am mortally tired."

"You're never too late. I always have one for you, Lady Mags," he replied with a wide welcoming smile. He fetched her a foaming mug of ale.

"I think that was my last job, Eddie," she said, handing him a copper. "I just don't have what it takes anymore. The little buggers almost had me. Water-sprites are a pain in the arse to deal with, even when they are only just hatched. The damned lightning amulet just didn't have enough 'oomph', this time. Of course there were twenty of them, so...."

"Huh...that is just what someone else in your line of work was saying earlier, in regard to retiring," he said, watching her reaction. "The old boy is thinking of quitting too; says his horse is tired. He is an old friend of yours."

"Who would that be? Most of my old friends are dead now," she said, curious as to who of her acquaintance could still be alive, much less be stopping over in Limpwater. "Everyone who is still alive lives here on Rose Street."

"Sir Julian Lackland is here for a day or two," he replied, and he saw shock and joy pass fleetingly through her eyes, followed by hope.

Quickly recovering herself, she said, "Ah, he was a gorgeous man, with a smile that could turn a woman's legs to jelly. Is he still alive, then? My brother told me he left New Bekenberg after Beau died, and told no one where he was going. Jules was worried about him because he was taking the loss very badly and was in a terrible state. If he is still in the business of rescuing people, he is alright then, I suppose."

"Yes, he is sort of working and looking to retire, perhaps to Limpwater," Eddie said, feeling a bit pleased with himself. "He's a little worse for the wear, his armor hangs a mite loose but he still has all his teeth."

She stood there for a moment; a hundred emotions swirling in her heart, and then drained her mug. "Well, as I said, I am mortally tired. I am going to head on home. Maybe I will stop in here for breakfast," she said nonchalantly. "See you tomorrow!"

"You might want to see him now; he is having a kip by the fire as we speak!" Eddie gestured toward the alcove before the great hearth. "Go on, I will just close up. You can let yourself out, when you are ready to leave."

As she walked hesitantly to where Julian sat napping before the fire, she remembered that special summer so long ago. She remembered how young and in love they were, despite the things that stood between them; things that were her fault and hers alone.

She remembered his golden hair shining in the sun as they lay on his cloak in a field of daisies, watching the clouds after a long afternoon of making love under the wide blue sky, that had nothing on the blue of his eyes; saw his perfect profile and his smile that took her breath away. *'Why did I let him go? Why didn't I take the chance when I had it? Why did I let my selfishness get in the way?'*

She had wondered that every night since he and Beau had ridden out of Limpwater at the end of the last good summer she had. She had lost them both forever when Julian had followed Jules to court, and Beau had gone with him.

Beau had begged her to come with them, begging for Julian's sake. But she couldn't see herself leaving the trade, even to be with them.

That peculiar nagging, wondering about all of her poor choices was why Mags had finally left the Rowdies. It was in Plimpton, Lanqueshire that her sword had begun to slow. Although no one else had noticed, Mags had and it had scared her. Fearing that her slow reflexes would be the death of a Rowdy, she had officially retired and come back to Limpwater to settle down.

She was vainly looking to recapture some of that golden summer. There was plenty of the old gang settled down in Limpwater, so that she hadn't been too lonely: Babs and Annie, Huw, Culyn and Belle and the grandchildren; Merry Kat and Slippery Jack. They all had their cottages near her own little house.

The trouble was, she was alone, and had been for all those years. Oh, lovers had come and gone, but none like Beau, and never a one to match her own dear Julian.

The sad part was that Beau and Julian had each other for all those years, and she had had neither of them, through her own fault. She could have had them both, but she had chosen to live without either of them because she could not give up the life she had as a mercenary.

Now Beau was dead, and it was too late to tell him that he was right. She had been in Plimpton when the news had come, and by then the funeral was long over, and Julian had disappeared. She had feared that he was dead; as did Mel and Jules.

Jules and Melvin De Portiers visited her regularly. Just last week, they had told her how worried they were about Julian being missing for so long. They had frequently heard rumors of a mysterious lost knight who went about helping people, but rumors often placed him in widely separate places at the same time. No one could say for sure who he might be; though they fervently hoped he was Julian.

Huw though, had sworn that the mysterious wandering knight had to be Lackland. "Who else could it be? So far as I know, he is the only elderly knight who has gone missing."

Jack agreed with him, saying, "It can only be Lackland, Huw. Did you ever know any other knight who would risk his life to save a cow from a nest of firesprites? Beau is dead, so it has to be Julian."

Mags sat next to Julian on the settee before the fire. She took his hand in hers, watching his face as he slowly opened his eyes. The joy that she saw there, once he realized who was sitting beside him, was heartrending in its intensity. Joy, hope, love and fear; all his emotions were raw in that still-handsome smile.

"Oh, Mags," he said brokenly, drawing her close and kissing her tenderly. "Mags, I have missed you so. Our Golden Beau is gone, you know. How he would have loved to see you, still so beautiful!" Now that he saw her again, he knew what it was that he had been looking for all those years; and she had been here all along. "My beautiful, beautiful Mags, no one could ever compare to you." He tenderly touched her silver hair, not realizing that a tear had streaked his seamed old cheek.

"Julian, will you marry me?" she blurted out. She was terrified that he might say no and that he was done with her and had other commitments. "Let me take care of you, let me give you what you should have had all along! Let me try to be as good to you as you deserve!"

"I will! Of course I will, though I have little to offer you but my heart, and a tired, worn-out horse who would like nothing more than to retire from the road," he replied, happiness roaring through his veins, making him feel alive again.

"I have missed you so much Julian! Don't ever let me go again," said Mags, holding him, and feeling all the pain and tiredness fall away. "I feel exactly the way your poor old horse does; and if you would like to share my cottage, we will all get along quite well, I think."

Eddie and Estelle stood in the shadows watching them, smiling so widely that their faces hurt. Holding hands, they quietly went to their bed feeling that the tale had ended well.

This time old Huw would be able to write a ballad for Lady Mags and Julian Lackland that ended

'and they lived happily ever after'.

Excerpt From

The Tower of Bones

The World of Neveyah

Book 1

By

Connie J Jasperson

Due September 2011

In the universe, all is not as it should be. The gods are at
war, and Neveyah is the battle-field...

Chapter 1

Staggering as he landed hard on his feet, Edwin Farmer looked at his surroundings, startled and completely disoriented. "What the...! What the heck just happened to me?"

Nothing was familiar to him. Judging by the position of the impossibly huge crescent moon, he thought that it must be the early hours before dawn, though only a moment before it had been mid morning. That was before he had fallen through the rocks and into this strange place.

"This is why Dad was acting so strangely this morning. Somehow he knew," Edwin said and stood, numbly looking around and considering his next move. He was still too stunned to think clearly. His low mutters sounded out of place in the dark silence of the prairie.

It had already been one of the stranger days of his life, and it had only just begun.

The day had started normally enough. Right after breakfast, he had loaded the cart with the bushels of apples as his father had asked him to do. Even though he was twenty years old, he always did what his father asked him, with no complaint; that was just the way Edwin was.

Edwin was not an unhappy person. On the contrary, he was actually quite cheerful. His one and only trouble had always been that there *was* no trouble in the peaceful village of Markett. As a boy, it had irked him that there were no marauding bands of Orcs to vanquish, no new worlds waiting to be discovered, no maidens worth the effort of rescuing in the entire town. As an adult, his bucolic existence was dull, dull, and dull. At times, the thought of spending the rest of his life on the farm toiling away in boredom, never having seen the world terrified him.

If the King's Army had been hiring, he would have joined up long ago. But there was no war in the quiet lands around Markett. The army had its pick of men and they were full up. Besides, enlisting in the King's Army was out of the question for the average young man, as it cost fifty golds to join the army. He and his father didn't really earn that much gold in a year, though they were not poor by any means. They simply were not rich, and only the rich could afford to send a son to court to serve the king.

The neighboring family, the Leggs, had sent their oldest son to the army, but they had sold their entire flock to earn the money for it; something Edwin would never ask his father to do.

He had pretty much made up his mind to become an animal-healer. He really loved the animals, and he had had a lot of experience at it. It was just him and his dad caring for all the animals on the farm. The neighbors often asked for his help when their animals were ill or injured. The local animal-healer said he had an instinct for it, and had offered Edwin an apprenticeship. It was not an adventurous occupation, but it at least it was not a boring one.

Though Edwin should have married and left home long before that morning, he had found that even the girls in Markett were boring. He had never yet met 'the one' at the market, though he dreamt of her nightly. He knew her face as well as he knew his own.

Unfortunately, all the girls seemed to want to settle down with Edwin. Everywhere he went, hopeful mamas pushed their eager daughters at him, pointing out their virtues. All they wanted to do was to get married and settle down to raise children and more farming, which he would have done, if only he were to be shown 'the one'. There was no challenge in chasing the girls of Markett; actually the challenge lay in escaping them.

Tall and quite muscular from hard work on the farm, with long, sun-bleached blonde hair and frank blue eyes, Edwin was not the best looking man in Markett, but there was something about him that women could not look away from. Hearts skipped a beat when he flashed that crazy smile that was the trademark of the men in his family. The girls couldn't help it; they were drawn to him like moths to a candle, staring and losing their train of thought when he entered the room.

The friendly-girls at the pub would not leave him or his father to sit in peace. They were free-women with few restraints, and the whole group of them invariably made a beeline to their table the moment they sat down; vying contentiously with each other for the privilege of sitting on their laps and generally hanging about them. For Edwin, it was embarrassing to no end. Over the last year, he had gotten quite good at pretending not to notice the problem, attempting to carry on as if there were no ladies draped across his shoulders. His father tolerated it with a grin, but he too declined their generous invitations.

Even though a simple evening at the pub with his father usually turned into a circus, his father had given him some good advice; smiling his sardonic smile and asking him, "Do you really want to have to explain to your wife about all the friendly-girls who know you by your first name everywhere you go?" Though Edwin did not feel comfortable asking his father how it was that he had come by that bit of wisdom, he nonetheless was careful to follow it since it made sense to him. Thus, due to the embarrassment of persistently being the center of attention, he had not gone out much in recent months and was currently feeling rather house-bound.

When he had complained about feeling somewhat caged, his father had just shrugged and said, "The Boar's Head is just down the road. We can have a pint of ale and then come on home, if you would like." But Edwin was no longer able to deal with his popularity among the free women and friendly-girls, and frankly his friends were glad that he was not there to steal their thunder. They found it difficult to compete, and that had caused some trouble, now that everyone was of an age to be settling down. Even his childhood friend, Josiah Legg, had felt jealousy toward Edwin, despite the fact that Edwin was not interested in dallying with just any girl.

All his life, he'd had a vision of the girl that he would marry, and he had never seen her in the Boar's Head Tavern. Nor did Edwin ever expect to find her there.

On that particular morning, as Edwin rounded the corner of the sheep pen, he had noticed that the gate was slightly ajar. Counting heads, he found that one of the sheep had escaped. "This is great! The sheep can escape, but I am still stuck here, rotting." Muttering to himself, he closed the gate so that the rest couldn't escape and set out to look for the stray.

Edwin stepped into the farmhouse to tell his father where he was going, and quickly made a lunch to take with him, since finding the sheep could take a while. In Edwin's opinion, sheep were sly, crafty creatures, and one never knew what to expect next from them.

His father looked up, with a sad, surprised look. He said, "A missing sheep you say. Umm... you do know that you were not born around here, right?" Edwin nodded, wondering what direction his father was going with that thought. John Farmer was not a man who made idle conversation. "I left home once long ago; it started by me following a missing sheep...I found myself somewhere far away, in another world, really. That is always the way it starts in our family."

Edwin just waited for his father to continue, unsure now as to what was going on with his Dad. *"Something is bothering him; he is not making any sense. He looks very upset, and I don't think it is just the sheep. Have we received bad news?"*

Unaware of his son's confused scrutiny, John Farmer looked out the window, thinking. He turned back toward Edwin, saying, "Look son; there is a lot that I haven't told you, and much that my father did not tell me. Please don't be too angry with me when you get to where you are going, it is just better this way. Do you understand what I am saying?"

Edwin nodded, completely confused. "I think so. Maybe."

His dad continued, speaking almost as if he were saying 'good-bye' to Edwin. "My own father was right: If you have no preconceived notions, you can accomplish so much more. It is just that I was unable to finish the job, and from what I have heard lately, you won't be able to either. Just do the right thing. You will know what that is when the time comes." His father's face, as he spoke, was inexpressibly sad; whatever had brought on this strange behavior had truly upset him. "I will be here when you return, no matter how long it takes you."

He stood and hugged his surprised and confused son. "I knew this day was coming, I just did not expect it so soon. Don't worry about me, I will be fine. Just take your time and do the job right. Say hello to Marta and Garran for me when you see them." After saying that, Edwin's father put on his hat and left to go to Markett with his wagonload of apples, leaving a rather stunned Edwin to find the missing sheep.

John held the reins as the apple-wagon rumbled down the lane, feeling depressed. He had a gut feeling that his son would be gone now, perhaps forever; but the bargain his family had with the Goddess Aeos required it, and John Farmer did not like long good-byes. As the wagon rumbled down the dirt lane that led into town, he was thinking, *"There is no missing sheep. I counted them half an hour ago and they are all there. This is how She calls us; placing the thought in the mind of the one she wants that a sheep is missing. The trail always leads to the same place. Aeos, Goddess watch over my boy. Don't ask more of him than he can bear."*

Along with that thought came the flood of painful memories, but no tears filled his eyes. John Farmer had cried himself dry of tears long ago. Even after all the years that had passed, no matter how he tried not to see it, in his mind's eye he saw Pauli's body lying battered and broken as the rest of them made the escape that he had given his life to make happen. John's stark face stared at the road as he wondered what sort of trouble his son was walking into. *'Garran or Marta will let me know what is going on...I hope. If I haven't burned all my bridges, that is.'*

Edwin stared after his departing father. *'That was strange. What the heck was Dad talking about? He actually hugged me! Something is going on, but...I will worry about it later.'* Edwin decided that, although he was having a strange morning, at least it made a nice change from the usual grind. *'I had better get going; sheep don't usually find themselves. I will make Dad talk to me this evening when he gets back from town.'*

Quickly placing some sliced bread, some cheese, two apples and a canteen of water in a knapsack, he left the house following the trail of the wandering sheep. The trail wound over every hectare of the farm, and he followed the errant sheep for nearly an hour until he came to a rock outcropping.

That particular outcropping was very familiar to Edwin, and brought back happy memories. Long ago as a child, he had often hid out there; it was a place where he had read and dreamt of doing great things. Many an afternoon had been spent leaning back against the boulders and watching the clouds.

However, today the old pile of boulders was a bit different from the last time he had been there.

A strange glow suffused the normally dark cleft in the boulders. As he stooped to see what was causing it, Edwin was grabbed as if by invisible hands and pulled into the glowing opening. The sensation was like being sucked through a bottle's neck. He did not even have time to shout before he found himself standing in the center of a dark, barren prairie.

Abruptly dropped on his feet, Edwin stood dizzily, trying to get his bearings. Wondering what the heck had just happened; he turned around and found that the door or whatever it was gone. His outcropping was gone; and nothing was as it should be.

That was how Edwin came to be standing alone in the center of the eerie, mysterious prairie.

The huge arc of the sky was dark and unfamiliar stars shone brightly, while a huge waning crescent moon hung high over the horizon, eerily lighting the plain that spread out before him. Trying to get his breath, he stared around himself, awed by the stars and the moon which illuminated the plain below.

'Amazing! I have never seen the moon so large; it is beautiful. It is easily twice the size of even a harvest moon back home.' Along with that thought came the realization that this was nowhere he had ever been. *'Where am I...? Somewhere else, just like Dad said.'*

Edwin turned slowly to get his bearings. It appeared that he was standing on a large rise in the center of a large plain. Until the sun began to rise, he would have no real idea which direction was which. Far off in the distance, he could see a campfire and some sort of camp. He began walking toward it, going carefully over the rough ground.

Strange shrubs and low scrubby trees appeared in the darkness as he made his way to the distant camp. The land around him was silent and no insects called; it was as if Edwin's presence has disturbed them.

He had been walking toward the campfire, for what felt like forever, and he had been feeling as if he were being watched for quite some time. The brush was low and sparse, but the ground was uneven. Edwin heard a noise behind him, confirming that he was being followed. Slowly he turned, hoping to see who might be stalking him.

Out of nowhere, he was attacked by some sort of misshapen animal that was about half his height. Struggling desperately, Edwin grabbed a stick and attempted to drive it off, but the crazed creature would not be diverted. Realizing that his life was in danger, Edwin somehow managed to kill the beast by bludgeoning it to death. With the handicap of his less than hefty stick it had been a very close fight, and Edwin was bloodied in several places.

'That was not that much fun! What the heck is this animal, anyway?' Edwin looked closely at the corpse, and saw the gleam of metal in the light of the waning moon. Upon closer examination, he found several pieces of strange money on the ground near the body where it had apparently fallen from the beast's clothing. The money was hexagonal, and had a woman on one side and a building on the other.

Both seemed to be familiar to him, but he could not remember ever having seen that sort of money before.

Looking again at the creature, he realized with horror that his attacker had not been a beast. *'This is not an animal...it is some sort of a person, but I have never seen this sort of person.'* He had never seen a person like the dead creature: its face was rat-like, with hands that had terribly sharp claws. It wore rudimentary clothing of some sort, though it was in tatters and rags; as if the clothing had been worn day and night for months.

Suddenly, Edwin felt a deep pity for the poor creature he had just killed. *'I haven't been here an hour and I have already killed someone.'* Sighing remorsefully, he put the money in his pocket. *"But if he didn't want me to have his money, he should not have tried to kill me. I suspect that I will need it more than he does now. I am alone in a strange world."*

It was a well known fact that people who farmed the land tended to be a practical sort of folk, and Edwin was as practical as anyone; more so than most in many ways. *'The poor thing must be some sort of robber, waylaying travelers. Too bad he didn't have a knife or something. I need a good weapon. But then, if he'd had a knife it would be me lying dead on the ground. What if he is not alone?'*

At that thought, Edwin had looked around until he found a heavy stick, one more like a good club, and began walking toward the campfire once more.

He was soon glad that he had found the better club, as he was attacked once more before he reached the campfire. This beast was like the first one, but was thinner, and more raggedly dressed. It had no money, and had been in many fights before it attacked Edwin; he could see healed scabs and scars on the poor thing. The pathetic corpse stirred a sense of compassion in him; sorrow that the wretched creature had been so desperate that it had to die in such a horrible way. Edwin also felt an unaccustomed sense of grief that he had been forced to resort to beating the creatures to death to save his own life. *'That is just plain wrong,'* he thought as he once more walked toward the campfire. *'Kill or be killed. That is no way to live. What sort of place is this?'*

From a safe distance, Edwin observed the camp, worried that it could be the lair of the strange creatures who wished to kill him.

A girl of about 18 years of age, clad in tight red leather trousers and a loose linen shirt with the sleeves rolled up to her elbows, was seated by the fire, meditating or praying. Red lacquered armor sat near to hand, waiting to be put on. She bore many tattoos of thorny red and yellow roses spiraling up her arms from wrist to neck on both arms, woven with runes for wisdom, strength and courage. A red lightning bolt was placed on her cheek, just before her left ear, and a single rune for wisdom graced her brow. Though he could not see them, red and yellow roses covered her thighs too, but one never saw them. Her long dark hair was plaited into two braids and coiled around her head like a crown. There was a fragile beauty about her, which was quite at odds with her sword that lay balanced across her knees in its sheath.

Deciding that she did not appear to be another enemy, Edwin moved into the light of the small campfire. His clothes were torn and dirty from skirmishing with the beasts and he was disheveled and bloody; both from the beasts he had killed and some of his own.

The girl looked up and said, "You are late, farm-boy. I expected you last night."

"I'm late?!? I'm almost dead! If you knew I was coming, why didn't you help me?" Edwin was exhausted and angry at her comment. He dropped down by the fire to gratefully eat his lunch, politely offering the girl an apple and some bread and cheese. "Wait a minute - how did you know I was coming? And who are you?"

"My name is Aeolyn Brendsdottir. You are here because you are the son of your father, and for no other reason. I have been sent to bring you to the Temple at Aeoven. But as to why I gave you no help on your way here, if you can't defend yourself then you are not the hero we are expecting! Others have been known to stumble through the portal. But your father will surely have told you of that, and of your family's bargain with Aeos." She seemed surprised that he had to ask. "This is the appointed meeting place."

Edwin did not know what to say to that. His father had never spoken to him at all about this place. "Not really," he muttered. "He has told me nothing of you or this place." He accepted the tin cup of fragrant tea that she handed him, wondering, *'Why? Why did he tell me nothing of this place? What have I gotten myself into?*

ABOUT THE AUTHOR

Connie J Jasperson lives and writes in the small quarry town of Tenino, Washington. She and her husband share five children, nine grandchildren and a love of good food and great music. Connie has worked as a field-hand for a Christmas tree grower, a dark-room technician, a hotel maid, a bookkeeper and also 'did time' in the data entry pools of several large corporations. She now is semi-retired and is writing full time. Currently in the works are several tales based in world of Neveyah, and a sci-fi romp based in the fictional Stump County.

Check out our other great books at your favorite retailer or:
www.fantasyislandbookpublishing.com

Made in the USA
Charleston, SC
02 November 2011